More Praise for *Empire Settings*

"A story borne of the spirit of Africa, depicting complex, lively, and vibrant characters who speak with passion . . . David Schmahmann's *Empire Settings* takes the reader on an amazing journey."
—Welcome Msomi, playwright, and chairman, Naledi ya Afrika

"David Schmahmann's story of a lasting love between a young white man and a young colored woman during the apartheid era is an intriguing overview of the whole social scene in South Africa at the time. It is a very good read."
—Helen Suzman, D.B.E., former opposition member of the South African parliament, recipient of the United Nations Human Rights Award

"Skillfully told, engrossing, and subtly wise, a novel that makes politics powerfully personal in its telling of the agony and still incomplete triumph of the new, multiracial South Africa."
—Will D. Campbell, recipient of the National Humanities Medal, civil rights activist, and author of *Brother to a Dragonfly*

"Danny and Santi's love is the story of South Africa, bound by past and present."
—*The Christian Science Monitor*

DAVID SCHMAHMANN was born in Durban, South Africa. He is a graduate of Dartmouth College and the Cornell Law School and has studied in India and Israel, and worked in Burma. His publications include a short story in *The Yale Review* and articles on legal issues. He lives in Brookline, Massachusetts, and practices law in Boston.

EMPIRE
SETTINGS

A NOVEL

David Schmahmann

A PLUME BOOK

My thanks are due to Steven Frank and Sandra Goldfarb,
who made introductions that opened the skies

My gratitude to Florence Tambone,
for reasons too numerous to describe, is boundless

PLUME
Published by the Penguin Group
Penguin Putnam Inc., 375 Hudson Street, New York, New York 10014, U.S.A.
Penguin Books Ltd, 80 Strand, London WC2R 0RL, England
Penguin Books Australia Ltd, Ringwood, Victoria, Australia
Penguin Books Canada Ltd, 10 Alcorn Avenue, Toronto, Ontario, Canada M4V 3B2
Penguin Books (N.Z.) Ltd, 182–190 Wairau Road, Auckland 10, New Zealand

Penguin Books Ltd, Registered Offices:
Harmondsworth, Middlesex, England

Published by Plume, a member of·Penguin Putnam Inc.
Published in a hardcover edition by White Pine Press, Buffalo, New York.

First Plume Printing, July 2002
10 9 8 7 6 5 4 3 2 1

Some of the material in this novel first appeared as a short story in *The Yale Review*. Lyrics from "Orphans of the Empire" printed by permission.

 REGISTERED TRADEMARK—MARCA REGISTRADA

The Library of Congress has catalogued the hardcover edition as follows:

Schmahmann, David.
    Empire settings : a novel / by David Schmahmann.
        p.   cm.
    [1st ed.—Buffalo, NY : White Pine Press, 2001]
    ISBN 1-893996-16-1 (hc.)
    ISBN 0-452-28327-2 (pbk.)
    1. First loves—Fiction. 2. South Africa—Fiction. I. Title.
    PS3619.C44 E46   2001
    813'.6—dc21   2001026785

Printed in the United States of America
Original hardcover design by Sheila Smallwood

Contents

For Sheila

Fill my soul, Africa
Don't let me go, Africa
Let me grow old, Africa
And remember me.

"Orphans of the Empire"
—*Johnny Clegg & Savuka*

CHAPTER ONE

Danny

I MET TESSEBA on a bus in Boston in 1978. She's the sort that peers over your shoulder when you're reading and makes some uninvited comment, and that's exactly how it happened. For a moment you resent the intrusion and sometimes you brush it away but sometimes you don't, depending on your mood. I've seen it replayed dozens of times since then, on airplanes and park benches and in waiting rooms. Tesseba has a disarming manner, which is why she gets away with it — that and a gamin face which is both mournful and exotic, and draws you to her.

So she leaned over and asked what I was examining so intently, and then one thing led to another. I was examining the difference between life and death. But how could I describe that to her?

It was wintertime and whether an almanac would confirm that it was especially cold that winter or not I don't know, but to me it was as cold as death itself.

"What are those?" she asked.

"Government forms."

"They look intimidating."

"They are, rather."

"What accent is that?"

Only a month, and already the question made me wary. What

started as a casual inquiry always invited a comment after it had been answered, an opinion, a probing to see where I stood, to see if I passed some sort of muster. And most people knew so little.

"South African," I said and looked out the window.

The wind could lift the snow up, I'd learned, twirl it, sweep it against your skin.

"Is that where you're from?" Tesseba asked.

"Yes."

"How neat."

"Neat?"

"It's an American word."

"I know that," I said.

"How long have you been here?" she asked.

And so Tesseba and I were on our way.

Even if it was not the coldest winter on record, what made it bone chilling was how unprepared for it I was. It hadn't been that many weeks before, after all, that I had been standing at the great picture window overlooking Gordonwood's swimming pool, watching the awnings flap, the leaves blowing across the patio, the goldenrod sending showers of orange buds over the grass. Death was everywhere, blood still on the walls almost, all life at a standstill.

It's where my thoughts were when Tesseba interrupted them.

❧

Tesseba has stayed with me for all these years, through thick and thin, or, more appropriately, through thin and thick. I'm not really wealthy now but when I met her I had nothing, not even a proper winter coat or insulated boots. Melted snow would creep in around the edges of my soles and squeeze about in my socks for hours until I was able to take them off. I had never seen anything like it. In Africa people didn't stow themselves in insulated rooms waiting for a thaw, the air was warm and moist, you feared snakes, perhaps, drunks, runaway buses, a rabid monkey taunting with acorns and squeals, but not the air itself, snaps of wind so sudden they made you gasp. In Africa you could make mistakes, missteps, somehow muddle through, but in Boston if you made a mistake you could die, freeze to death or worse, fall without any hope of being stopped or saved.

Tesseba had a strange little loft apartment in the middle of nowhere when I met her. Even today I don't know what the area's called. You go over a bridge and across an expanse of warped asphalt and then you come upon a scrabbly hodgepodge of half-used warehouses and half-filled tenements. A number of artists lived in the warehouses, and Tesseba was one of them. I think her rent was thirty-five dollars a month. It sounded almost as cheap then as it does now.

"What are those forms?" she asked on the bus.

"Asylum papers," I said.

"What sort of asylum?"

I knew what she was thinking, toyed for a moment with the prospect of leading her on, letting her think I was some kind of lunatic. But it wouldn't have worked. Alongside her picture in a Providence high school yearbook — straight hair, smooth skin, closed-mouth smile — is the entry: "Semper Fidelis." Knowing Tesseba now I don't think it would have changed how she regarded me.

"Political asylum," I said.

"Wow," she said. "Were you a political prisoner?"

"Not exactly."

"Is that one of the ways you could get to stay here?"

"Yes," I said. "I just came from a legal aid center."

"Is it hard to get?"

"Yes."

"Is it the only way?"

"The other way is to marry an American," I said.

I know as I look back on it that I said it with a touch of mischief, an edge.

"I'd marry you," she volunteered.

"You don't even know me," I said.

"I know enough," she said. "Not marry marry. Just marry. Maybe marry marry. I don't know about that."

It's peculiar, really, how after an exchange like that nothing is barred even as it was one of those conversations that could also have ended in nothing. We could have reached her stop and she could have stood up and left the bus and we could never have seen each other again, the whole exchange nothing more than an odd moment, something on the margins of memory. But instead when we reached her stop I got off with her and we walked, without commenting on what we were doing, down the barren street and across the lot to her building.

"Do you want to come up?" she asked.

"Sure," I said.

"Where do you live?"

"At the Y," I told her. "I'm hoping to get a place when things are more settled."

"You could stay here, if you wanted," she offered.

I looked up at the building with its dirty brick face, boarded windows, rusting fire escape.

"How can you make an offer like that?" I asked. "You only just met me and you're making all sorts of offers. I could be anything. Somebody who really needs an asylum."

"Sure," she said. "But you aren't."

"How do you know?"

"Am I wrong?"

"No," I said. "But you could be."

"Have you looked at yourself in a mirror lately?" she asked.

She took my hand and led me to a window beside the building's entrance.

"Look."

I saw myself and then next to me a dark, pretty girl wearing blue jeans and boots, a coarse woollen scarf wrapped around her neck, a heavy blue jacket. Behind us were parked cars.

"Not at me," she said. "At you, with your neatly parted hair and little blue blazer."

"So?"

"I'm not wrong about things like this," she said.

Her apartment was narrow and long with a floor to ceiling window at one end and a steel sliding door at the other. The roof was very high and run with pipes and long-abandoned pulleys, and for lights there were canisters the size of dustbin lids with large glaring bulbs that you turned on and off by pulling on a rope. There was a knee-high refrigerator in one corner and a little gas stove with its own cylinder in another.

"This is quaint," I said.

"Quaint good or quaint bad?"

"Is this meant to be a place to live?" I asked. "I mean, are you supposed to be living here?"

She was taken aback.

"Of course I am," she said. "I have a landlord and everything. It used to be a warehouse where they kept stuff. Sometimes you can still smell the things that have been here. But of course it's an apartment."

I thought I may have offended her. She walked to the window and began to lift it.

"I didn't mean to criticize."

The air smelled vaguely of sawdust, that and seawater. It was all somehow familiar.

"My father had a warehouse like this in South Africa," I said. "He exported things to Europe and America."

"What kind of things?"

"Things," I said. "Cloves, ivory, wood, pepper."

"Does he still?" she asked.

"It became difficult with the boycotts," I said. "And he died last year."

"I'm sorry," she said. "Is your mother okay?"

"She's still in South Africa," I said. "She can't leave yet."

"Why?"

"She just can't."

"Sisters and brothers?"

"Just my sister, Bridget."

"What does she do, Bridget?" Tesseba asked.

I paused.

"Bridget's in jail," I told her.

❦

Whatever it is I have with Tesseba, whatever we started that day, it's almost twenty years now, the twenty years I have been an American, or in America, and Tesseba enters every measure I make of my years on this continent. Almost everything I have seen I have told, at one time or another, to her. It is her face that draws each of my days to a close. But even as we stand in the terminal waiting for the flight from London, the one that will bring my mother and her odious husband Arnold, I look across at her and wonder what it is that holds us together.

"They're late," she says.

"Maybe they missed the flight," I suggest.

"That's wishful thinking," she says. "Nobody's come out from London yet."

A woman pushes a trolley through the international arrivals door and Tesseba asks where she's coming from.

"Madrid," the woman says.

"What was the weather like?" Tesseba asks.

"Nice. Like here," the woman says.

Before I know it they're speaking Spanish, Tesseba and this woman, and I turn away. Tesseba's people are Spanish, or Catalan, she likes to say.

"It's not their flight," Tesseba confirms when the woman has moved on.

"I gathered that," I say.

7

"Are you annoyed about something?" Tesseba asks.

"Of course not," I say. "Should I be?"

"Don't play semantic games," she says. "Sometimes you get the look."

"Don't start, Tess," I say. "We've got a week filled with domestic debates ahead of us. We don't need to add our own."

"Don't you start either, you," she says.

We smile. It is impossible not to love Tesseba, I think.

The international arrivals doors open and out come my mother, Helga, and my stepfather, Arnold. Tesseba sees them first and gestures in their direction, and then I see them too. They're not hard to spot, of course, Helga with her inappropriately jet-black hair and excessive makeup, Arnold with his silver beard and monocle. He's also in a wheelchair for some reason and for a moment I feel concern. Not for him. For her.

But he looks exactly the same as usual and no one has said anything about an accident or an illness. The man is almost eighty but he can outwalk me. They're arguing, you can see from the agitated expression on my mother's face and her pursed lips, so involved in whatever it is they are bickering about that they forget even to look up and find us. But eventually Helga does and she sees me, and then she sees Tesseba. I can tell she is surprised. My mother has long since lost the ability to dissemble.

"Darling," she says extravagantly as they reach us. "How lovely of you to pick us up."

"I said I'd be here," I say.

"And Theresa," she adds. "What a nice surprise."

"It's Tesseba, Ma," I say.

It is no coincidence that the first words out of her mouth are bound to make Tesseba uneasy. I look across at Tesseba in her turquoise shirt and white canvas pants, at her long hair hanging in loose curls down her back. Her hair is threaded with silver now, not enough to change its chestnutty look but enough so that the silver strands stand out, reminders perhaps that she is no longer a girl.

"Hello Arnie," I say. "What's with the wheelchair?"

Almost in unison my mother and Arnold tell me to be quiet. There's a porter wheeling him and from the way they glance over at him there's something they don't want him to know. He's a black teenager with an earring.

"I can take you to the curb only," the boy says.

"That'll be fine," Arnold says.

He fishes extravagantly in his jacket for his wallet, pulls it out, and from a thick wad of notes peels off a single dollar bill.

"Thanks, kid," he says.

The boy is temporarily taken aback. He takes the dollar as if it were dirty and pushes Arnold across the terminal in silence.

"We'll go and get the car," I say.

"He can walk," my mother whispers irritably. "Why isn't Bridget here?"

"Leora had a gym meet," I say.

"Oh," my mother says. "I guess Tibor didn't want to go by himself."

There are a dozen ways I could respond but I say nothing. I made a vow with myself years ago that I would stop arguing with my mother. For the most part I have been able to keep it.

After my father died and we lost Gordonwood my mother moved with Baptie, the Zulu housemaid, to an apartment on the Durban beachfront and they lived there together, in their separate worlds but somehow dependent on each other, until Arnold came along. I know she was unhappy — I was here, Bridget was in London — but it has always been inexplicable to me how she could have married this man. Money isn't everything and never was to her before, but so far as I can see it's all Arnold has to offer, and his bombast is very difficult to take. He's going on now about a Bentley he used to own in Durban — I have no idea how he's come to the subject — and I'm only half tuned in until I realize it's a bridge, of sorts, to some other topic. He's been broadly hinting for weeks that a large part of the reason for their coming to Boston now is that there is something important he wants to discuss with me. He has refused to be more specific on the phone.

"I wonder where that Bentley is today?" he says. "Probably still going."

No one responds.

"Some African gentleman is probably reveling in its pleasures," he says with a sigh. "Along with everything else."

Helga can't resist taking the bait.

"Well, don't they deserve something too?" she demands. "Haven't they been shut out for long enough? I can imagine you'd have a thing or two to say if you were in their shoes."

"Mom's so excitable these days," Arnold says. "I keep telling her nothing's worth getting so heated up about, but she doesn't listen."

I cut my mother off before she can respond.

"Why were you in a wheelchair?" I ask.

10

He's walking quite normally beside me now, carrying an overnight bag in one hand and a walking stick under his arm.

"I'll tell you in a minute," he says. "But you must remind me later to tell you what arrangements I've made for you in Africa. It's critically important for Mom."

I don't know what he's talking about and I really don't want to know what it is that Arnold thinks he can do for any of us. He's filled with offers, my mother's second husband, but he never delivers on any of them. And when it comes to Africa there's something about it I guard, something private, something I want him to stay out of.

"Why the wheelchair?" I ask again.

"It's quite simple really," he says. "You call the airline and tell them you can't stand for more than a few minutes at a time, and they lay on a wheelchair for you. You should try it. When everyone else is standing around and waiting, you sit in comfort and then they wheel you right to your destination. I mean, you pay for it, you might as well get all the service you can."

"Except that it's not honest," my mother says to no one in particular.

"Mom disapproves," he continues, "but —"

"I do not," my mother interjects. "You do as you see fit. I only said —"

"I'm teaching your mother how to travel," Arnold interrupts. "For instance, she always packs far too much. I say, the difference between a tourist and a traveler is the amount of clothing they pack. When we left London —"

"I suppose you think I never traveled before I met you," Helga snaps.

"It's the little tips that make all the difference," Arnold continues. "Like ordering kosher food on the plane. It's always better, and usually served first. Mom ate all of her own and most of mine."

I notice with a strange sense of satisfaction that his cravat has come loose at the back and flaps about his neck like a flag.

"Will you cut your cackle," my mother says.

"Please," I say. "Will you both please."

"Mom just won't learn," Arnold says.

I see Helga clench her fists at her side, shake her shoulders in frustration.

At last we reach the car, Tesseba's new Mercedes, and she unlocks the doors and goes around to open the trunk. Just as she passes out of earshot my mother hisses: "You might have told us she would be here. We've brought nothing for her."

And Tesseba, in an instant of privacy as we close the suitcases in the trunk, asks: "Didn't you tell them?"

❦

I sometimes wonder what Tesseba must think — really think in recesses of her mind she doesn't disclose to me — of this lumbering entourage.

Her family lives in Providence, her parents and two brothers and an extended collection of aunts and uncles, several grandparents, constantly drifting through a rambling clapboard house behind Brown University, where her father teaches. Her grandmother speaks no English and is hard of hearing, but Tesseba makes herself understood and when it comes to me Grandma's filled with handclasps and arm squeezes and knowing nods.

Usually Tesseba goes to see them on her own but when I go with her I am struck by how effortlessly they all seem to pick up where they left off. There are no extravagant greetings or effusive goodbyes, and yet their very casualness confirms that their separations are transient, unimportant, that they are never far from each others' thoughts. The speeches they make on Christmas Eve and the special cakes they bake for Easter, the aunties in black dresses and uncles with gnarled hands, these are alien to me and yet very much a part of her.

Perhaps it is the unabashed foreignness of her family that makes Tesseba seem so American.

"Music video," she explains to her grandmother. "*Niños escuchando musica de video. No esta supuesto aser una estoria.* Not supposed to be a story."

Grandma chuckles, takes Tesseba's hand, nods vigorously at me. "*Una chica buena,*" she says. "*Una mujer fuerte.*"

And though all along a silent censor wonders what I am doing among them, they have come to accept me, her family, even her brothers Marco and Ric. You can sense it in the offhand way they greet me.

"Yo, Danno," Ric will say, scarcely looking up. "Take a load off."

"Hi Ricky," Tesseba behind me might say, throwing into his lap some flyer she's picked off the grass. "Is that Tia Dodo's car out front?"

"Close, Tata," Ric will respond. "They're both green."

On the Fourth of July her father and brothers wrap themselves in red, white, and blue aprons and cook paella for their neighbors and friends. They dig a pit in the yard and fill it with coals, and on a pan the size of a manhole cover they build a mountain of rice and shell-fish and tend it with spatulas as big as shovels. Ric, standing for a moment to the side as he drinks a beer, puts his arm around Tesseba.

"Do you think we've made enough?" he asks.

Tesseba takes his bottle, sips from it, gives it back.

"Not if you're expecting the National Guard."

"What kind of food did you have in Africa?" he asks me.

I'm not sure how to answer this. Baptie made us roasts and shepherd's pie, macaroni and cheese, even knishes and pickled herring. Sometimes she made curries, milk tarts, *koeksisters* soaked in honey.

"Pretty much the same as here," I say.

"What about ostrich eggs?" he asks. "I hear they're huge. Taste like chewy omelets. Got to get me one of them ostrich eggs."

"Nope," I say.

"Lion stew? Pickled tiger? Braised elephant?" he goes on.

"Afraid not."

"Wildebeest burgers? Rhino dogs?"

"Only on special occasions," I say.

"What kind of Africa did you live in, anyway?" he says and goes back to tending the paella.

"Do they have something like Independence Day there?" Tesseba's father, sensing that Ric has been too brusque, asks. "I imagine they have something similar."

"The Day of the Covenant I suppose comes closest," I tell him. "It's the day God cemented his alliance with the Boers by helping them to wipe out a Zulu army."

"God's proving pretty unreliable, if that's the case," Ric says from the other side of the charcoal pit.

I stop talking. It seems so odd to be discussing this in a garden in Rhode Island.

"You celebrated that?" Tesseba, glancing at her brother, asks.

"What do you think?"

"Do you miss it?" she asks. "South African holidays or whatever?"

"No," I say.

And that is true, but it's not the complete truth. Sometimes when I'm making a note in my diary I can't help seeing that it's May 31 and thinking that in Durban they're celebrating Republic Day, or December 16, the Day of the Covenant. I just do. July Fourth, for all the hoopla at Tesseba's parents, isn't there inside me. What is especially ironic is that in the new South Africa the days I remember aren't holidays anymore either. Only for me. Days to remember and then pointedly to disregard. When I glimpse Nelson Mandela's face I feel pride in him as if he were somehow mine too, but also misgivings, am swept aside by events that affect me deeply, and also not at all. In the photographs and news footage I search the out-of-focus faces for one that is familiar, something I might recognize. It is never there.

Tesseba paints when the light is right, talks to her cats, sings songs to herself with words she plucks right from the air. She once said that before she met me she was happier than she has been since, not because of anything I have done but because of how I think.

"And there's no going back," she added. "Nothing that has happened can be undone."

I do not understand how this can be so, how I can have made her less happy and yet have kept her, how it is that she makes me feel blessed and yet at times trapped too. It is an odd sensation, though, trying now to imagine a free-spirited Tesseba mixing paints, hugging her brothers, wrapping a gift, and also oblivious to my existence. In fact, it is impossible.

❦

Tesseba starts the car and we move slowly through the lot to the airport exit. Arnold is sitting beside her, his arm draped over the back of the seat, his fingertips just touching her bare shoulder. I am in the back with Helga.

"Nice car, this," Arnold says. "How much do they cost these days?"

He is diabolical. He knows that this is not Tesseba's kind of car and so he wants to know the circumstances in which I have bought it for her. He also guesses, correctly, that she does not have the slightest idea how much it costs. You just have to look at Tesseba to know that.

"I don't recall," she says.

She searches in her bag for her purse as the attendant waits, and then, just as she finds it, Arnold takes his wallet from his jacket and without opening it offers to pay.

"It's okay," Tesseba says, and he puts his wallet away.

"Just a range," he says.

"What?" Tesseba asks.

"A range. What cars like this cost. Not this car. Just in general." Helga senses that something is awry.

"Would you mind turning off the air conditioning?" she asks. "You Americans think nothing of going from the heat into a freezer."

"Just turn it down a bit," Arnold says.

"Off will do fine," Helga snaps.

And so it continues the whole way home.

This is the thing with Tesseba and me. We're married and have been for years, but we're not really married either and most people, ourselves included, don't know what to make of it. I accepted her offer, in the end, the one she made on the bus, the one to marry her but not marry marry her, and so we went through the whole elaborate affair with the justice of the peace and the witnesses and the affidavits, and there wasn't much need of further charade except that we had to stay together for several months to convince the immigration people that our marriage was real, and those went by very quickly.

"You can leave anytime you want, you know," she kept saying after that. "You're not obligated to stay just because you think I did you a favor."

"Do you want me to leave?" I'd ask.

"You'd know it if I did," she'd reply.

At some point we began sleeping in the same bed, and then eating together, going places together, and without ever declaring ourselves, deciding to be man and wife, we fell into a gap somewhere between strangeness and intimacy, something like old friends, distant relatives, former lovers. I can't say how it would have been if things had been different at the outset, if I had met her under different circumstances or if she had not made her offer or if I had not accepted it, but it's all so mixed together now I can't parse out any one piece of the puzzle and say how it would stand all on its own. In a supermarket a good-looking stranger strikes a conversation with her while I am distracted and when I turn back I see that he is admiring her, seeking a response, and I am jealous. I do not always want the things that I have come to take for granted, but something within me says I would have difficulty doing without any part of them.

I do know one thing for sure, though, and it is the one thing I have never mentioned to Tesseba. On the afternoon I supposedly married her I was in love with someone else, and I have been in love with someone else every moment since then, and no matter what happens, what I do, what time passes, my love remains snagged on a person other than Tesseba. She is someone whose name, except perhaps inadvertently or in passing or in some other innocent context, Tesseba had never heard until that last visit to London, and the saying of it, what happened after that, changed something between Tesseba and me that has never quite changed back.

I am talking about Santi. She is framed by shadows as I see her, with stripes of moonlight cutting through the staves of the fence and crossing her face and cotton dress. She stands expectantly, her hands in mine, waits for me to say something, to find some solution to the crisis I have created for her.

"This is not over," I had told her. "We will find a way."

The sky of Africa is a dome which holds only us, Santi and me, until the hedge shudders and someone whistles. There is a mystery in it, in the things that might have happened and that did not, and I have never stopped thinking that at the heart of the mystery, if I had ever made the journey to the heart of the mystery, I would have found a good piece of myself.

❦

"When are we seeing Bridget?" Helga asks.

"Heavens, sweetie," Arnold says. "Your kids have their own lives. They can't just drop everything because their mother comes to town. I specifically told Gregory not to come to the airport."

"As if he would have come anyway," Helga says.

"They're coming as soon as Leora's gym competition is over," Tesseba says quickly.

"What is it?" Helga asks. "Something important?"

"It's a match between several high schools," I say. "She's very good, Leora. With any luck she'll make an Olympic team before she's much older."

"Bridget would have made the South African team," Helga says immediately.

I could kick myself. I should anticipate better by this stage.

"Really?" Arnold says. "The South African team?"

He knows why she didn't. He's heard the story a dozen times. He just wants to string it out, make sure we don't pass too lightly over Bridget's little tragedy.

"They should be over by six," Tesseba says.

Helga can't leave it alone.

"Yes, she would have," she insists. "To this day I don't know why she allowed herself to be derailed like she did. She was as talented as any kid in the whole country. The whole country. Achh," she says bitterly and turns to look out the window.

"She was," I agree.

She's very thin now, my sister, Bridget, sticklike almost, and sometimes as I watch her moving about her kitchen or involved in conversation I am struck by how it seems almost as if two people have inhabited her body, the gymnast walking about Gordonwood in leotards, stopping every now and again to perform snatches of a routine as it comes to her, and the toneless mother, unflappable, unemotional, perhaps a little disengaged.

We're close in a way, Bridget and I, but not like in the early days in Boston. Back then, not long after she had married Tibor and when I was still doing odd jobs to support myself, we shared a kind of bleak, black humor that was lost on both Tibor and Tesseba, a cama-raderie that dissipated as we settled down to our lives as they now are.

"Baptie," she'd call when we were done eating. "You can take the dishes now." And when only silence came back from her cramped kitch-enette, that or the sounds of Tibor clunking around at the sink or mak-ing coffee, pointedly ignoring us, she'd add: "That lazy, cheeky girl."

It was back then that Bridget asked me about Santi. For a mo-ment I was surprised that she knew anything about Santi and me and what had happened, but then I felt relieved too, happy, in fact, to hear it all said. Before too long though I heard a skepticism in Bridget's voice, an unexpected iciness that made me want to shut the subject down, then and forever.

"Are you sure you know everything you should about this girl?" she asked.

"What are you getting at?" I demanded. "What is it that you think I should know that I don't?"

She didn't want to press it, Bridget, didn't want to answer.

"Who she really was," was all she would say.

"I don't know what you're implying," I told her. "But I suspect you're disapproving for very unattractive reasons. I thought we'd left that a long way behind."

"Of course I'm not," she insisted. "In any event, it's water over the dam."

It isn't, really, at least not for me. But if I were to tell Bridget to-day how big a role Santi still plays in my life I know how she would react.

"If she really meant that much to you, you would have done something about it long ago," she would say.

"I always thought I would," I'd have to tell her. "If it weren't for Tesseba I would have. And I can't say I still won't."

"So maybe you will then," would be Bridget's eminently sensible response.

But nothing has kept me from daydreaming. I once thought, especially when I first came here, on the flight that brought me from Johannesburg, for instance, or on the morning I first landed in Boston, that it was only a matter of time before I saw Santi again, that once the turmoil was over, transitions completed, we would have our chance, she and I, together. I would see her again in some airport somewhere, watch her as she came towards me, we would embrace in full view of everyone, unleash our questions and our answers in hurried "but I thoughts" and "didn't you knows." She would sit beside me in a car, we would hold hands, we would eat and we would drink as freely as if this were all unremarkable, I would touch her knee, she would brush my hand, we would, eventually, leave our bed perfectly tussled, all openly. What was taboo would be commonplace, except to us, especially not to us.

But so much happened, and though I believe as Bridget does that in the end you do what you really want to do, sometimes there is not such clarity about what your heart seeks that allows you to act with certainty and resolution.

⊰⊱

I grew up in a town called Durban which is on the Indian Ocean and in a province which the Portuguese explorer Vasco da Gama called Natal because he came upon it on a Christmas morning. It already had a name, of course, something like "Place of the Zulus," or KwaZulu,

21

and in the new South Africa it is called KwaZulu-Natal. It will, in all likelihood, eventually be called again, more simply, KwaZulu. It is, after all, interlopers aside, the place of the Zulus.

I could say it is a vapid swamp of a place, a rundown little backwater with yellowing beaches and torpid palm trees, toneless high rises, Victorian buildings, a strangely dated gentility in some things and a frontier roughness in others, but that is only part of it. There was once a colorful market, beaded rickshaw men, a colonial ceremony to civic events and a hierarchy set in stone, but these are, I am told, discarded or in flux or gone, deemed unsafe or incorrect or impolitic, and that is another part of it. We lived at Gordonwood, a dilapidated mansion high on a ridge overlooking the city, quite separate from it in some ways, separate from it and completely entwined at the same time, and that is another part of it. My grandfather was rich while my father died defeated and disgraced, when I was seventeen I fell in love with someone I was forbidden to love and I let her go believing it was for a short while only and for the best, and then it was all so hurried and disjointed and unraveled I cannot remember any of it without bitterness, and that may be the rest of it. Bridget has some of the details, Baptie others, Helga, to the extent she can remember anything clearly in the face of Arnold's relentless onslaught, knows it all better than any of us do. But what Helga knows is now quite inaccessible.

One of the things Arnold does is prevent us from delving into the past. We are so busy listening to his banter, waiting while he and Helga skirmish, that there is never an opportunity for us to reflect together, to talk openly once and for all, about anything. What Arnold hears he will surely abuse and repeat and belittle. And so we just sit and listen and wait, and at the end of each day we go to bed exhausted, taunted further by Arnold's whistles as he showers and changes, prepares to take his place beside my mother in some bed or other.

I do not know what Helga thinks, really, even as I guess at what she is thinking.

❦

As we reach the gate at the edge of my house a great tiredness sweeps over me and then I see that it has affected the others too, that Helga's eyelids are flickering, that even Arnold has become quiet. I turn to look at my mother and see her looking out the window, faintly perspiring, one arm on her green cosmetic case and the other on the armrest. I cannot help wondering what my father would think if he were to see her now.

Tesseba reaches under the dashboard to activate the gate and we pause as it swings slowly open.

"Wonderful bloody things," Arnold says.

"It is convenient," Tesseba says.

"We should get one for the house in London," Arnold says.

Helga comes to life.

"We don't have a gate in London," she says.

"For the garage," Arnold says.

"What do we need it for?" she asks.

There's a certain aggression in her tone. They're like terriers, these two, always on the lookout for a chance to scuffle.

What they don't know, of course, is that the whole subject of gate clickers has its own history with Tesseba and me. Perhaps it is intuitive with Arnold, his ability to sense one's pressure points, never to miss an opportunity to ferret out one's discomforts. Tesseba's clicker was one of the things she stacked in a pile on my side of the bed on the day she said she was leaving. I remember looking at it and wondering when she had unscrewed it from her car, that day, or the day before, or when.

"I can't live like this anymore," she'd said.

"Like what?" I asked. "What's changed to make you suddenly unhappy?"

"It's just all wrong," she said. "And maybe it's my fault, including what happened in London. But I'm tired of this, of pretending to see things the way you see them, that we can go on living like this, like friends who sleep together, that we're beyond making the normal promises that marriage is meant to be about."

"What more do you want?" I asked. "We are married. We're beyond questions of promises."

"No, we're not," she said. "I'm only thirty-nine and I'm not beyond anything. I'm young enough to look for the things that will make me happy."

"What more is it that you want from me?" I asked again.

"I don't know," she said. "Certainly I don't want anything you don't want to give. But if I were to say what it would feel like I would say that I want you to leap off a bridge for me, not to settle for me. I want you to choose me, to cherish me, to love me without holding yourself back."

"I don't know what you mean," I said. "I'm not the type of person who leaps off bridges. You know that I love you."

She shook her head.

"That's not what I'm saying," was all she would say. "I have to sort out what I want and then I have to get it for myself."

Things have a way of developing a momentum of their own and even if it sounds unduly passive there's a certain comfort in just letting them take their course. I can't say I even felt sad as she walked around the bedroom checking the closets for the things she wanted to take. It was more a sense of numbness, some kind of resignation.

"You really can stay here," she'd said that first day when I met her on the bus and she'd taken me to her loft behind South Station. I was so young then, thin, in gray flannel trousers and brown lace-up shoes, a navy jacket with only a sweater underneath, a tie. Her face then was as smooth as a child's, innocent, I think now, like a child's.

"How would that work?" I asked. "How would you have privacy?"

"I'll get what I need," she said. "The building's half empty anyway, except it isn't heated on some of the floors."

"You make it sound like a challenge," I said.

She looked at me for a while without saying anything and then pulled off her boots and crossed the room to the little stove.

"What will you do if you don't get asylum?" she asked.

"I don't know," I said.

"Will you go back?"

"No."

"Do you want to stay for coffee or something?" she asked.

I think it was at that moment that I realized how truly innocent her offers were, that I could say no and leave her forever and that I didn't want to. There was Santi, yes, but she was so far away, back where it was warm and where she knew the streets, recognized faces, where she was in danger too but a different kind of danger, not the kind that threatened at any moment to wipe clean a slate with everything she knew written on it. And it had always been impossible. By what miracle would it be possible now?

And so on the day Tesseba left I found myself thinking, lying on our bed in an empty room: Maybe now I have what I have been waiting for.

Tesseba pulls the car slowly up to the house and parks it beside one of the stone pillars at the entrance.

"What arrangements have you made with Gregory?" Arnold asks as he hauls himself up from the car and runs his eye over my house.

"I said you would call him when you were settled," I say. "He should be at home now."

"How is he?" Arnold asks.

Gregory is Arnold's son from another marriage. He lives on an estate west of Boston and I never see him unless Arnold is in town. We have an understanding, Gregory and I, that under different circumstances we might have been friends but that as it is, it's impossible. The stresses of our connectedness are simply too great.

"He's fine so far as I know," I say.

"You two don't see much of each other?" Helga says. "You're stepbrothers, after all."

"I'm a little too far along in my life for new brothers," I say.

"Nonsense," Helga says.

I can see that Helga is watching carefully as Tesseba takes keys from her bag and opens the front door, leads us all into the house very much as a hostess would, as she would if she were indeed leading guests into her own home. Arnold is about to say something but my mother clasps his forearm and squeezes it sharply.

We follow Tesseba indoors.

"It's exactly the same," Helga exclaims. "You've changed nothing."

"Danny doesn't like change that much," Tesseba says wryly. She looks at me knowingly. "He likes things predictable."

"There's nothing wrong with that," Helga says.

Tesseba is about to respond but just shakes her head.

"I'll go make some tea," she says.

Arnold crosses the room, lifts a small statue from a shelf and examines it carefully. He is a caricature, I swear it.

"Where did you get this?" he asks.

"You gave it to me," I tell him.

It's like some sort of game, every time they come here.

"Do you know what this must be worth today?" he asks. "Have you any idea?"

"None at all," I say.

"Two thousand if it's worth a penny," he says. "Maybe three."

"What counts isn't what it's worth," Helga says. "It's that you use and enjoy it."

She straightens her hair in a mirror, looks quickly in the direction Tesseba's gone, comes right up to me.

"What's going on with you?" she asks. "We thought this was over at last."

"Ma, don't do this," I say. "Tesseba and I will sort things out ourselves."

"Would I interfere?" she asks hotly. "You're not a spring chicken anymore and neither is she. So what is it you're doing with your life and with hers?"

"Now is not a good time to discuss it," I say.

Arnold is watching us avidly.

"You should always treat others the way you would want them to treat you," he volunteers from across the room.

"Are we going to have some time to ourselves?" my mother asks.

"Of course," I say.

"I want you to listen to what Arnie has to say," she whispers urgently. "On another subject. It has to do with my father's money."

"Oh?" I say.

"Yes," Arnold says, walking across to us.

He's an old man and when it suits him he professes to be infirm. But he hasn't missed a word.

"If you don't do something quick, old Walter's fortune will be the dowry of piccanins," he says.

"Please don't talk like that," I say.

"I'm serious," he says. "Cattle feed."

The phone rings; it's Bridget.

"Darling," my mother shouts. "Where are you?"

"I think I'll call Gregory," Arnold says loudly. Instead he wanders through my house, lifts things off shelves, appraises.

"Your clock's slow," he says as he ambles back into the foyer. "The one next to the stairs."

"It's not slow," I say. "It's stopped."

"You shouldn't keep something around that doesn't work," he says.

"It only needs to be wound," I say. "There's nothing wrong with it."

This is not true. I have noticed that the clock seems to be broken.

"I'm going to help Tesseba," I say.

"What time is Bridget coming?" Tesseba asks when she sees me. She is setting snacks out on a tray.

"How on earth did things get to be like this?" I ask in response.

⋯

You start with this big house on the top of a hill. It is a craggy, African hill of a thing, red-earthed, yellow-grassed, barren looking. You add several other houses, smaller and more modest with Morris cars and an Austin or two parked outside, and of course groups of servants sitting in the shade. You can add a very blue sky, heavy-handed sunlight, a great ball of steam that builds over the Indian Ocean and slowly unwinds over the city. Its leading edge reaches into the sky like a pillar of light, but as it unrolls it licks the whole plain and leaves behind a sluggish sheen. Mirrors cloud, bricks moisten.

I don't know who built Gordonwood, what this person could have had in mind when he appropriated a piece of wild land on a ridge, decided that it was destined to be his, and set about building a house quite maladapted to ordinary living. What kind of lord he wished to be, what kind of overwrought European contraption he dreamed of planting on a craggy African hill, and why, we didn't think to ask. Gordonwood looked like a castle, a relic from another time, another continent certainly, even a fortress with its malformed turrets and wrought iron mantels. It didn't belong where it was but, like so many things, after it became ours it did begin to belong and even to seem, somehow, inevitable.

I learned later, of course, that it never really was ours either. My grandfather paid for it as a gift to my mother, though one that came with many strings. All I saw of this was the way he would inspect it each time he came to visit, make the same ostentatious tour of his collateral, tapping on walls, looking in closets, picking at loose pieces of stone. He would sniff, crumble a piece of masonry between his fingers, throw it angrily into the garden.

"Madness," he would say. "Arrogance."

At dusk the house looked its best. That is when its imperfections were masked by shadows, when mud stains on the walls looked like patches of shade, when the red ants crawling about the verandas got lost in the sheen of the oxblood polish. And when it rained and water fell about in sodden ribbons the air inside became moist too, moist and sweet. From deep within the wooden beams, fragrances of polish and resin, years of careful dusting, seeped out, filled the house with a rich and distinctive fragrance.

"You've got to see the view," my father would say to anyone who visited. "This you've just got to see."

He would lead them up a winding little staircase to the cupola on the roof and tell them where to stand. First you see the lawn below, a tree shaped like an elephant's leg, and then your eyes move out over the unwieldy hedges, the rooftops in the distance, plunge off the ridge through a sheath of heat and mist to what looks like a tray of miniatures set on a ledge far below complete with toy trees, a railway line, the green oval of the racetrack at Greyville. On some nights you can see even farther, over the city, the buildings at the shore, the looming forested bluff on the far side of the bay, out beyond the misty deck lights of the ships waiting to enter the harbor, out, it seems, to where the earth curves and then drops from reach.

"I love this place," my father says. "It is a treasure."

"Maybe, Div," my mother replies. "But we need a place to live, too."

"Doesn't this do?" he asks. "It lacks for nothing."

"My father thinks otherwise," she says.

"That's his problem, isn't it?"

"I wish it were that simple," she says.

Arnold, on seeing a picture: "Rather shabby, don't you know. Had a painter once could do marvels with decrepit old arks like that. Name was . . . well I've forgotten it, don't you know."

On a school cricket trip to Rhodesia we travel for two days by train, from Durban to Pietermaritzburg, past Mooi River, Ladysmith, into the Transvaal, and then across the border through Botswana and into Rhodesia. At the South African–Botswana border the master gathers us all in the dining car.

"We are crossing out of South Africa in an hour's time," he says. "Then we'll be in Botswana for almost a full day before we reach Rhodesia. Botswana has an African government and while we're there you must watch what you say and how you speak to any official who boards the train, whatever his color. You are not at home now. Do you all understand?"

"Yes," we say. We are a little puzzled but not alarmed. What could happen?

Not more than an hour across the border we pull to a stop at a station that looks like nothing so much as a corrugated iron shed, a shelter for garden tools. From nowhere hawkers appear, they and groups of black children barely dressed and persistent in their demands for coins.

"*Baas, baas,*" they say. "Five cents, please. You got five cents?"

It is dusty outside and there is no shade anywhere. Inside the train it is gritty too and the windows are lined with sand. All one can see is bare earth, a scattering of scrubby bushes, no signs of settlement.

"Bugger off," someone in the fifth form shouts.

"Watch it," a prefect reminds him.

I see some of the senior boys huddled in the corner of our compartment lighting matches. They rush to the window, fling out a handful of pennies. As the kids rush to pick them up, they burn their hands.

"You're a bunch of fucking sadists," my friend Rupert says.

"What's that language you used?" a prefect asks.

Rupert says nothing. For the rest of the day he is confined to his compartment. Early that evening we cross out of Botswana and back into white Rhodesia and the warning is, presumably, lifted.

❦

Arnold finds us in the kitchen.

"What mischief are you up to now?" he jokes. "Faster, please," he adds, clapping his hands. "Work faster."

"Why don't you keep Mom company," I suggest. "Tess and I are just getting some tea and sandwiches together."

Arnold walks over to where Tesseba is standing, puts his hand on the back of her neck, peers over her shoulder.

"We've been eating since we left Sloane Square," he says, picking a piece of smoked turkey from the wrapper. "Mom and I don't need to eat again."

"It's all here anyway," Tesseba says.

Tesseba's opinion of Arnold has, of course, evolved since the night she met him. She doesn't like how free he is with his hands and she's more than weary of the constant bickering. Unlike me, though, she refuses to place blame.

"They're both damaged," she has said more than once.

I know too much to argue with Tesseba about other people's behavior. She is usually right. But my father was so unlike this noisy charlatan.

"You want to know something else?" she asked me.

"What?"

"You may be the first man I ever met who wants me to dislike his parents," she said.

But it is Tibor, Bridget's husband, who has called it most accurately in my opinion. When we first met Arnold — all of us, Bridget and Tibor and their daughter, Leora, and I that first time in London, that foolish expedition before we knew better when we agreed to let Arnold pay our way over for their wedding party as he's never failed to remind us — Tibor's concern turned out to be far more accurate than either Bridget's or mine.

"He will ruin her personality," Tibor said solemnly. "A woman can't live with a man like that without becoming submerged."

He was right, of course. Tibor often is. He is a Bulgarian and much older than Bridget, and there are times when I think I respect him more than any other man on earth. This doesn't mean we're unfailingly honest with him, Bridget and I. He knows some things, about Bridget's going to jail and my father's sudden death, for instance, but he doesn't know how he died, or why he did it, and we're so careful when we talk of my grandfather that I wouldn't be surprised if Tibor pictured him as a pleasant old man with a genial manner and white hair. One thing about Tibor is that he doesn't ask questions. He listens, nods, occasionally makes an observation.

Perhaps this is because of his profession. Tibor is a psychologist and he works as a vocational guidance counselor in the local school system. This also means that they don't have much money, Bridget and Tibor, and they live in a shabby little house a few blocks from the school. They never talk about money, though, but I notice things, like how many winters Bridget has worn the same coat and how cobbled together Leora's outfits sometimes seem.

"Come with us to Loehmann's," I said to Bridget once. "Tesseba's talked me into sitting on the husbands' bench by the door while she scavenges."

Bridget looked thoughtful.

"I don't think so," she said.

"Let me treat," I said. "I can't think of anything I'd prefer than to watch the two of you pick through the chaos and come up with outfits that look good."

"You don't need to make offers like that," Bridget said. "Tibor and I manage fine."

"I don't need to but I want to."

"It's okay, really."

"Can we take Leora at least?" I asked.

"Leave it," Bridget said, and there the matter rested.

In one sense I don't really care what Arnold thinks of me and Bridget and my family, but in another I obviously do. When Tibor offered to fetch them from the airport in his crumbling station wagon I said no, I'd do it, and when Bridget suggested we eat at her house, at the Formica table in her kitchen with its sticky countertops and broken telephone, I said no too.

I suspect a large part of the reason for this is that Arnold knew my father. If he wants to see how strong Silas Divin could have been, let him come to me. His weakling son Gregory has lived off trust funds all his life. My beautiful house I built from scratch.

❦

We can't get him out of the kitchen. My mother is still on the phone with Bridget in the hall, and Arnold is lurking around, watching what we're doing, commenting, helping himself to bits and pieces of food.

"Harrods is an amazing store," he says. "There's nothing you can't get there. I don't think you have anything like it in America."

"I'm sure we do," I say.

All of a sudden I'm a xenophobe.

"Really?" he says vaguely. "Of course now the Arabs own it, but then they own half of London anyway."

He pauses.

"Do they own much here?"

"I don't know," I say.

Tesseba arranges several plates on a tray and carries it out of the kitchen and into the study. The moment she's out the door Arnold moves right next to me and puts his hand on my shoulder.

"It's very important that we talk," he says.

"We will," I say, moving away. "You just got here. There will be plenty of time."

"I don't think you get the urgency of the situation in South Africa," he says. "Now that the euphoria there has died down people are beginning to realize that the place is in the hands of a bunch of chimpanzees. I'm well aware of your family's noble sentiments and all the rest of it, but the fact is that the place is falling apart and it's only going to get worse. Your grandfather's trust is over at last, thank God, and unless you do something soon you're going to lose it all. It doesn't matter to me, of course. I've done all the things I need to do. I'm set, and Gregory's set, and his children are set, and probably his grand-children too. I say this for you. For your own good."

"Arnold," I say impatiently. "I'm not going to talk politics with you. And I'll say again what I've said before. My grandfather's money in South Africa belongs to my mother and is looked after by profes-sionals. The law says you can't take capital out of the country. There's nothing I can do, and there's nothing I want to do."

"That's where you couldn't be more wrong," he says. "She's in the hands of certified idiots. If she weren't they'd have found a way to get her money out of South Africa years ago."

He helps himself to a slice of melon.

"Look," he says. "Don't you watch the news? There's a break-down of law and order. The Reserve Bank's become the private reserve of the schwartzes who run the place. The economy's up to crap. One of these days whatever they haven't stolen they're just going to confis-cate."

I ignore him for a moment, get to work tidying the kitchen, try to let it all go, try to stay calm.

"You're naive, man," he says. "I hate to say it, but you're naive. Like your mother."

I stop moving. It feels like I keep taking it and taking it but there must be a line drawn somewhere. I hear Tesseba walking back from the study.

"Just do me one favor?" I say.

"What?" he asks.

"I know you're a racist pig and it goes right over my head," I say. "You're comfortable being a carpetbagger and I'm not and there we just have to agree to differ. But do me one favor. Please don't talk like this, or about any of this, in front of Tesseba."

"For Pete's sake, why not?" he asks. "They're not your assets in a divorce."

My insult has gone right through him, though I know he'll remember it. When he strikes back it will be shrewish, and my mother will pay for it.

"I've asked you not to do something and that should be the end of it," I say sharply as Tesseba comes into the room.

She senses, of course, an atmosphere.

"I just don't see it," Arnold says and walks towards the door. "I'm only trying to help."

"What was all that about?" Tesseba asks quietly.

"God only knows," I say.

Arnold doesn't know it, and I would never give him the satisfaction of telling him, but in a way I've known him all my life. There was a time, if the truth be told, that I envied him. He owned a string of factories that made shoes and tents and plastics, not only in South Africa but also in other countries, in Rhodesia and the Congo and

Zambia, even in Europe. Everyone in Durban knew who he was in his shining Bentley with its uniformed chauffeur, with his beard which was then tinged with silver rather than perfectly white, his huge house near the British Governor General's overlooking Mitchell Park. When my mother made her hopeless run for Parliament he was there, a big donor in his silk hat and perfectly pressed trousers, paying courtly compliment as my father watched quietly, Tibor-like, from the sidelines. Arnold could not have agreed with a thing my mother represented then, given the contempt for Africans he expresses now, but his support was doubtless carefully considered and entirely personal. Perhaps he was hedging his bets on the apartheid issue, appearing to condemn it as he profited so richly from it, or perhaps even then he thought that somehow, someday, he might have the chance to call in his chits against my mother herself.

But she welcomed his support, I remember that, feted him, complimented him in public, happily accepted the money and the endorsements. There was a sense of a huge restrained power in it, no doubt, in the crisply maintained mansion, the fleet of cars, the way vast wealth accorded him the best tables in restaurants, the royal box in theaters, brought him to sit applauding on the stage at political rallies where he gained merit even as he did not accept a syllable of what was being said. In the old white South Africa, perhaps more so than elsewhere, money bought mystique.

I dreamed about my father last night, a dream I have had before, that he is not dead at all but instead abandoned and desperately needy in some faraway place. In my dream I am an adult, not much different in appearance and circumstances than is true, but the years seem to have passed without a thought of him until, in my dream, I come upon him suddenly and without even realizing at first who he is or why he looks so familiar. And then, just as recognition sinks in and I understand what I have to do, I awaken and the chance to do anything slips away.

—❧❧❧—

"Bridget will be here at six," Helga announces.

"That's what we told you," I say. "How did Leora do?"

"I forgot to ask," my mother says. "I'm sure she did beautifully."

"She's fabulous, Ma," I say. "Really fabulous."

"And why shouldn't she be?" Helga asks. "She's Bridget's daughter."

"She also works very hard," I say, defending my niece now against my mother's onslaught. "You wouldn't believe how seriously they make kids take their athletics here."

"They didn't in Durban?" Helga challenges. "Bridget spent her whole youth in the gym."

She pauses.

"Until she threw it all away."

"It's different," I say. "More scientific now. Very competitive."

My mother ignores what I have just said. She looks over her shoulder and then says quickly: "I want you to listen very carefully to what Arnie has to say. He knows what he's doing."

There is an urgency to her manner, as if an opportunity is slipping away even as I delay.

"What new could he possibly have to tell me?" I ask. "I've heard all his stories at least twice, and know more than I'll ever need to what he thinks on most subjects."

39

Arnold is somewhere else in the house and Tesseba is not in the room. My mother and I have come upon a moment of privacy and I find myself prying for a glimpse of the old Helga. She ignores my comment even as she seems momentarily more relaxed in the peace that comes of not having Arnold around.

"Apparently he and his cronies have set up a way of getting money out of South Africa legally," she says. "He's gotten out millions already. Millions. And ours sits there like a pile of shit."

My mother swears often. I think it is a pattern she has come upon as the easiest way to emphasize something before Arnold cuts her off or deflects what she is trying to say.

"Like shit," she repeats.

"Not legally," I say.

"Almost legally," she says crossly. "In any event they're all doing it and there's no reason we shouldn't."

"If it's illegal there is a reason."

"It's for you kids," she says. "Maybe you don't need it but Bridget could use it. When I see how little she has, it makes me sick."

"She's happy, Ma."

"Tibor has nothing," she says. "And he'll never have anything. And my father's millions are there for the asking."

"You're allowed to take some of the income out," I say.

"I don't care about me," she says. "In any event it's *babkes*. Nothing."

"But you have enough, don't you?" I insist, a little concerned. "I mean for your own needs."

"I don't know what enough is these days," she says. "Arnold makes it sound like I contribute nothing. I don't care about that. What

I care about is you kids. I look at how easy Gregory has it and it makes me sick. That little bastard hasn't had to work a day in his life and Bridget struggles and has nothing and you work like a dog, and all the while my father's money sits there. Arnold tells me that even with all the frittering away, the trust still has more than forty-five million rand in it. That's over six million dollars. My father came to South Africa as a boy with nothing, not speaking a word of English, and by working like a dog and denying himself everything he built a little empire. So whose is it now? Not ours? Arnold's? If it's not ours who owns anything?"

She pauses, on the verge of tears, takes a tissue from her pocket.

"I'm not saying it's not ours," I say without conviction.

"That's nice of you," she mumbles.

"It would be nice if we could legitimately get it out," I say. "And if it were possible Nerpelow would have done it a long time ago."

"Nerpelow's a senile old man," my mother says of my father's lifelong friend and lawyer. "Listen to Arnie."

She's crying now, desperate. Her tissue is a shredded mess.

"You kids break my heart," she says. "I raised you too decent for your own good."

"I'll listen to Arnie," I say. "Does anyone ever have a choice?"

She pauses, surprised perhaps at my concession, and then she smiles.

"He really is something else, isn't he?" she says. "What did I think I was getting myself into?"

A glimpse of the old Helga too, then. And I cannot help thinking what effect it would have on my mother if I were indeed somehow able to rescue some of this great bounty for her and for Bridget, perhaps even for me too though I can't think how it would change anything in my life. Perhaps, I think, Arnold would treat her with more respect or at least stop his bullying if she could show, somehow, that for all his bombast she once was, or could have been, or is, independent of him.

❧❦❧

We sit in my study and drink our tea, pick at the sandwiches Tesseba has made for us. Tesseba has long, slender fingers, wears many silver rings, a silver bangle. She jingles softly as she eats, holds her sandwich sideways and bites off the corners, listens without saying much.

"I feel like a visitor in this house," she has said more than once, and there in the armchair she does look like one, like someone who is not in her own room but has settled comfortably into someone else's. She has long, brown legs, a slender waist, a face that is often somber but is also wonderfully appealing. Her eyes are dark, her hair perhaps too long, her nose narrow and straight. On her face now too are signs of the faintest creases, vague little lines at her eyes, a shadow that runs from the edge of her mouth down to her chin. I can't see age in myself, but I do see it reflected in Tesseba's face.

Once, a long time ago, after I'd found a place of my own and Tesseba's loft had become her private retreat, somewhere she went to paint or to be alone, I was in an elevator when a striking woman caught my eye and held it unabashedly through a drop of thirty floors. When we reached the ground and everyone else had stepped out only she and I remained, and when I asked her to have a cup of coffee with me she accepted.

She was in a similar field professionally, and quite irreverent. Her name was Linda. We took the afternoon off and ended up sitting on a seawall below the Kennedy Library exchanging intimacies with a candor that surprised me. I told her about Tesseba, she told me about a man in her life, but we ended the day at a motel in Quincy anyway, made love awkwardly, and when it was over lay on the hard bed with its starchy sheets and talked until it was quite late.

I arrived home after midnight. Tesseba was in bed reading, a mug of peppermint tea at her side.

"I was worried," she said. "Where were you?"

"At a meeting," I told her. "It ran over. We went out for something to eat."

"Are you okay?" she asked. "You look tired."

I said I was fine, went into another room, undressed, showered, came to bed. And it was as I slid in beside her that I realized she had no suspicions at all, would no sooner have guessed what I'd done as have done it herself. As I moved up close to her, felt her stomach under her nightgown, her breasts, her unsuspecting throat, I knew I could not do such a thing again, that it would change me irreparably to see her face as she learned that I may not be who she had thought, that it was too troubling even to imagine how she might look if ever she were to suspect it.

"Is everything all right?" she asked again as I held her, turned her on her back, leaned over to kiss her face.

"Fine," I said. "Everything's fine."

⋙⋘

"Of course she's a lovely girl," Helga says to me as she unpacks her suitcase.

Arnold and Tesseba are downstairs on the patio. Arnold is already on his third scotch, Tesseba, as usual, drinking cranberry juice.

"But after that whole business in London we thought it was over."

"So did I," I say. "Obviously it isn't."

"If the two of you don't make each other happy, you're both well out of it," she says, looking up from her suitcase.

"It's more complicated than that," I say.

"For one thing," my mother begins and I know immediately what's about to follow, "she can't have children."

"She can't. But that's not the reason."

"And you always wanted children, didn't you?" she perseveres.

She is correct, of course. I regret giving her this information but at some point it seemed a good idea to prevent further tactless hints about babies. I wish I'd kept quiet.

"You don't leave a woman because she can't have children," I say.

"Of course not," my mother says indignantly. "And Arnie and I think she's very nice, don't get me wrong. It's just that this on again, off again business is for the birds. Last time we spoke it was over."

"It was," I say. "When we got back from London we separated. She left."

"And then?"

"She came back."

"And what was supposed to have changed in the meantime?" she demands.

I remain silent.

"Well, she must love you, that's all I can say. And you should consider her interests too," Helga says.

"I do."

"I don't mean materially," Helga adds suddenly. "I know you're generous. But maybe if you left her alone she would find a more appropriate match."

"Maybe," I say. I'd be a fool to be complicit in this discussion.

"I've always wondered," my mother goes on, "whether she's sophisticated enough for you. Here you are, a successful professional, and she's the same scruffy little thing in beach pants and a tee shirt."

"I wish you wouldn't say things like that," I tell her.

And then I notice that she is weeping again, tears cascading down her cheeks. She half turns, dramatically so that I will see both that she is crying and also that she is trying to conceal it from me.

"I just want my children to be happy," she says. "Is that too much to ask?"

When I was a boy my mother was quite a political figure in left-wing circles. She was the one they called on when a clear liberal viewpoint was needed in political debates or when a biting speech was required at one or another of the protest rallies that invariably followed the passage of the ugly laws that flowed from the white Parliament in the 1960s. Her speeches were punctuated by laughter at her mimicry and sarcasm, and even the conservative newspapers seemed to have a soft spot for her, to report fairly what she had said, even to add a remark or two about her poise or her wit. Once she was arrested and briefly detained for violating the security laws and a crowd of students protested in front of the prison and had to be dispersed with dogs and truncheons.

As I watch her unpack, a look of determination on her face as she decides what must be ironed and what need not be, I recall the look of sad amusement and irony that would cross her face as she listened to someone spouting racist claptrap, and the slow, deliberate way she would begin her response so that her adversary barely knew the point at which the discussion's tide had turned. It all seems, in my shadowy guest room, like a very long time ago. A year or so after my father died she resigned from the university and withdrew from public life, and when I left to come to America she sold our house and moved into a little flat far away from it. But back then, when young people still crowded into her office for advice and counsel, what she thought I thought too.

Now, of course, there is only Arnold. I lounge in an armchair and listen to her as she talks, half to herself, about what she will wear and what she plans to buy, a suit at Escada, whatever she can find at Loehmann's, down pillows she thinks she will find at Bloomingdale's, velvety towels from Saks. When I call her in London, Arnold, if he is not watching television, listens on the extension and interrupts frequently, keeps us captive as we wait to continue whatever it was we were discussing when he interrupted. Sometimes I feel flashes of anger that are almost uncontrollable but I have learned to curb myself. When I am rude to him he takes it out on her in long, carping sessions of recrimination and threat.

She asks for more hangers, and then for an iron, and begins to press the clothes she has decided are creased. We talk about people we know, relatives who are ill, news from Durban.

"Why are you silent all of a sudden?" she asks.

"No reason," I say. "I like watching you work."

46

"I know you better than you think I do," she says. "You have a disapproving look that gets stronger each time I see you. You're my son so I don't really mind it whatever your thoughts may be. Just don't underestimate me, that's all. Things are not always what they seem."

And then, without warning, Arnold tumbles into the room to see what we are doing.

Another dream I have, and consistently these days, is of the boys I grew up with in Durban. I dream that we have been separated by the years but that somehow I have come upon them all again, all gathered together in a room. Philip, who I heard has gone quite gray, sitting with his head of white hair and young face talking to Ricky, now a surgeon, or Paul, who was once considered a genius. I ache to talk to them, to remind them who I am and to tell them what I have become, but they are offhand, busy, talking among themselves, not interested. And then, just as I begin to break through to them I sense that our reunion is ending even as I have so much yet to find out and to tell. It fades, I scramble, and then it ends and I have learned nothing, imparted less.

Helga is lifting a wrapped package from her case and she turns to present it to me.

"A small gift from London, darling," she says. "If you don't like it we can return it."

"If they'll take it back when we get home," Arnold chimes in.

"Of course they will," Helga shoots back at him. "They know us well there."

"Remember what happened when you tried to take that little print back last week," Arnold says sanctimoniously. "The fuss you made in the store. I'm not going through that again."

"Please, guys," I say. "I love it and I'm keeping it."

Only then do I unwrap it. It is ghastly. Some person has apparently thought it would make interesting art to take an old hubcap and plaster it with colored paper. It looks a little like a bad Halloween mask or an advertisement for Mexico. The colors are garish, overlapping, tinselly. I am not good at dissembling, but I try.

"What an interesting idea," I say. "The colors are beautiful."

"Are you sure you like it?" Helga asks uncertainly.

Arnold takes it from me.

"The wave of the future, this sort of art," he says. "It's all the rage in Europe now. Probably will be very valuable someday."

I feel very weary. At that moment Tesseba enters the room.

"How beautiful," she says, and comes to stand next to me. I hand it to her and she examines it, turns it over to see how it is made, holds it up to the light. "What a fascinating idea."

"And the girl's an artist. She ought to know," Arnold says to Helga. "I told you it was a good purchase."

I watch Tesseba carefully. She seems actually to admire it, which I find inexplicable. Later she tells me that she really does like it.

"I wouldn't have bought it myself," she says. "But it is original. And it's beautifully made."

Arnold begins pointing out further features of the hubcap to Tesseba as my mother and I watch. She turns to me anxiously.

"You really do like it?" she asks again.

"I said I did and I do," I say.

"We didn't bring you anything," Helga says to Tesseba, "because, well, to be frank, we didn't know you would be here. But we'll buy you something before we leave."

"Don't be silly," Tesseba says. "I'll look at this and pretend it's mine too."

"But it wasn't meant to be," Arnold says quickly, putting the hubcap down on the bed. "We'll buy you something just for yourself. What would you like?"

Tesseba does not reply. Even she has her limits. She shrugs her shoulders and walks from the room.

There are things that at times make me feel very remote from Tesseba. I am reserved and cautious while she is impulsive and disorganized and it startles me to see how easily she is disappointed, though she seems incapable of holding a grudge. She is always animated, people love her, she engages the attention of children like no one I have ever seen. At her family's gatherings the neighborhood children can't get enough of her. They draw around, sit so close on the bench their legs rub against hers. They watch her eat.

"I don't want to eat the toes," she says when she reaches the end of her lobster, and she pulls the legs off one by one and slams them down in my plate. "You eat them."

"Lobsters don't have toes," the children shout.

"What are these then?" she demands.

"Legs," says one.

"Fins," says the other.

"Toes," Tesseba says triumphantly.

When a tray her mother is carrying begins to wobble, Tesseba, as if prescient, is up and at her side to steady it. In the sun her hair glistens.

❧❀☙

"Tell me something," Arnold says to me as we walk to the corner to see if we can find a store with a London newspaper. "What do you see in her?"

"We have a lot in common," I say, determined not to let him get to me. "She's a lovely person."

"I can see what she gets from you," he adds, scarcely listening. "But what's in it for you? I mean, she's not pretty or anything."

I keep walking, notice that they have started construction on a little bandstand at the far side of the village green. I always thought a bandstand on the green would be a good addition. Now in the summer we can have concerts and performances.

"She makes me happy," I say after a pause, and I picture her face, her dark eyes, her high cheekbones and sallow skin. Somehow the memory makes me sad. I have not wondered if she was pretty for a long time. By some measures she is. By some she is not.

After Tesseba left me I would sit at my desk and look out the window, daydream about the possibilities her leaving presented while at the same time unable to plan a single day without her. And even as it seemed irrational, absurd even, for the first time I felt homesick beyond description, not for any particular place or time or even for any person, just homesick. The years were going by, it seemed, and my stranding in America rolled on and on without hope of resolution. Each morning I would awaken, eat, battle traffic on highways that never looked quite right, were somehow reversed, would begin the daily rituals of tracking and selecting investments, charming my clients, and yet even as it all seemed to be working I could not shake the feeling that one wrong step and I would be out again, in the street, worse off than when I started. My ivory elephants, the carved head on my shelf, my shining stinkwood desk, all these trophies of my ephemeral successes would be a mockery then indeed.

Tesseba, only Tesseba, had seen it all, knew how it had started, how it all fit together, what lay beneath this polished floor. I'd call her up and she would answer, happy to hear my voice even when she realized that I had called with nothing new to say.

"I'm going to make myself beautiful," she told me on the phone. "And I'm going to find another boy."

"How are you going to make yourself more beautiful?" I asked.

"I'm going to cut my hair short. And I'm going to buy accessories," she said.

"Accessories?" I asked, surprised. And then we both laughed. Tesseba's sense of the absurd and mine converge.

Her car broke down and I surprised her with a new one, shining and expensive and beautiful, and she accepted it with surprise and charm, but sometimes when we spoke it became bitter, and then we did not speak for weeks. One night I came home and saw her car parked outside the gate, her hunched figure on the portico by the front door, and she was back. I woke her up and welcomed her back but without any sense of elation.

"This is only temporary," she said, her voice groggy, still half asleep. "One day you'll wake up and I'll be gone."

"Come inside," I said. "Where I live is home for you too."

The clicker she left on the hall table and it stayed there for several weeks before I realized she was waiting for me to reattach it. I did it one night when she wasn't home.

❈

In the afternoon we all go for a drive. Helga does not like to walk and Arnold says he has arthritis, and so we do not walk much. I show them the mansions behind the reservoir, Frederick Law Olmsted's, Isabella Stewart Gardner's, those of others whose names they will not recognize, Payne, Cabot, Sargent. As I describe what we're seeing I find myself being quite proprietary, discussing batty Mrs. Gardner and her monster collection of art as if it and I were all part of the same tapestry, the Cabots and Lodges and I, all sharing more than just having passed briefly over the same ground. Tesseba, dangling earrings and tasseled jacket, takes my hand and smiles.

Later we all drive to the Wayside Inn, where Longfellow is supposed to have stayed, for dinner. Waitresses in colonial dresses serve us popovers and corned beef, and all through dinner we listen to Arnold. He compares the houses to those he has seen in England which are bigger and better, the restaurant to one he ate at in Cornwall, criticizes the wine, insists on taking the bill and then pretends he can't read the price so that all can hear what he is paying. Tesseba and Leora exchange a smile, Tibor eats his stolid meal. Helga — so smartly dressed, elaborately made up, carefully groomed — says almost nothing.

Things change so much in the course of one lifetime. People who were once intimate become strangers, places that one had never once imagined become home. One can feel, at times, like a spectator. As we eat I begin to think about this matter of going back, retracing steps, revisiting images, faces, left undisturbed for half my life. Someone says something to me as we eat but in my mind's eye I am wondering about Santi, where she is, what became of her life. I hear a scraping sound that startles me but it is merely a woman at the next table brushing by and I settle back into my reverie. Arnold drones on and on and for once I am glad of it. To see Santi again, I can't help thinking, would be to throw light on a shadow that has followed me without fading.

Later, as I prepare for bed, I come upon Tesseba standing at the window and slowly brushing her hair.

"I don't mind having your folks here," she says. "In a way it's all sort of endearing."

"They might be endearing if they weren't my family," I say.

"But they're a part of you anyway," she says. "And watching you with them makes me feel very protective."

"It does?"

"Well of course it does."

As she bends forward to sweep the hair from her shoulders I find myself drawn to her. A filament of shadow traces the muscles of her calf and thigh. Her hair hangs like a rich curtain. I walk behind her and touch the shapes of her back with my fingers.

"I'm not finished," she says and then, when I do not stop, she adds: "Sheesh. It's either feast or famine around here."

And on my mother's first night with us I have another dream, one that brings back something I have not thought of for years. I come home from school to our house high on the ridge and find it empty. The servants have finished their chores and are in their rooms, Bridget is at the gym, my father is at his warehouse, my mother at the university. I go to the kitchen, where Baptie has left my lunch under a fly screen, fruit and juice, a sandwich, and when I'm through I wander about the house, read, hit a ball against the wall. But as the afternoon advances and the house cools and darkens, in the hours between sunset and night when turning on the lights will not brighten the rooms

and yet they are all quite gray and bleak, I lie on my bed, still in my
school uniform and brown sandals, just to wait. Time passes, but
slowly and aimlessly, I may hear footsteps downstairs, see a shadow
pass my doorway, but I am immobilized by despair, can do nothing
other than lie and wait.

It is this waiting that comes back as Helga and Arnold lie snor-
ing in the next room. Moments before I awaken, images of the people
who populate my life float through the air, approach my bed, then
leave me untouched. There are schoolboys in gray safari suits, road
crews chanting in Zulu, Baptie washing herself from a bucket. Only
when Helga comes through the door will it end, the house be lit again,
the bottomless isolation end.

As I sigh in my sleep, long for what I cannot have, weep almost
from sadness, Tesseba stirs and I awaken, my dream still vivid. I watch
her beside me, dark haired, unkempt, far removed from me, and turn
towards her to press myself against her warm body.

I would wake her if I knew what to say. I would close this gap between us, this little chasm that grows as I approach it, shrinks as I
draw away, close it and discard it and not think of it again, if only I
knew how.

CHAPTER TWO

Helga

I KNOW MY CHILDREN better, I think, than I know myself. As we walk from the customs hall I am momentarily distracted but then, looking out over the crowd, I see a face I partially recognize, and then fully recognize, and then I see Danny too standing to the side.

My understanding was that this supposed marriage to Tesseba, especially after what happened on their last trip to London, was dead and buried. To my mind the girl's behavior, whatever the provocation, was unforgivable. You just don't do that sort of thing to a young man, in full view of his parents and involving the police and who knows who else, disappear in a strange city and leave him half frantic for two whole days. Thank heavens Arnold knew some people and was able to smooth things over when we found out what was really going on.

"Hello Ma," he says jovially, but I know my son.

There's what I can only call a sheepish look on his face, the kind he used to get when he hadn't lived up to his own expectations and then tried to pretend that it really wasn't that important to him. Like, for instance, when he and Bridget both did gymnastics and she began truly to stand out, when he decided he didn't like the sport after all. He did respectably, of course, but Bridget was, quite simply, exceptional.

Danny's a tall boy, over six foot, like Silas, but he's always been very slender. He also dresses well, my Danny. Among the raggedy Americans with their frayed tennis shoes and wrinkled shirts he looks cool and groomed.

I wondered why Bridget wasn't there.

"Leora has a gymnastics competition," Danny said. "Bridget and Tibor are there to give her support."

Is this a slap at me, I wonder, because I so often wasn't there when Danny was a boy? I entertain the notion, and then I dismiss it. I just don't like it when someone I expect to see waiting at an airport is missing. It concerns me, panics me, even though air travel is so commonplace nowadays one is almost expected to take a taxi. The days when we'd stand at the edge of the Durban tarmac, waiting for the plane to break through the clouds and take its final turn over the sea before landing, when arrivals by air from Johannesburg or Cape Town were significant events, are long over. But my children are always there waiting when I come to Boston even if air travel is now rushed and impersonal and lacking any sense of occasion.

I must say that I also usually meet my kids at Heathrow when they come to visit, but it's much more complicated in a city as complex as London, especially when they come with children and spouses and, in Danny's case, with what have you.

"Tesseba," I said and then, for want of anything else to say, added: "How nice to see you."

It's because of Tesseba, I have no doubt, that Danny is looking uncomfortable. She's one of those people, for me at least, whose face I associate with a mixture of feelings not all pleasant. She's a scruffy little thing, if the truth be known, long and gaunt and with blue bags under her eyes like she needs a good night's sleep or at least someone to take care of her. I wish she'd get her hair cut too. She has a mother somewhere. Doesn't her mother tell her these things?

"Hello Helga," she said and kissed me on the cheek.

I'm too old for this kind of ambiguity. Either the girl's my daughter-in-law or she isn't. If she is I'll come to terms with it. If she isn't, I'd like to know it too.

I don't know what it is with Danny, what he's still doing with her. She's no beauty and okay that's not everything but she's also a strain to be with. She has this distant, critical look she gets around me, as if we're somehow a totally abnormal group of people. I don't think that's so. And Danny keeps saying she's an artist but I've yet to see anything she's done.

Danny looks so much like Silas. As we drive from the airport I wonder what Silas would make of all that's happened, what he'd think of his children, what he'd think of me.

"I like Boston," I say. "More than any other American city."

"Why?" Tesseba asks.

She is driving a new car that I can see must have cost a pretty penny and there can't be any question about who must be footing the bill for it. Danny likes nice cars, he's got a shining maroon antique himself, and I know he's generous, but I wonder whether it's not guilt that drives his generosity in the case of Tesseba. It's different for a girl. A man can flit about almost forever and still have options at the end of it, but Tesseba's given twenty years, on and off, to Danny, and she's not a youngster anymore. In fact I wonder why she's put up with it, this marriage of convenience they didn't even tell me about for years that then somehow turned into a partnership. I feel sorry for her even as I wish she and Danny would leave each other alone.

"Oh," I say, "a lot of it probably is because Danny and Bridget are here. But it's not unlike Durban in some ways."

"Durban?" Danny says. He turns towards me with something like scorn on his face. "Durban and Boston? What could they possibly have in common?"

"They're both port cities," I say. "More English than their surroundings. And historic."

"I can't think of two more unlike places," Danny says.

You tend to take things from your children in a different way than you would if they came from someone else. I'm not going to argue with him. We've just come three thousand miles and I haven't seen my children for months. Every time I leave them, in fact, something deep inside tells me that this could be the last time. Anything can happen.

"I lived my whole life there," I tell him. "You left when you were still young. Perhaps that's why we have such different perspectives."

"It is a coincidence, isn't it," I hear Tesseba say, trying to smooth things over, "that you and my dad are both historians?"

I've heard this about her father before but I can't remember from whom. Maybe we've had this discussion.

"I haven't taught for a very long time," is all I say.

I wish I'd had a chance to teach at an American university. Perhaps if we had left South Africa when I wanted to it would have happened. This was in 1948 and the Afrikaner nationalists had just won the first postwar election. Their victory in that election was my first wake-up call, the moment when I realized that the sleepy indifference of white privilege came at a price and that the price would get steeper and steeper with time. Everyone was apprehensive, not about racial issues — that came later — but about the Afrikaners themselves, what they had in mind for the country.

"At last we have our country back," they kept saying, and for me that left one open question: If this was their country, where was mine? It was not easy to forget how hard these same people had pressed to desert the British Empire and get in bed with the Nazis. The war had only been over for three years, after all.

"Let's leave," I remember saying to Silas. "Before we have a family and it becomes impossible."

"And where would we go?" he asked. "I don't know why you want to go and be a stranger somewhere else. This country isn't perfect, but what country is? Life is good here. This is where we belong."

"We could go to Palestine," I used to argue. "We're needed there. We can build our lives and a new country at the same time."

I remember the blank look that would cross his face as I talked, and after a while I just let it drop. The point was that Silas didn't share my apprehension, my sense of unease about the country's future that began about then and that never went away. And you have to be very sure of yourself to uproot a man from everything he knows and, let's face it, at twenty what did I know of Palestine? Or of America, for that matter.

I used to think that perhaps the time would come when he'd change his mind, another, more opportune time, but of course it didn't happen that way. I felt like a canary in a gold mine, sensing something toxic and yet confined to my cage.

My father saw it differently.

"Only the cowards run," he'd say whenever I raised the subject.

I'm not sure what my father would say if he were alive today. He came to South Africa looking for a brighter future than he'd faced in Czarist Russia, and landed in Durban on the day Britain joined its four southern African colonies into a new country, the Union of South Africa, on May 31, 1910. He wondered, my poor father, virtually penniless and speaking perhaps a half dozen words of English, what the fuss, the flags, the crowds in the street, were all about. He once told me that on that first day in his new country he thought life outside of Russia resembled a carnival.

And now so much else has changed that it's difficult to imagine how one would explain it to a person who wasn't there to see it all unfold.

⌘

Distances mean nothing to Americans. What would have seemed like a whole expedition in South Africa is merely the distance Danny drives to work every day. By the time we reach his house somewhere miles from Boston the long day, and the jet lag, and perhaps the excitement itself, has wearied us all. I know I could have nodded off.

It pains me how hard my children have had to struggle. I thought on the day my father died that all this was behind us, that the kind of problems Silas was never quite able to shake were, at last, a thing of the past. So far it hasn't turned out that way, but it still might. That, if the truth be known, is a large part of the reason why we came to Boston now. It wasn't the best time for us to get away, otherwise.

"Your house looks as beautiful as ever," I say as a majestic gate swings open and we pull into his driveway.

"Thanks," he says. "Nothing's changed since you were here the last time."

Nothing has changed but there's something about how the place looks that makes it obvious to me that my blase son has gone out of his way to make things look good. You can see the lawnmower lines still fresh in the grass, that there isn't a leaf out of place, that the front porch has been recently polished and that not a soul has set foot on it since the polisher was lifted away.

"You always had such good taste," I say. "Even as a boy your room at Gordonwood was nicely arranged and always tidy, which Bridget's never was. Do you remember that old oriental rug you found in the cellar and restored yourself?"

"Of course I do," he says. "Remember that strange little stained glass window above my bed?"

"Was it stained glass?" I ask. "I thought it was just painted."

"No. It was stained glass," he says.

I don't argue with Danny about things like that. He's got Gordonwood laid out in the most minute detail in his mind, and though I think his memory exaggerates there's usually a kernel of truth in all he says. I don't give it all much thought anymore. What would that achieve? I didn't even know I had photographs of Gordonwood and then one afternoon Danny found them in an album in Sloane Square and spent the afternoon transfixed. And poor Baptie's letters, from what I can see, he just about enshrines.

I find Boston humid. Not unlike Durban.

"Are you okay?" Tesseba asks.

"Why, dear?" I say.

"You look a little tired," she says. "Would you like some tea?"

"I'm just happy to be here," I say both with and without conviction. "I'd love some tea."

She checks some envelopes on the hall table as if they may be hers, goes off to the kitchen to see about tea. It's not lost on me that she treats this beautiful house as if it were hers.

"Is she back living here?" I ask Danny when she's out of the room. I mean, either she is or she isn't. Things like that aren't a secret matter in this day and age.

"She still has a studio downtown," he says.

Perhaps it is none of my business.

"That doesn't mean she doesn't live here," I say. "Does she?"

"We're back together, Mother," he says.

It might have gone on except at that moment the phone rang. It was Bridget.

Bridget breaks my heart. Perhaps that's just something that happens with parents when they have high hopes for their children and things don't turn out as they might have. Bridget would have made the South African Springbok gymnastics team, no doubt about it, if she'd stayed with the sport. It would have made her life so much easier if she had. Instead I watch her struggle, clean up after her slovenly husband, listen to Leora's insolence, and I could die for her. Doesn't she notice that the man's left patches of stubble on his face? Didn't they have deodorant in Bulgaria? Apparently not.

"Mommy. You're here," she shouts into the phone. "I'm so happy."

"How are you, darling?" I ask. "How's Leora?"

"We're all fine," she says. "I'm sorry we couldn't be at the airport. Leora's been in a gym meet. She did beautifully."

"How wonderful," I say. "When are you coming to Danny's?"

"We have to go home and change," she says. "And then Leora has to do something at her school. And then we'll come right out."

I want to ask what could be so important that Leora has to do at her school that it can't wait until later, but I resist the temptation. I know how it would be interpreted.

"How are you, darling?" I ask again.

"Fine," she says. "We're all fine."

This may sound odd given all that's happened, but I'm not sorry I didn't raise my kids in America. It's not only the obvious dangers, the ones one reads about like violence and drugs, but the subtle differences that make me say this. American kids — kids like my granddaughter, Leora — are far too self-involved. Leora's obsessed with gymnastics in much the same way Bridget was but there was something so much more innocent about Bridget's sport than there is about the carefully orchestrated performances Leora's trained to put on. There's no innocence to it. I don't know why, but although I'm thrilled by her achievements I'd have to concede in my private moments I'm not too *interested* in them either.

I'm also not wild about being called "Gammy." It's an Americanism, I understand, but it makes me sound like I've got an incompetent limb or something, to say nothing of the slightly contrived way it sounds coming from the mouth of an adolescent girl. And American women have such high-pitched voices, by and large. You'd have thought, given Bridget's clear voice and Tibor's bass, monosyllabic grunts, that Leora would have had a fighting chance of sounding different. Well, she doesn't. Maybe it's something in the air or the food, or from watching television.

Leora gets her height from Silas. Silas was very tall, taller actually than either of my children, with good posture and a fluid, graceful manner. He asked me to marry him on our first date but it took me eight months to say yes and even then I wasn't sure I was doing the right thing. These days I see Silas in my kids and in Leora all the time. Sometimes it's all I can see in them. Danny, for instance, holds his cup exactly as Silas did, the graceful fingers looped around the bowl, the index finger barely touching the handle, the pinky under the base. I can't take my eyes off him, him and Tesseba, as we sit drinking our tea in the room they call his den.

I'm not exactly sure, to be perfectly truthful, what Danny does for a living.

"I manage money," he tells me when I ask. "I help people decide where to invest."

"But what exactly do you do?" I ask. "I mean, if you said you were a stockbroker, that I could understand."

"It's different here than in South Africa," he answers.

I still don't understand what it is he does, but it doesn't sound very useful. Perhaps it's my own bias. How can a man live his life simply making money without wondering where it all fits in, what he's really doing, and why. Even at my age I'd like to feel useful and although Arnold will never understand it that's why I don't like living in London. Our lives there are so insular and anonymous, completely marginal. We know nobody except former South Africans and a few others we've run across over the years, and we fit in nowhere. Sometimes I'm almost inclined to say I'd prefer to go and face the music in South Africa than to continue traipsing about like flying Dutchmen. Arnold makes a joke out of any suggestion that we go to Israel, but I'd still go there like a shot. I mean, how much theater and how many museums can a person see? Once I was useful. That is what makes me feel especially useless now.

◆◈◆

It's hard to believe, I know, especially in light of all that's happened, that not too long ago, in the thirties and forties, there was a sense of inevitability about race in South Africa, an assumption shared by almost everyone, as basic as the sun rising and setting, that white people would govern the country for as far into the future as anyone could see. For a long time I didn't even know a white person, or a black person for that matter, who didn't accept this as a fact of life. General Smuts's policy of an indefinite white trusteeship over the country was accepted in the circles in which I moved — Anglo-Jewish, economically ascendant, first generation — as more than reasonable. This doesn't mean that growing up I didn't notice things or wonder about them, obvious injustices, ugly incidents. But I said and I did nothing.

Everything changed in 1948. The Afrikaner Nationalists were adamant that the whole world had to be viewed through the prism of race, and not only race but religion, too. The gradual changes that had seemed inevitable under General Smuts — a process by which somehow, as the country developed and opportunities grew, some sort of racial accommodation would emerge — came abruptly to an end, and it was jarring. The new prime minister, Malan, was an anti-Semite and a race baiter and his attitude towards Africans verged on contempt. Nothing seemed quite so cozy or inevitable anymore.

And then, in 1953, in the first election after the Afrikaner Nationalists came to power, I went, largely out of curiosity and without

65

telling Silas, to a rally addressed by a woman named Margaret Ballinger. She had formed a new political party that advocated the revolutionary concept that every person regardless of their color had a right to vote. Given that Africans outnumbered whites by four to one this meant of course that she was advocating the frankly sacrilegious notion that Africans could, in fact should, run the country. People thought she was nuts and I knew what Silas would have said, let alone my father, but there was something about this that made sense to me.

There had been quite a bit of racial unrest too that year and the press was still free to print what African leaders were saying, and their account of their grievances had a big impact on me. I mean, as a Jew and with memories of the Holocaust still fresh how on earth could one justify the assumptions on which all South African politics rested? I began to wonder whether there wasn't something profoundly wrong with everything I had always believed to be so obviously right.

I stood at the back of the largely empty hall and listened to her and I knew then that of course she was right, and in retrospect this seems almost trite but for the place and the time it was nothing short of an epiphany, that the point wasn't skin color or race but one's character and what one made of one's opportunities, and that the sooner the government realized that by denying Africans schooling and property and the right to move about and to work and to speak they were imprisoning us all and that the sooner this ended the sooner we would all be free, the whites from fear and the blacks from the tyranny it had bred. It wasn't going to be easy and it wasn't simple, but it was obvious. Everything else led only into a morass.

Out of respect for Silas I didn't join her party, or even say anything about it when I got home. But I had no doubt what I believed.

⬥❦⬥

When Bridget finally arrives it's getting dark and I could use a nap. But just the sound of the car in the driveway, the crumble of the gravel and the whistle of something in its engine, reinvigorates me. Bridget is like fresh air to me, her face a panorama of memory.

"Mom," she shouts as I open the door. They're walking up the path from the car, first Bridget then Tibor with Leora trailing behind.

Tibor stands back as we embrace, kisses me on the cheek.

"And Leora, my darling," I say. "She's shot up, must be almost five feet already."

"Hi Gammy," she says.

"My God," I say, breathless. "You're a giant."

"She gets stretched out on the beams," Bridget says. "Just hangs there by her hands and then pulls out like taffy."

"Enough," Leora says. She's obviously not thrilled about her height.

"It's gorgeous," I say.

Bridget was a beauty when she was a child but Leora looks too much like Tibor to say the same of her. With her height, her long legs, her cascading blonde hair which doesn't come from our side of the family, she's not going to be short of admirers.

"She won, you know," Bridget says. "Highest marks on the uneven bars, second highest on the mat, second highest on the horse. First overall."

"Congratulations, darling," I say and try to kiss her again. She shies away but surrenders her cheek.

"Hi Tesseba," Leora says.

67

You can tell from the way her face lights up, how Tesseba responds, that there's something going on between these two. I don't know what it is — perhaps it's how uninterested she is in the normal conventions — that seems to endear Tesseba to children. I have no idea how it plays when Danny needs her to be a real hostess. You can know your children so well and still not have a clue why they choose the people they do. Right now she's still in a tee shirt and cotton pants.

"Well, did you?" Tesseba asks.

Leora smiles irresistibly and shakes her head.

"Did you what?" I ask.

"Nothing," Leora says.

"Girl stuff," Tesseba says, smiling.

"Did you what?" Bridget asks. She's not thrilled about this secret dialogue.

"Nothing, Mom," Leora says impatiently.

I see Danny look at Tesseba. This is my kind of look he gives her, a subtle signal of disapproval. She looks at Leora, who shrugs.

"Her hair," Tesseba says to all of us. "She was going to ask you if she could highlight the pieces at the top."

It's not such a big thing, of course, but I wonder what it is about her that makes Tesseba privy to this big secret no one else is.

"You want to highlight your hair?" Bridget asks. "Why?"

"Do we have to have a general debate?" Leora asks, and pushes her way past us into the house.

Bridget wasn't like that. In fact I wonder where it is that a twelve-year-old girl even gets the desire to color her hair. Perhaps it's a good thing for children to know their own minds. And in America what else is there to occupy an adolescent girl than the color of her hair?

I suppose I have to take responsibility for Bridget's life being as scratchy as it is. Tibor's stolid manner must have made him seem like the Messiah when she first met him in London. But when I was notified that she was being released from jail in Pretoria I packed her clothes in a suitcase and took the first flight up there from Durban. Once they were done releasing her I put her in my rented car and drove her straight to the airport — no ifs, ands or buts — and put her on the first flight out of the country. I may learn slowly, but I learn well.

"I've been thinking about seeing Gordonwood every day for six months," Bridget told me in the car. "And there are people I'd like a chance to say goodbye to. Why can't I just go home for a few days, and then to London."

I can't recall if I even responded, just kept driving along the freeway to the airport.

"Is this really necessary?" Bridget kept asking. "It's over. They won't come back now."

"You're going," was all I said. "And you're going today."

I remember that the next flight left in forty-five minutes and that in that time I had to buy her a ticket, check her bags, find the gate, and then push her through it. She walked onto that flight in the same clothes she'd walked through the gate of the prison two and a half hours before. It's what one does to protect one's children when that's all there is one can do.

"This is too much," she kept saying as we stood by the gangway.

"It can't go on like this," was all I said. "You have to go."

I remember shoving money into her hand, a phone number to call when she landed, some other things. I'd arranged it all with only one thing in mind really, to get her out, out, as far away as I possibly could and with no delay. Let them come back with some further banning order or new arrest warrant and I'd laugh because the only part of me that remained vulnerable would be in the air and on her way to England, far beyond them and the chaos they wrought.

I stood at the window on the second floor of the terminal and watched as they unlatched the plane from its mooring and edged it off on its way. I knew what my daughter must have been thinking as she looked back and saw the country slip away beneath her. It probably mirrored what I felt as I watched the craft take her away from me and everything that was familiar to both of us. And it wasn't the first time either. It was only three months earlier that I had done the same with Danny. But a mother knows when things have run their course, and the morning the police came to arrest my Bridget I knew that they had run their course for us, that everything that was to happen to my family in South Africa had happened, and that all that was left to do was to leave.

We should have left a generation ago, I kept saying to myself as I stood at the window. We have been here but not here, within this place but not a part of it. We have been like spectators at a play who find themselves dragged onstage as the action unfolds, unwittingly and without guile, but onstage nevertheless and confused about their lines. And I should have seen coming what came for my kids. If Silas and I had left when I wanted to, before the kids were born, it would all look quite different now. You can't prevent your kids from following their instincts just because you want to protect them. In the end I'm not all that sure it's the right thing to do anyway.

When they came for her, Bridget went to the door, if you can believe it, in leotards and with an apple in her hand. She was still holding the core when they loaded her into their wagon.

❧

I only went to university and got my degrees when the children were old enough to be left alone with Baptie. This was in the early sixties when the outside world was just vaguely aware that something unsavory was going on in South Africa. In fact, the government was in the process of enforcing a segregation harsher than anything we'd seen before. The premise of it was that South Africa was not a country at all but a random collection of tribes that had accidentally been mixed in with each other. Their mission, so the government said, was to unscramble this three-hundred-year-old egg by moving the members of each African tribe, very much against their wishes, and plopping them down in racially distinct enclaves situated in the middle of nowhere. There, and this is the best part, they were told to start their own countries, no less, from scratch. South Africa proper, along with all its mines, its factories, its banks, its cities, its universities, and the rest of it, was, by coincidence, where the white tribe's "country" was going to be. Anybody who opposed this scheme, they insisted, was an agent of the Soviet Union. Well, almost.

It was ridiculous. In retrospect I'm not sure how we even accorded this absurdity the dignity we did by arguing against it, trying to point out its flaws, discussing endlessly in all-white debates its rationales and its weaknesses. The fact is that although you won't find many who'll fess up to it now, most whites went along with it happily enough.

71

When I started at the university it still had nonwhite students. Shortly afterwards the government ordered that they had to be expelled, including a few students I had become quite friendly with. I had never felt such outrage.

"We have no choice," the university's smug chancellor told us. "It is the law."

"How can you obey a directive that is so unjust towards your own students?" we demanded. "Stand up to this. Try to stop it. Disobey."

"There are nonwhite universities and white universities," we were told in tones so condescending it makes me angry even now to remember it. "Government policy is that groups should not mix. And only youth speaks of breaking the law."

It wasn't that alone that spurred me into doing something. It was a collection of little things and trying to recount which one, or which several, precipitated my decision to get involved wouldn't serve much purpose. I'm not even sure I'd get the chronology right. When a group of parliamentarians broke away from the moribund opposition to form a multiracial political party, I joined it. They didn't advocate a universal color-blind vote, they were too pragmatic for that, but I believed their approach would in the end achieve the same thing. Even when all but one of them lost their seats in Parliament in the 1961 election, I stayed involved. Then things just escalated until the party became my main interest and its members my closest friends.

I went from attending meetings and holding signs to hosting meetings at Gordonwood and serving on committees, and then to a point where I was speaking at rallies and being looked to for advice. I don't think, looking back, that in the end we had much of an effect.

In the end it was the Africans themselves who forced the showdown. But those were still the most interesting and productive years of my life.

In 1966, the party asked me to run for Parliament.

"You have no choice," several people in leadership told me. "You speak so well and you think so clearly. We don't think anyone has a better chance of getting in than you do right here."

"My children are too young," I told them. "And my husband needs me at home."

"It's a chance that won't come around again," they said. "If you win you will make history."

"I'll discuss it with Silas," I said.

It's difficult to describe the election now. Back then it seemed a matter of darkness and light, good and evil, but in retrospect it all seems so parochial what with six or eight thousand white voters in the whole constituency, hand-addressed envelopes, one little campaign office on a side street off Essenwood Road. We spent the days calling people on the voters' list, arranging house meetings, going door to door, trying to win people over one by one.

There was a time when I thought I had a fighting chance but I soon realized that the whole thing was doomed. The sixties was a time when other countries in Africa were becoming independent and one after another sinking into chaos, proving correct, so we were told day after day, every doubt white voters had ever had about Africans and their capacity to run things for themselves. Not only that. There had been something close to a national uprising in South Africa itself in 1960 and the government made sure that people were scared half to death of what might happen if they lifted the jackboot for even a second.

In the end people wouldn't give us a chance. I mean even Silas, who really was so decent in his own life, didn't support me. In all honesty I don't even know how he voted in the end. He was actually quite liberal in so many respects — for instance he didn't have to think twice about whether I could run for Parliament once I'd told him I wanted to — but when it came to race issues it was like speaking to a somnambulant.

"Why rock the boat?" he used to ask me. "Blacks here have it better than they do anywhere else in Africa. They come pouring in from Malawi and Mozambique, places they run themselves, looking for work, not the other way round."

"That's a false argument," I used to say. "This is a wealthy country and those other places aren't. We all have higher standards here and it isn't lost on South African blacks how great the discrepancy is."

"They're higher because the whites bring European ways," he'd say.

So figure this out. Silas was the first white man I ever met who addressed every black man as "Mister" as a matter of habit, and I never saw him treat an African without respect or any differently than he would a white. At his business, his African employees loved him, came to him constantly for advice, for loans when they needed *lobola* to get married, and when he died, as we stood around his open grave, the Africans who were gathered in the street outside began to sing a burial song and I never heard such sorrow, not before and not since.

"Just leave things be," he used to say. "Leave them be. Don't rock the boat."

"The boat is going to rock, Div," I used to say to him. "Whether you want it to or not. The question is when, and will we be prepared."

"No, it isn't," he would say.

Of course he was long gone when things changed.

⟡

The first time I met Arnold's son, Gregory, a boy who's managed to marry twice and both times women of breathtaking plainness and immeasurable wealth, I made the mistake of asking what it was he did for a living. Arnold never had said, though I might have guessed.

"As little as possible," Gregory replied.

As if that weren't enough to teach me to stay out of it I asked Arnold how that could be.

"How can someone do nothing all day?" I asked. "What does he do? Go to PTA meetings? Fetch and carry the children? What sort of a life is that for a man?"

Arnold can be malicious. Perhaps it was then that I realized how difficult marriage to him was going to be, the true price of all this ostensible comfort.

"Look," he said acidly. "At least my son knew enough to keep himself out of trouble."

It's unfair, truly it is, to compare Gregory to my children. I can just see — and from the little anecdotes Arnold drops from time to time this doesn't take much imagination — Gregory as a child in that mansion near the park, going to Michaelhouse, the most exclusive boarding school in Africa, drifting into Arnold's businesses, traveling, consorting with wealthy girls. For some people it is all so easy. When the easy life in South Africa ended Gregory came here, to Boston of all places, and with Arnold's money stolen from the country in the dark of night the transition has been seamless.

75

Sometimes I wish it could have been that easy for my children too but then I think of Gregory, smug little arse that he is, and I take the wish back. I'm not sorry for anything that happened, anything at all. Both my kids left South Africa heartbroken and I do feel bad about that, but in some ways, believe it or not, especially when I think of Gregory, I'm almost proud of the kind of trouble my kids got into.

❧

I raised my children in a poisonous environment but I always believed that the environment couldn't poison them if they were decent people with good values.

Even so it takes more than that. Take the relationship between Danny and Eben. Eben is Baptie's son and he's a year or two younger than Danny. I understand from Baptie that he rose quite high in the KwaZulu government and I'm almost afraid to ask what's happened to him now. The whole KwaZulu setup was an apartheid creation even if it did give blacks some semblance of a say in running their own affairs.

"Can I bring Eben up to play in my room?" Danny asked once and it created a dilemma, for heaven's sake.

"Why don't you play outside?" I asked.

"We don't want to."

So what is it you say to your ten-year-old? That it's not fair to bring this boy from a poor African farm into your bedroom? That it's unwise to immerse him in the things you take for granted because the time will come when he has to leave? That he may remember the experience with a modicum of bitterness?

Instead, of course, you say nothing.

The next thing you see, then, is your son with his gleaming brown hair sitting on the carpet of his bedroom playing cars with a little African boy, and the most noticeable thing in it is that the African's wearing clothes you'd given away because they were too shabby. Not hand-me-downs. Castoffs.

You ask: "Are you having fun?"

And then Baptie's at your door, in her apron, a wooden spoon in her hand.

"I don't like," she says.

"What don't you like, Baptie?"

"I don't like Eben to come in the house. Why they can't play in the garden?"

"It doesn't matter," I say.

"I don't like," Baptie repeats.

I don't like either. But what was I supposed to do?

Danny had a birthday party one of those years, perhaps his ninth or tenth, and Eben was in town. A group of Danny's little school friends came over for a birthday party, Jell-O and streamers, a cake, a clown, I think, and then after it was done they went off to play in the garden while I sat with some of the other mothers talking about nothing in particular. Until Baptie came running in.

"Come quickly," she said.

You didn't have to go far from the front door to hear the shouting or to see that it was Eben who was the cause of it, that Danny's school friends had barricaded him in Silas's tool shed.

"What's going on?" I demanded.

"We're just playing," one of the brats said.

"It doesn't look like Eben's having much fun, though," I said.

I looked at Eben, trying hard not to cry, imprisoned behind the barred doors of the shed.

"Where's Danny?"

He wasn't in the fore of the little white lynch mob but he wasn't helping Eben either.

"Eben's your friend," I said to him. "How can you do this?"

"We were playing," I heard again.

"I'm very disappointed in you," I said, opening the door and letting Eben run off to the kitchen.

That night I got Danny in his bedroom. It was his birthday, but after all this was a serious matter.

"What possessed you?" I asked.

"I don't know."

This was more like my Danny. Unbearably contrite.

"Did you apologize to Eben?"

"I can't find him."

"Did you try?"

"Yes."

"What possessed you?" I asked again.

"I don't know," he said. "It just happened."

"That's no excuse."

And then, to my relief, he turned on his stomach and began to weep and I thought, thank heavens, thank heavens, things aren't so bleak.

I don't remember another instance after that of Danny and Eben playing together. And when Silas told me about Danny and the young servant girl from next door I knew that even the most decent of children is vulnerable in ways a mother can't begin to contemplate.

◦◦◦

When Danny finished high school he was drafted. It was something all the boys had to do, serve their year in the army. I had no truck with those mothers who tried to get their sons out of going.

"You live here," I would say. "And whether you agree with the government or not, you share in the fruits of the land. It's your turn to give something back. And it's only a year."

Some of my friends were quite vehement in disagreeing, but I did not back down.

"We can't believe it's you who's saying these things," they'd argue. "Helga the great liberal. Helga, Alan Paton's big buddy. If you're so keen on sending your son to serve in the Afrikaner army be our guest, but don't try and make us do likewise."

"I don't want to send him," I'd say. "But it's the law. And besides, it'll do our little Jewish princes a lot of good."

"You sound like an anti-Semite," they'd argue.

It went on and on and got nowhere. Some of them sent their boys overseas, others tried for these ridiculous medical exemptions, drawing compliant doctors into a web of intrigue that showed us all up in a bad light. I wonder how many letters from doctors named Berkowitz and Jacobs and Levy the army authorities got. It made me sick.

And, to my regret, Danny and I clashed on it. The truth is things haven't been the same since then.

"It's only a year," I remember insisting. "Be a man."

"This is ridiculous," he would argue. "Why are you so adamant that I serve in this pathetic army?"

"You've never been so politically motivated before," I would point out. "Suddenly you've decided that the system is intolerable."

"Do you know what they do?" he'd whine. "They go into the townships and brutalize the people who live there. They say they're keeping peace on the borders and instead push around rural blacks who have no stake in things one way or another."

"You can rationalize anything if you really want to," I told him. "I'm not having any part of any attempt to get out of it. You're going."

"What I don't understand," he kept saying, "is where this vehemence comes from."

"If you live here, you have to go," I said.

In the end Danny went. He was so angry with me in the days before he left that we barely spoke. While he was gone he didn't write at all and rarely called until later when he had no choice.

⟶❦⟵

It was while Danny was away that Bridget ran afoul of the Security Police. To this day I don't know how it happened. The university, after all, was my turf. I knew that the Security Police were all over the campus but I also knew which organizations to stay away from and which were relatively safe. I encouraged Bridget to get involved with the National Union of South Africa Students, not because they were exempt from police scrutiny but because they were a known quantity. You could navigate along with them while still staying out of trouble.

What happened was that after the Soweto riots in June of 1976 everything changed.

"Debate between white people isn't relevant anymore," Bridget said one evening. I'd asked her to come to a protest meeting with me.

"What would you like us to do instead?" I asked. "Go to Soweto and stand in front of the tanks?"

"If that's what it takes," she said. "Your eyes are closed to what's really going on here. It's a total waste of time trying to persuade white people to change their minds when in the end what they think doesn't matter."

"What does matter, then?" I asked. "You may not care what they think but nothing will change unless the white electorate changes its mind. Change is not going to come about by violence."

"Why not by violence?" she demanded. "The whole system's violent."

"Oh do be realistic, Bridget," I said angrily. "Are you going to pick up a rifle and take them on?"

"Perhaps," she said. "Others have."

"I'm not going to discuss it with you if you're going to talk like a fool," I told her. "If you want to get yourself killed or thrown in jail keep right on the way you are. The situation doesn't need martyrs and God knows it doesn't need zealots either."

But my Bridget, who once had been so reasonable and moderate, wanted to do things her own way and I sensed, though I did not try and stop her, that I would not have been able to anyway. When she stayed out late I worried, when the phone rang at night I jumped, only when I heard the engine of her little car pulling into its shed in the yard could I turn out the lights and sleep.

One night, waiting for her, I was reading a book when Silas came in and sat on the edge of the bed. The sounds of singing were coming across the lawn from the servants' quarters, melodies that came in and out with the wind. Perhaps it was the sounds that brought to mind what he wanted to tell me.

"What is it?" I asked.

"I worry about the kids," he said. "Young people see things in absolutes. I worry about them losing perspective."

"She's young," I said.

Even while one is worrying one takes for granted, I suppose, especially when one reaches a certain age, that each day will be pretty much like the last, that the chance of something terribly disruptive happening is slight. One takes some comfort in it.

"It's not just Bridget," Silas said. "It's Danny too."

"What about Danny?"

"There's something I want to tell you," he said. "Something I promised Danny I wouldn't."

"What is it?" I asked.

And that's when he told me about Danny and what had been going on in the servants' quarters in the dead of night. It's not as if one didn't know these things were possible but as I listened to him I felt a sinking inside, a feeling of failure, of helplessness. Of all people, I remember thinking, it wasn't like Danny to take advantage of someone or to show such poor judgment.

"How do you know all this?" I asked him when he was done.

"It doesn't matter," he said. "I'm not sure I did the right thing about it either. But it's too late now."

I'd have done what he did, I believe, but how does one know for sure?

"Do you know what I've been thinking increasingly of late?" Silas asked me that night.

"No," I said.

"We should have gone to Israel," he said.

-⊶⊷-

Arnold has a glib, easy manner, is able to defuse animosity with his coarse and ready ebullience as quickly as he is able to create it. People who don't know him well come to feel an almost paternal affection for him, can disregard the stream of childlike boasting and enjoy his attention, his jokes, his advice. Arnold knows what he is and what he isn't and somehow he's come to accept it all.

Not my poor Silas. When I look back on the things that brought the end for him I am struck over and over by how unimportant they are, how little they count. I can't tell now why I fell in love with Silas, whether there was a time when I didn't love him, why I feel so drawn to him now that he is gone. What I can say is that whenever I think of him it is with a sense of waste, wasted opportunity, wasted talent, wasted love, wasted time. If I could only do it again I would say leave it, just drop it, just come with me and be with me and together we will find whatever it is we need. Of course that isn't what happened.

I knew Silas was having money problems but the truth is I paid no attention to them. When Europe and America started putting restrictions on the import of South African goods, of course it had an effect on him. And we lived well, but not extravagantly. The circles we moved in demanded that we maintain certain standards. The way I saw it, if we'd stayed in South Africa for the flesh-pots I didn't expect not to have them. I also assumed, quite frankly, that even if Silas was stretched thin from time to time, ultimately my father's money would be mine and things would fall into place.

But towards the end which I didn't know was to be the end he would come home so weary and withdrawn he scarcely had the energy to talk.

"What is it?" I'd ask.

"Nothing," he'd answer, and then he'd climb up to his study, pore over his ledger books and old papers, smoke endless cigarettes.

"Our expenses are overwhelming," he said more than once. "This house. The servants. The cars. It's just too much. It's not sustainable."

"So where would you like us to live?" I'd ask. "A little flat somewhere? From Gordonwood to a three-room walk-up?"

"No," he'd say. "But I can't keep up."

"I'm not budging," I'd tell him. "You chose this house and we've built our lives around it. This is where we live and this is who we are. You can't suggest now that it's all been a sham. If I need to I'll go to my father for help."

"Don't do that," was all he said.

Why did I say things like that? It's too late now.

I arrived at Gordonwood one afternoon to see my father's car and driver parked outside the house. It was a weekday and I was a little alarmed. I went in and found him sitting in the living room, both hands on the head of his walking stick, glowering.

"What the bloody hell is going on here?" he demanded.

"Hello Pop," I said. My father's outbursts were not entirely foreign to me.

"Did you hear me?" he said. "Do you think I'm an idiot? An imbecile? A moron?"

"What on earth are you talking about?" I asked.

"As if you don't know," he snorted.

"I don't know," I said. "Why don't you tell me."

You didn't cross my father. He wasn't a tall or an imposing man but he had a fierce temper, an irrational streak that made it preferable in almost all situations to mollify rather than to confront.

"You don't know what this is?" he demanded.

He pulled a piece of paper from his pocket and showed me.

"You don't know?" he asked scornfully.

I didn't.

"Well, what the bloody hell is this, then?" he said, turning the page.

It was a signature page and on it was Silas's signature and mine. Except it wasn't mine.

"Well?" he said.

I didn't know what to say. I had to speak to Silas, and yet I recognized, even in the bad forgery of my name, Silas's handwriting.

"I don't know what it is," I said. "I sign things for Silas all the time."

"You don't know what it is?" he said. "You give away your home and you don't know what it is."

"Give away my home," I said. "What do you mean?"

"This is a mortgage," he said. "On your house. Which you signed for your husband's business. Which the bank is calling. Which by coincidence I found out about first."

I'm not stupid and in the end there wasn't that much to understand. What wasn't clear was why he had done it, why he hadn't asked me. Why he had cheated.

"Let me speak to Silas," I said. "Let me find out what it's all about. There's an explanation."

"I'm sitting right here," he said, tapping his stick into the carpet, "until I get an explanation from your husband directly."

"Don't do that, please," I said. "Whatever it is, we'll sort it out. But the kids will be home soon and you'll accomplish nothing by making a scene of it."

He harrumphed around for a while and then stalked out, leaning into his stick, got into the backseat of his car and slammed the door shut, looked away as the chauffeur backed up the drive. In retrospect I should have let him stay, at least until he calmed down. Instead he went straight to his lawyers and we've been living with the consequences of what he did ever since.

⁓

I didn't say anything when Silas came home. I remember that as he came in the front door he was carrying a piece of stone, something that had fallen off one of the walls around the house, contemplating how he could repair it, not with proper masonry and chisels but with glue and plaster, chicken wire, gray paint. I felt sad for him even as I felt betrayed, angry enough to kill.

He went upstairs as he usually did, to his little study at the end of one of Gordonwood's endless, warrenlike passages. I imagined him there, crouched over his worktable, still in his suit, his tie tucked into his shirt, patching and gluing, propping things up to dry, working with his carvers and sanders and an array of makeshift tools. When he came downstairs for dinner he was still in his suit trousers and white shirt, his tie still tucked in at the second button. Silas didn't have leisure clothes, not even one of the elegantly patterned sweaters and softly folding cotton pants of which Danny has such a collection.

His thin hair was tousled. There was a speck of glue on his arm.

"Where's Bridget?" he asked.

"I'm not sure," I said. "At the university still."

He looked at me carefully, shook his head.

"I worry about her," he said.

"I worry about all of us," I said.

I hadn't planned it this way but for whatever reason his concern for Bridget brought it out, a wash of fury and doubt I'd thought I had under more control. I must have railed at him for the better part of an hour.

The thing about Silas is that he was not disingenuous. He had no explanation other than the obvious, no rationalization to offer, nothing to help palliate my anger. Not even an attempt to apportion blame.

"I was going to lose everything," he kept saying. "Everything we are."

He had a way, Silas, of running his palm, the flat of his hand, across the top of his head when he was at a loss. He kept doing it and each time he did a tuft of thin white hair would jump back out, stick out at the side like a feather. His hands were beautiful, even to the end they were beautiful, and as he did it I felt so sorry for the man, such great pity, that my anger began to evaporate even as I tried to hold on to it. That wouldn't have been true if he'd tried to justify himself, but he didn't.

"So what do we do now?" I asked. "How bad is it?"

"It's worse than you think," he said, and if it had been bad before, it was then, really, that the nightmare began.

"How worse?" I asked, my throat dry, my voice lost somewhere in uncertainty.

"There may be problems with the books," he said.

He didn't have to say more, and I wouldn't have let him.

❧

It got in the newspaper, of course, my celebrity, such as it was, saw to that. Even Danny saw it in an old *Natal Mercury* when he walked into a rundown little store in Matubatuba where his unit was doing maneuvers. Silas wasn't exactly arrested but he was called in for questioning by the fraud squad and it was all so painful I don't even remember one day from the next, how it all played out, who came and went, who stuck by us and who didn't. I was at his side, of course, dutiful, photographed, subdued. Nothing would be the same again, that was clear. I knew of course that my political life was over. What I did not know was how much else was over too.

And then he died. I remember this much. I was sitting in my study trying to read a book. It was a June evening, cool, almost midwinter. We'd had a trying day, more inquest, more explaining, more stolid ledger books with their impenetrable figures, but at last it seemed to be settling down. The sun had gone down over the harbor, Baptie had just served dinner, a quiet dinner, Bridget was out. We tried to talk about little things, Silas and I, but mostly we were silent. He was in his suit trousers as usual, his white shirt, his tie tucked in at the second button.

"What do you plan to do tonight?" I remember asking.

"Paperwork," he said. "Maybe I'll clean some of my collections."

I remember that after dinner I felt — or maybe this is only in retrospect that I remember it — a sense of calmness settle over the house. It was usually so cold in winter, drafty and dank, but on that

88

night it wasn't cold at all. Crickets chirped. Leaves brushed against the windows. Silas's collection was eclectic, trinkets he'd gathered over the years from shipments he'd received, things made of sandalwood and ivory, carved of stone, woven of silk so fine you couldn't even see the threads. Occasionally he'd inspect what he had, lift some of the pieces from their cases with hands as delicate as a bride's.

And then, suddenly, from the other end of the house there was a loud sound, like a bang, and for a moment I thought nothing of it, that something had dropped, a rock or a brick, or that a branch had snapped, and then I panicked, felt cold and exposed, put my book down and started to walk in the direction of Silas's study, and then to run, but by then nothing could make a difference. His head was on his desk, his mouth pressed open by an inkwell, his gun was on the floor.

I know Danny doesn't accept this, even as I look across the room and see him talking with his sister, turning to Tibor for concurrence. Tell me I'm deluding myself and I'll answer that one needs more proof than we have, something far more definitive, before reaching a conclusion such as the one Danny says is so unassailable. Silas was a careful man but on this one night of all nights he was too distracted to be careful enough. Or so I say, and will until the day I die.

But that wasn't all either. Just when you think things can't get much worse, they get worse again. There was so much bustle that night, with people coming and going as if Gordonwood no longer had a door, Bridget and one of the boys who was interested in her driving up to Ladysmith to get Danny, doctors and policemen and photographers everywhere, that I almost overlooked my father leaning on his stick in the living room downstairs. Somewhere in the confusion I'd called and asked him to come over and he had arrived, uncharacteristically unkempt and somehow disoriented in the backseat of his big American car. When he learned what had happened he slumped in a chair and began to sob, a gritty, heart-wrenching sound that was unbearable to hear.

And then several weeks later he had a stroke, and though he lived for a few more months — with one brief exception on a night a week before he died — not another sentient sound passed his lips.

⬦⬦⬦

Leora and Tesseba seem inseparable. I've just arrived and my granddaughter has done the minimum necessary to be polite, but now she's huddled on a couch with Danny's supposed wife and they're talking in a way that isn't exactly secretive but it would be difficult to know what they are saying without too obviously intruding. It's the price you pay, I suppose, for living so far from your children and theirs. If I had a choice in the matter I wouldn't have let it happen this way.

Leora turns around on the sofa so that her back is to Tesseba, and Tesseba begins to braid her hair. I could braid her hair if she'd ask.

"Braids like that are quite fashionable in London now," I say. "Perhaps your mother will let you come over at Christmas and you can see for yourself."

"To London?" Leora asks.

"Yes," I say. "There's plenty of room."

"I don't know," Leora says thoughtfully. "I'd like to come but that's when they're probably holding tryouts for the regionals."

She looks at Bridget for assistance.

"We can talk about it," Tibor says. "Christmas is a long time away."

You really do lose control when you get older. There was a time when the offer of an overseas trip would have made any of these kids jump through the roof with excitement, but now as I offer it it's as if I've done little more than throw a wet bundle into the middle of the carpet. It lands, spreads, seeps, is ignored.

"We'll pay, of course," Arnold says.

Danny stiffens visibly every time Arnold opens his mouth, never looks him in the eye, works to change whatever subject Arnold brings up. I know what my son thinks of my husband, and as far as Arnold is concerned Danny is an ingrate. I'll never make peace between these two. I heard Arnold say as much to Gregory on the phone. I don't know what they were talking about but Gregory must have mentioned Danny for some reason and then I heard Arnold say: "I'd be very careful dealing with him if I were you."

I can't say if Danny and Gregory would have been friends without Arnold's interference. All I know is that they're not and that Arnold's contribution was not positive. Arnold tends to sow discord, though. It's sort of his trademark.

"We'll pay, of course," he says, but that's not exactly what he means and we all know it. What would happen is that Bridget would make the reservations, Leora would come, and then nothing would be said about who was paying for the tickets. He'd slough me off if I brought it up, would wait for Bridget to do it, not once or twice but several times, and then if he did ever pay he'd do it with a flourish and only when other people were around, pull out his stupid Swiss checkbook, the one that lets you choose the currency as well as the amount, insert his monocle, ask several times exactly how much it was for.

"So Gregory's children will buy a little less gasoline," he'd say as he handed his check over. Sometimes he'll even ask for it back saying he thinks he made a mistake, make whoever's been supposedly lucky have to go through the ritual of handing the check back and then getting it again, saying thank you twice.

The only problem is that my children don't ask for money. They learned soon enough what accompanied each of Arnold's offers. So he makes his offers now with impunity, chuckles benevolently, and for years no one's taken him up. People who don't know the routine think he's generous with my kids. I don't think he's given either of them a bean for years.

And the odd thing is that I thought I was preserving something by marrying him, not changing as much as I obviously have.

❦

My father's stroke didn't kill him, turned him instead into a rambling infant, incontinent, belligerent, sometimes even dangerous. We brought him to Gordonwood because it seemed the only place he could be, set him up in a wing of his own in the house, kept around-the-clock staff to tend to his needs. It wasn't an easy time, though perhaps in retrospect it did deflect some of the sadness that followed Silas, kept us too busy to dwell on more sorrowful things.

"I'm going to Israel," he might start saying at three o'clock in the morning, trying to climb from his bed, to pull whatever garment he could reach over his pajamas, to find his way to the door.

"You can't go to Israel tonight," the nurse would say. "It's too late."

"I'm going, damn you to hell," he'd shout. She'd ring for me and then soon enough the whole house would be up, trying to soothe him,

92

to put him back into bed, to convince him that he really could go if he wanted but only in the morning, when it was light, when the planes were flying.

Of course in the morning he'd have forgotten all about it. And the odd thing is my father wasn't even a Zionist. When I first suggested I wanted to go to Palestine his response hadn't been equivocal at all: "Don't expect to hear from me if you do," he'd said.

Perhaps the hardest night of it all was the one he woke up weeping, perhaps the most lucid night of them all, told the nurse to fetch me, specifically: "Fetch Helga," he said, and then sat crying on the bed much as he had on the night Silas died. Except that this time he called the nurse over too, ordered her to get a pen and paper, and then when she was sitting ready on a chair next to his bed he tried to dictate something to her. I now know, though I didn't then, what it was all about.

"I, Walter Paladin, being of sound mind," he said, his voice unusually sonorous, like he was reciting a poem, "now want to make a proper will. I revoke all earlier wills, and want to make a proper will." He paused.

"Did you get that down?" he asked the nurse.

"Yes, Mr. Paladin," she said.

I think she was taken aback by the lucidity, by taking instructions from a man whom minutes before she had been handling like an infant.

"In my proper will," my father continued, "I want everything I have to go to Helga. Outright. Everything to Helga. No trust."

And then he sighed, leaned back, started weeping again.

It goes to show, though, how you never know how things are going to end. It's one of Danny's pet themes these days, that the unthinkable becomes commonplace as you get older. But who would have thought that my father would die at Gordonwood, a place he hated, and in such an infantile state. It happened without warning a few nights later, as the nurse was feeding him, death descended like a bird and swooped him up. And it was hard, burying him, not to think of Silas whom we'd buried so short a time before. When we closed the casket on my father we closed it again on Silas, buried Silas all over again.

It's then, really, that morning my father was buried, that I remember as the last calm patch before the real storm broke. Not long afterwards they arrested Bridget, and then when Danny came back from the army all I could think about was how to get him out of harm's way. And then when both Danny and Bridget were gone, suddenly I was completely alone.

And, of course, there were issues with money. On the afternoon my father found out about Gordonwood he'd revoked his earlier will and made a new one, one that made it impossible for us to touch his money for years and years, put it into a trust that allowed only a trickle, enough to sustain myself but not much more, until the children were almost themselves middle-aged. It's over now, of course, at last. Now, for the first time, the money is truly ours.

I was ready to challenge it at the time, brought in the nurse and her notes, her sworn statement that in the midst of all the dementia this was, indeed, a lucid moment. But the lawyers, and especially Nerpelow, Silas's old friend, talked me out of it.

"We know it's true, you and I," he said kindly. "But you have to anticipate how others will see what you're asking me to do. They will bring in doctor after doctor to rebut what this one nurse says, and your motives will be questioned and challenged. And I can't promise that your own credibility won't be questioned, especially now, or that Silas's ordeal won't be dragged into it. I can't let you do this."

I know that in America if you get one legal opinion you don't like you simply go down the street and get another that you do. It doesn't work like that in South Africa, or at least it didn't then. So I listened to Nerpelow and allowed this great sum of money to be locked away, released in a trickle as needed, enough to keep body and soul together, not much more.

I sold Gordonwood and started gathering my things and preparing to start again. I remember those last nights at Gordonwood, after someone had committed to buying it, after all the servants except Baptie had been given their severance and told to leave, much of the furniture earmarked for sale or already moved out. I was scared, frankly, living alone in that rattling old house and asked Baptie if she would move from her room in the servants' quarters and take one of the suites upstairs. She agreed, though she was uneasy about it at first, and it worked out very well. Of course it was illegal to have a black woman living in my house but it was strangely comforting, knowing that there was some life in Gordonwood beyond my own.

I'd auctioned off just about everything, the grand piano from the ballroom, the collections of pure silver place settings from my father's old house in Durban North, Regency and Empire and Colonial, the faux antiques he'd bought and given me when we moved to Gordonwood, so much more. They set up a little red marquee on the lawn and an auctioneer came over to sell it off by batch. I couldn't watch. I left Baptie to see that the auctioneers got what they needed and buried myself in the library up at the university.

I remember the last night we spent there, Baptie and I. Almost everything was gone and so we sat on the little patio overlooking the pool and picnicked on chicken and salad off the wrought iron table we were planning on leaving.

"Wait one moment, Madame," she said, and before I knew it she had wandered off into the pool house and turned on the little lights Silas had placed in the gazebo behind the hedge, the lanterns he'd built to line the walk.

"It looks too beautiful," she said when she came back. "This is how memory should be left."

⊸◌◦

It is amazing, really, how quickly the time went by. Danny was here, Bridget was in London, I was in this tiny little flat down on the Esplanade overlooking North Beach. I decided to stop teaching at that point. My heart wasn't in it, giving lectures in halls filled with unfamiliar yet knowing faces. I felt ashamed, really, not so much by what had happened to Silas and how my publicly impeccable life had been shattered, but by myself, by how everything had become so reduced, Gordonwood to this little flat on the beachfront, a family to Baptie and me, a measure of stature to a measure of nothing. I seemed to be losing touch with my kids, what they were doing, to be out of touch in general.

I decided to get my doctorate then, and that was a saving grace. I started doing research on King Shaka, analyzing the political structures that supported his reign, and it was engrossing. I'd stay up late working, my mind at KwaDukuza in the midst of an *indaba* rather than in my study high above the Indian Ocean. Sometimes it was only Baptie arriving with tea at midnight that reminded me it might be time to go to bed.

"You should go to bed, my Madame," she would say.

"What's the time?" I'd ask.

"Midnight," she'd say. "Very late."

"I lost track of all time."

"Yes," she'd say. "You live like an orphan."

And that was when Arnold entered the picture. I had heard that his wife had died. It was in all the newspapers, of course, a big event given his prominence and her social do-gooding. I didn't really know him well, though he'd been quite a booster when I ran for Parliament. I think, knowing now what I do about him, that he may have come forward then for other reasons. I didn't leave any room for ambiguity then, but he was quite a philanderer, I'm told, in his younger days.

He called one evening out of the blue.

"This is Arnold Miro," he said. "You remember me, I hope?"

"Of course," I said. "I'm so sorry to hear about Zelda."

"It's been a year, already," he said. "It was tough at first."

"I know how it feels," I said. "But it slowly gets better, doesn't it?"

"Life goes on," he said.

He asked about my kids, where I was living, what I was doing, and all along I knew why he had called, that sooner or later he'd edge into a subject I wished he wouldn't. Other men had asked me out in the months since Silas and I'd said no.

"So here's the point," he said at last. "I think you and I should go out to dinner, talk about these things, all that's happened and hasn't happened. I think it's time."

I hesitated. He could hear it.

"It can't do any harm," he said. "Listen. If you prefer, why don't you invite me over for tea one evening. That's only polite, wouldn't you say?"

Of course I had to. Not inviting him over then would have been rude, as if I expected something unseemly, in some way even hoped for it.

I made Baptie stay late that night. She sat quietly in the kitchen while Arnold and I chatted. I liked knowing that she was there.

"You can let the girl go to bed, you know," he said at some point. "The poor thing doesn't have to be your chaperone."

I didn't let him touch me, of course, though he would have been perfectly prepared to stay the night if I'd given him half a chance. The next morning he sent this enormous bowl of roses, thirty-six red ones if memory serves, and the whole apartment smelled so strongly of roses for a week it became almost nauseating. Then he called and asked if I'd have dinner with him and I wasn't so sure, but he called again the next morning and the morning after that and eventually I said yes.

And I suppose I began to think, for the first time since Silas had died, about what it might mean to have a man in my life again, not any man either but a man like Arnold. He took me to restaurants that Silas and I rarely went to, spent on wine what I paid in rent. It wasn't the money that turned my head, even the things that it bought, but the spending of it, the ease, the sense of assurance and even entitlement. You could say that Arnold acted as if he belonged, and people treated him as if he did.

And what the heck. I had fun, too, fun in a way I somehow hadn't with Silas.

"When was the last time you saw the Victoria Falls?" he asked one afternoon.

"Who knows?" I answered. "When I was a girl."

That night we were on a plane to Rhodesia, in separate suites at the Victoria Falls Hotel, dining on a balcony overlooking the Zambezi.

"Let's gamble," he said.

There was a casino there, a little thing now that I've compared it to others but not like anything I'd seen before.

"I didn't bring clothes for that," I said. "You go."

Situations like that are an invitation to Arnold. Within minutes there was a knock on the door and an English dressmaker was standing there, complete with sewing basket and fabric.

"If you can put something together in an hour," Arnold told her, "I'll pay you whatever you ask. And if my sweetie likes it, I'll double that."

So I was taken in. I became a habitue of Victoria Falls and Plettenberg Bay, Sun City and Mauritius, places I'd never much thought about. The chauffeurs and Rollses didn't impress me, or the mansion behind Mitchell Park, or the office on the top of Durban's tallest building with its movie theater and marble bathroom, but I was taken in by the ease of it, the absence of turmoil and struggle.

And one other thing. Arnold asked often about my children. I could tell he wasn't close to his son and he seemed almost to take pride in mine, in Bridget's courage, in how Danny seemed to be picking himself up by the bootstraps and starting over in Boston.

"I look forward to meeting your kids," he used to say. "If they're anything like you they must be exceptional people."

Bridget was with Danny in America by then and that Christmas we went to them in Boston. Arnold had just bought the house in London and we were going there afterwards. But on our first night in Boston, in the presidential suite of the Ritz-Carlton Hotel, he asked me to marry him.

"Life will be paradise if you will live out the rest of it with me," he said.

I looked at him carefully, the silver beard, the strange monocle, the silk cravat, and I knew even then that I would never love him. The expensive excursions had grown thin, the excesses had become wearying, the fawning and scraping by those who knew his reputation had become, of all things, irritating. But we'd just left my kids downstairs in the hotel, Bridget climbing into Tibor's rusting car, Danny going back to some little warehouse apartment, and I thought that perhaps as Arnold's wife I could give something back to them, two parents, a point of reference, and yes, perhaps some material help too. It's not easy watching your children struggle when you're sleeping in a penthouse hotel suite and have just treated them to a dinner you know they could not possibly have afforded themselves. No one had to live with him except me, and what a difference it would make if he was anything like what he seemed to be.

So I said yes and a number of years have passed again like they always do and I've learned things I wish weren't true but they are and that, as they say, is that.

But what's happened now is that the balance seems on the verge of tipping again because I know Arnold's lost a fortune in currency-swapping deals he spends so much time on the phone orchestrating, and Gregory's demands haven't decreased. I wonder if he has ten percent of what he once did now that the South African currency's crashed and so many of his own assumptions have proved invalid.

And I've begun receiving these unspeakably polite letters from South African bankers and currency officials and it seems that some change in South African law allows my father's trust to end early. I called Nerpelow to ask him to look into it and he's given me some surprising reports.

"The amounts have lain fallow for quite some time," he says in his careful, dry-throated voice. "Your father was of course a wealthy man when he died, and his trust has not quite kept pace, but your assets are still quite considerable."

"How considerable?" Arnold asks into the extension.

"Quite considerable, Mr. Miro," Nerpelow says.

"Can you give us a ballpark?" Arnold asks.

"If you'd like me to, Helga," Nerpelow says. "Of course it's rather vague given that the money's invested in disparate vehicles."

"Please," I say. "Approximately."

"Approximately forty-five million rand," Nerpelow says. "That's just over six million dollars. A considerable sum."

"It's all mine?" I ask.

"Except for some minor taxes and other matters, yes," he says.

"How much of it can she take out of the country?" Arnold asks.

"There's the problem," Nerpelow says hesitatingly. "As you may know, Mr. Miro, one can't take capital out of the country at all. If that weren't the case every cautious person would remove a certain portion of their holdings from the country until things settled down and the economy would be gravely damaged."

"What are the limits on the income one can take from the country these days?" Arnold asks.

"Two hundred thousand rand a year," Nerpelow says. "About thirty thousand dollars."

"That's still the limit?" Arnold shouts. "They keep talking about raising it."

"I'm afraid there's not much likelihood of any further changes of substance until the economy improves," Nerpelow says.

"I'll look into it," Arnold says and I hear the phone in the other room click.

"I would advise you to be very careful," Nerpelow says before he hangs up. "If you choose to come back you would be a very wealthy woman. If you don't, as always, I'm here to render any assistance I can."

That of course sets Arnold off on a flurry of activity. There have been calls to and from South Africa at a furious rate, numerous meetings with men I've not met before, lots of planning and decisions to be made.

❦

Arnold's approach, I can tell right away, is not going to sway Danny.

"It's not for Mom and me," he says. "It's for you kids. A fortune's going begging. Mom and I are too old for it to do us any good, though of course there's no question it's her money while she's alive. But it's you who've got to go to South Africa to salvage it."

"We don't need it," Danny says. "We've lived all these years without it. Perhaps they'll change the law at some point and we can get it out legitimately. I'm really not interested in doing anything illegal."

"If you don't go," Arnold says, "they'll steal the lot. Bridget can't go and Mom would be in over her head."

"I would not be in over my head," I retort hotly. "But it's the kids' money, and Danny knows about these things."

"They'd eat you alive," Arnold taunts.

I'm about to respond but Danny speaks first.

"It's blocked money," he says. "We can't take it out of the country so what's the point of going? To count it?"

"Don't you believe that for a second," Arnold says authoritatively. "There are ways. Everybody does it. I'll put you in touch with people. And," he adds ominously, "you'd be an idiot not to do everything you can to get your money out. There are plans afoot to nationalize the lot. Where are you likely to see six million dollars again in this lifetime?"

"They can't just confiscate our things," I say. "Surely."

"Every last bean," Arnold assures. "Your father's fortune will become the dowry of piccanins."

"I asked you not to speak like that," Danny says sharply.

This business of smuggling money from South Africa is an obsession for people like Arnold. They chatter about it at cocktail parties, boast of their exploits, how much they have got out, how little it costs.

"You hand a suitcase full of rand to a courier in Johannesburg on a Tuesday," I heard him say once, "and by Thursday morning your banker's calling from Zurich to tell you that a deposit in dollars has been made to your account. I tell you, it's as if God made the conversion."

It's tough to think of money that could be ours being lost while people like Arnold manage, so effortlessly it seems, to salvage theirs without even a trace of anxiety. Arnold says he got his out in exactly the same way he's arranged it for us. If only Danny could be persuaded.

Later that night, when Arnold's in the bathroom, Danny comes by my room to say good night and I see that it's something different than I had thought that's troubling him. He kisses me on the forehead, asks if I have everything I need, gives me a book he says I'll enjoy.

He lingers at the door on the way out. It's at moments like this, those rare times when we are alone, without Arnold and Tesseba, Bridget, Leora, that I wish my Danny and I could truly connect again. I'm not asking for the world, for him to understand me perfectly and me him, just for moments of clarity, true understanding, an exchange of the kind of uncritical affection I know we're both still capable of.

But the moment is, like all others, evanescent.

"What is it?" I ask. "Quickly, before Arnold comes back from the bathroom."

"Do you really think it's worth it?" he asks. "This crossover into Arnold's world."

"What are you talking about?" I ask.

"This detour into currency smuggling," he says. "Taking the low road in South Africa, after all we've been through."

"It's time something went our way," I say. "And it is our money."

And it is. It should be.

It's as if we've earned it in more ways than one.

CHAPTER THREE

Bridget

"I DON'T KNOW ABOUT your television," my mother says. "Is there no bodily function that's too personal to discuss on the air? Nothing any more that's considered perverted?"

"What are you talking about?" Danny asks.

"That overweight black woman," my mother says. "I was watching her this afternoon. Opal somebody. You wouldn't believe what she had on. Men who dress as women. In broad daylight with not even a hint of self-consciousness. Can you believe it? How can they face their parents?"

"Oprah Winfrey?" Leora asks.

My mother looks at her doubtfully.

"You're allowed to watch her?"

"Give me a break," Leora says.

"Well are you?"

"What's to watch?" Leora answers.

"And I saw," my mother goes on, on a roll now, taking Leora's arm firmly to keep her from interrupting, "on another show, that a man who abducted and hurt a young girl had already been convicted of the same thing and spent a total of five minutes in jail. Literally five minutes. I mean, has this country gone mad?"

"It's like that," Danny says.

"I mean," my mother says turning now to Tibor, "you work in a school. Have I gone mad, or has the world gone mad? Since when have children had the right to carry guns into a classroom?"

"It's not a right," Tibor says. "People are trying to stop it."

"No," my mother insists. "I heard that it was a right. That they have a constitutional right to carry guns into their classrooms and to leave them loaded on their desks. How can anyone teach under those conditions?"

Fortunately Arnold walks into the room and asks what we're discussing. So the story has to be retold and soon enough he's hijacked the conversation and has everybody listening to him talking about something completely different. Unlike Danny, though, I don't really mind. I just tune out and take a break.

"Doesn't Gammy ever say anything nice about anybody?" Leora asks me when we're alone.

"She's had a difficult life," I say. "Just be tolerant."

"She makes things difficult for herself," Leora responds.

⬥

My mother insists that she's pleased Danny and I grew up in Africa. This has something to do with knowing when to use a fish knife and transvestites on television, and also with my mother's conviction that there's something American about the way in which my daughter's so very impatient with her. It is true that life felt different in Africa, somehow more predictable and sensible. We wore uniforms to school, shop attendants were generally polite, there were no muggings, everyone knew where they belonged. But the world hasn't stayed like that anywhere, least of all in South Africa. You'd hear English aristocrats, I'm sure, expressing similar complaints about vanished standards. The problem is that my mother's not an English aristocrat, though at this point in her life if it were Arnold who said she wasn't she'd probably take issue with it.

Tibor says that while Danny and I were growing up, white Africans lived in a pocket of time that doesn't fit any logical sequence and I think that's right. My grandfather came to South Africa from someplace in Europe where life must have been terrible. He arrived when he was nine or ten, worked behind the counter of an uncle's store, eventually opened his own, bought some property, became rich. But he didn't seem to have learned an awful lot from his own experiences, least of all about things like respect for the underdog.

"What's the matter with your driver?" he'd ask my mother when Ambrose would pick him up for Friday dinner.

"Nothing so far as I know," my mother would answer warily.

"Stinks like a pig," my grandfather would say. "He doesn't have soap?"

"Of course he does," my mother would say. "It's just very hot out."

"They all stink," he'd insist. "Like pigs. Tell him to take a bath before he drives me home."

"I'm not doing that," my mother would say. "I'll take you home myself if you'd like."

And my grandfather would growl, perceptibly growl like an angry dog, curse under his breath.

"Like animals," he'd mumble.

It wasn't much better at his flat either. He lived in the penthouse of this high-rise building on the Marine Parade overlooking the North Beach, and although the view was nice the price you paid for it was that everything was always damp, the windows steamed up and the fabric on the couches clammy. Until I first flew in an airplane it was the highest I'd ever been. You could see right out to the horizon from his balcony, farther even than you could from the very top of Gordonwood.

We'd have to go there for lunch every Sunday and although he had several servants, a cook and a housemaid and others, it was always disorderly and disturbing. Everything was burned — from the clear soup to the custard, or raw, or stale, and we'd have to eat it, Danny and I trying not to make faces or to laugh, taking just enough not to seem rude. Food came to his table in bits and pieces, the servants shrank from him, even my father would get a wry smile on his face, a look of total resignation.

"You get out of here," my grandfather would growl at his cook after he'd called her in to criticize the food. "Get the bloody hell out of here."

"Don't talk to her like that, Pop," my mother would say. "Just don't."

"She's useless," my grandfather would say. "Why God made that species is one of the mysteries of the universe. When I'm dead, it's the first question I'm going to ask."

"Provided there's someone there to ask," my mother would say. "Not just a little red chap with a fork."

"Funny," my grandfather would retort, hacking at his meat. "You'll be there too."

After lunch my father would have to play *klabbejas* with him while we sat, my mother, Danny and I, on the veranda overlooking the sea.

"Can we go yet?" we'd keep asking.

Later, in the car on the way home she'd say: "It's your future. Not mine. One day you'll be pleased you made this effort."

My grandfather used to tell about the time he flew from South Africa to Europe. It was after the war and he went there to see what was left of his family after the Holocaust. They were all gone, of course. The worst of it was that when he finally got to the town where he was born the gentile family who'd moved into his parents' house wouldn't let him inside.

But there's another part to this story that puts it in a uniquely African perspective.

"We left Johannesburg in the morning and went to Salisbury," he'd say. "And they refueled the plane and we went to Nairobi. You could go to Nairobi from South Africa in those days. The British still had civilization there. After we landed I felt the airplane rolling but no noise at all and I looked from the window and there on the ground I see fifty schwartzes with ropes pulling us into a hangar. I turned to the man sitting next to me and I said: 'Did you see that?' 'Yes,' he said. 'Overnight the whole plane they wash by hand with sponges.'"

My grandfather would laugh.

"I looked carefully in the morning to see if maybe in Kenya at least they knew to clean properly. Sure enough, it was better before they touched it."

I have other African stories too. I heard a while ago that a woman who lived next door to us at Gordonwood was killed by a lion. I don't know how in this day and age a Jewish woman gets to be killed by a lion, but each time I picture it I see this affluent lady, bangles on her arms, carefully sculpted hair, going headfirst down a lion's throat. And

I wonder what she was wearing, what happened to her shoes. Or about my cousin Janice, who's a doctor in Soweto. She's very liberal, Janice, almost gave my uncle Barnes an ulcer when she told him she was a socialist, but one evening she was driving back to Johannesburg and a black mob surrounded her. Some hooligans wanted to pull her from the car and necklace her then and there — kill her by putting a burning tire around her neck, my first cousin, Janice — but then someone she'd treated at Baragwanath Hospital recognized her and they let her go.

I saw a book once in a bookstore called *The House Next Door to Africa.* I didn't read it but I keep thinking about the title. It describes where I grew up.

❦

From the day I was born until I began university the only Africans I knew were servants, ours and other people's. I've racked my brain to think of exceptions to this because it's so odd, not knowing any Africans when you live in a country where they outnumber you so completely. But it's true. That's what apartheid was all about.

The servants' quarters at Gordonwood were on the other side of the swimming pool, down a slope of lawn and out of sight behind a hedge. There was a wooden trellis, like an archway, built into the hedge, and if you went through it you'd be in another world, on a little path with gray flagstones and granadilla vines overhead. At the end of the path was a row of seven rooms, their walls splashed with mud, one for each servant and an extra room or two for storage. At one end of the row was the bathroom with its concrete floor and corrugated iron roof, and at the other end a toilet. There wasn't a bowl there, just a porcelain hole in the ground. The whole area smelled of urine, urine and antiseptic and rotting granadillas and paraffin stoves. It was from these rooms that the servants trudged each morning, over the flagstones, through the arch, across the lawn, to take care of us. The sun would come out, send orange flashes across the pool, and while we lay in bed there would be all this industry going on, the pool being cleaned, breakfast made, clothes folded.

Baptie's room was on the end of the row where the ground sloped, and as it subsided one of the walls had begun to slant so that eventually there was a six-inch space between one wall and the other.

"Don't things come in?" I asked her.

"What do you think?" she said, her hands on her hips.

"It's not my fault," I told her. "Don't blame me."

"I blame this stupid house," she said. "Always breaking, falling down, leaking. Look at this bloody wall."

"Can't my dad fix it?" I asked.

"You can fix it by pulling down the whole house," was all she would say.

I remember how at the time of the Sharpeville massacre they closed the school and everyone's parents came to hurry them off home. There were soldiers in the streets, tanks too, driving up Old Fort Road and then turning onto Berea and disappearing off in the direction of Kwa Mashu. We knew what was going on but only vaguely, that somewhere out of sight crowds of Africans were trying to march into town. I pictured them moving in a solid column, chanting, dancing, waving sticks and spears. Perhaps it's because I wasn't old enough to be scared that I wasn't. I also knew that if nothing else, Baptie would keep them at bay.

That night, the night the Sharpeville massacre happened, I lay in bed thinking about the servants and their falling down rooms. My mother told them to stay inside the house until it was over and so they moved their things into the kitchen and spread mats on the floor when it was time to sleep.

When all the lights were out I went downstairs and asked Baptie to come and sleep on my bed with me, but she wouldn't.

"Your mother won't like," she whispered, pushing me away. "Go sleep by your bed and I sleep by mine."

⬥

I can't say when it was that Baptie came to Gordonwood. I know she came after Danny and I were born but to us it seemed as if she had always been there. She used to shrug off the question with an impatient laugh.

"Who cares about such things?" she'd ask. "I came and that's what happened. You were so small then you could fit into a shoe."

When we were growing up, when my father was alive, Baptie was both a servant who disappeared with the others into her mud-caked room each evening and also an enforcer of rules whose word stood against any child's. There was never any doubt that she was upright, had integrity, was scrupulously truthful, but she was also at least in part incoherent. Danny and I may even have found her frightening as we listened to her stories of miracles from the dark and unreachable place she called The Great Valley. These were filled with the supernatural — always an enchantment, changes in identity, confusion in the heavens — and a casual acceptance of sudden death and deformation.

As she told her stories it was as if she herself became transformed, an accessory to a random and malevolent order.

Now a lifetime later Baptie is a piece of my family as real as if we were bound by blood. And we of hers. She even insisted that her grandchildren be named for us. So her son Eben's first boy they called Silas, and then the first girl Helga, and now there's a Bridget and a Danny too, a whole little family of Zulu Divins wandering around Gingindlovu, where they live. I don't know if it's sad or if it's humorous, but it's true anyway, one way or the other.

Danny's so into trashing my mother these days I don't know how he remembers things but I know I'm not receptive to attempts now to rewrite how it was. She just wasn't around much when we were growing up. I don't mean to be unkind but the fact is that you don't become a celebrity by staying home with your children. My mother insists this isn't true but it was Baptie who raised us, really, my mother popping in to take part in the high points, the gym meets and piano *eisteddfods* and parent-teacher conferences. There were times when I'd sit on my bed, just sit there doing nothing, yearning for her to come home.

"I was aware of everything that was going on in my home," she says authoritatively. "Everything. What Baptie did, she did on my instructions."

Danny and I don't disagree with her. What would be the point? It was Baptie who was the last person we'd see before we left for school and the first we'd see when we came home, Baptie who set lunch under a fly screen, left out clean clothes to change into. Each afternoon she'd fold my gym clothes over the back of my dressing-table chair with as much care as if she were clothing a mannequin, and then stand behind me braiding my hair as I warmed up, sinking as I went down and then rising to tiptoes as I rose. When she'd had enough she would hit me softly in the small of the back and say: "Stop your nonsense. Your braid will look like a bus ran over."

So she had all this patience but also a streak of violence that to this day I can't really understand. She had a vegetable patch behind her room and one day a couple of dogs started fighting there and destroyed much of her crop. I remember arriving home at the end of the chase, when she'd cornered one of the dogs and was approaching it with a stick.

"Bloody hell," she was shouting. "Devil."

"Stop it," I said and ran up to her, tried to grab the stick.

She shook me off as if possessed.

"That bloody dog ate my garden," she said and began to light into it with the stick, striking it over and over as it cowered and yelped, eventually limped out of her reach and started off up the drive with its tail between its legs.

"You can't do that," I cried, outraged. "You can't just hit an animal like that."

"If someone doesn't like," she said, running off to resume her chase, "let him come and tell me."

"You don't treat living things that way," I insisted. "You just don't."

"You don't know nothing about living things," she shouted. "You don't even know to catch a bus. If Ambrose get sick, you stay home forever."

When I went after her, tried to grab the stick, it was as if she didn't recognize me. If I hadn't backed off she'd have hit me as readily as the dog, banged me about until I yelped as loudly. Or maybe she wouldn't have and it was all a bluff. You didn't test Baptie on things like that. But I remember wondering while it was going on, Baptie swinging her stick, me trying to hold it, how little I really knew her, how far apart we really were.

In the winter when it got dark early and gym practice didn't end until after dusk, she would come with Ambrose to fetch me because my mom didn't want me to ride alone in the car with a black man after dark. They would wait outside, the two of them, Ambrose in his white coat and cap in the front, Baptie in her pink uniform in the back, and when I came out the door she would look both ways carefully, gesture frantically through the window when she thought it was safe to cross.

"You don't have to do that," I said once. "I can cross the street, you know."

"You can cross," she agreed. "But what if there is a car you do not see?"

And when I got into the car she would always ask: "Did you have a nice time in your exercise?"

And I would say: "It was okay."

Then she'd hand me a banana or a bottle of milk, put a sweater around my shoulders, tidy my braid.

"You spend too much time in your exercise," she'd say. "It is only like a game. Not like a job."

"Is Mom home?" I'd ask.

"Maybe soon," Baptie would tell me. "Eat your fruit."

❧❦❧

My mother ran for Parliament when I was eleven. She stood for a party that wanted to give Africans the vote and even some of her close friends refused to vote for her. Some people said it was a lost cause from the start.

"These things need to be said," she'd reply. "Whether or not I actually end up in Parliament is irrelevant."

I'm pleased she has this to look back on. It must have been a thrill to address rallies, appear on the same platform as the archbishop of Natal and the chancellor of the university, be on first name terms with Helen Suzman and Alan Paton and Desmond Tutu and the rest of them. But it is startling to have your mother's picture plastered on telephone poles and nailed to palm trees all about the city. Sometimes I would be sitting on a bus and we would pull to a stop and there her face would be, staring right in at me from a campaign billboard. It's something you don't ever get used to, having your mother's face pull right up to a bus window, serene, smiling, wearing a familiar string of pearls. It was funny too because although the teachers in my school were supposed to stay neutral, those who agreed with her couldn't stop themselves from letting me know and those who didn't became so stiff and formal with me it sometimes seemed they were in danger of snapping.

"I don't understand this business of putting your face on a board and hanging it in the street like that," Baptie would say. "What good is there in that?"

"She wants to go into the government," I'd tell her. "To change the way things are in South Africa."

"How will she change things?" Baptie would ask.

"To be sure black people are treated fairly," I'd say.

"The Boer is the devil," Baptie would say simply. "They do not know how to listen to people who say things they do not want to hear."

"She can try," I'd tell her.

"And if she wins," Baptie would say, "does that mean she will fix the walls in my room?"

"It doesn't all come down to something like that," I'd say.

"So what does it come down to?" Baptie would ask.

It was all a long time ago, of course. Back then my mother seemed capable of anything, of answering every question I asked, of saving the country itself. When the police raided because they thought Africans were living in the servants' quarters illegally she would wrap herself quickly in a coat, stride across the lawn, take them on angrily.

"What is it?" she would demand.

"There are people staying here illegally," they would say sullenly. "We are checking passes." And then, weakly, they might add: "It's for your own safety."

Sometimes I would watch with Danny from the balcony, see her standing there at the end of the lawn, gesturing, the policemen looking away, trying to stand their ground. There would be vans with blue lights flashing, noise, the servants standing in a group behind her as if she, and only she, stood between them and terrible hardship.

"This is not a cat and mouse game," they would say. "We warned you before. If there are people here without passes, we will take them."

"I don't like when the Boers come," Baptie would say. "They don't know anything."

My mother is quite overweight now but she's still perfectly proportioned and quite limber. It's not all that long ago that she stopped playing tennis and I don't think I've seen many people more competitive. She'd climb the fence before giving up on a lob.

That's how she fought her election too. Nobody actually expected her to win but in the end she came closer than just about any other liberal in the country. This had a lot to do with her district, which included the university, because the students really took to her, but a lot also to do with how hard she worked. After the polling booths closed the votes were counted by hand and it took until midnight to finish, but when the results were announced on the steps of the polling station people were really surprised. It was a rout everywhere but less so in my mother's district. When they gave her numbers there was a cheer that went on for ages. You would have thought she won.

"Next time," they kept shouting. "Just you wait."

After the election things really took off for her. No one wanted the campaign to end, in part because it had been fun and in part because everything else was so desperate. You would read every day about forced removals of African villagers and detentions without trial, and there were also real absurdities like the time we weren't allowed to compete in a gym meet in Rhodesia because the English team had a West Indian girl on it. It sounds nothing so much as bizarre now but South Africa didn't have television in the 1960s and there was censorship of everything so you got to see the world through this parochial little prism and it made things seem as if it were you who was the odd duck and all the rest of it perfectly normal. So you sought out and stuck with people who were like-minded.

In any event, after they closed the campaign office the same people who had worked in the election began coming to Gordonwood to help prepare for the next one. They would come down the drive and you would see them, and not only those who were coming for the first time, walking across the lawn and looking up in amazement at the turrets and balustrade.

"What they want?" Baptie would ask. "All these peoples."

"They're students," I would say. "They're Mom's supporters."

"All they do is drink my tea," Baptie said. "Then they eat everything like cockroaches."

Sometimes I would help Baptie wheel in the tea tray. Like most African women in domestic service she always wore a uniform which consisted of a pastel-colored coat dress and a white pinafore, that and a white scarf, starched and folded neatly over her hair, something we called a *doek*. My mother didn't like her working in the house without her *doek*, as if there were something improper about her neat little rows of braids.

"You know Bridget, don't you?" my mother would say, introducing me. "And Baptie of course."

"Good afternoon, ma'am," Baptie would mutter as she poured the tea.

It didn't last long if you plot things against a lifetime, but that was my mother's heyday. Night after night my father would be working at his desk upstairs, Danny and I would be doing our homework, and downstairs my mother was presiding over this buzz of activity that had her at its center and visions of a different country keeping it aswirl. When they weren't stuffing envelopes and updating voter lists they'd be going from house to house canvassing for support, and always when they came back for tea they'd be filled with jokes and strange stories.

"Change will come," my mother used to say, "with or without our efforts. About that there is no doubt. But how soon it comes, and how things will look afterwards, those are things we can affect."

And everyone at Gordonwood believed her, everyone except Baptie.

"What change?" Baptie asked her once. "What exactly will be in this change?"

"A new way of life in South Africa," my mother said. "A way to share what this country has to offer."

"I don't need," Baptie replied, shaking her head.

※

There's not much left of my mother the celebrity, the confident public speaker, bane of the local police. She's well preserved for her age, though, my mother. I'm not sure she would accept that as a compliment — she'd want to be told she was well preserved for any age — but it's true. She has this thick head of hair, a soft skin, a nice figure. She used to dress beautifully too but now she's so constantly under assault by Arnold that she seems to have lost her confidence, to be unable even to make the most simple decision.

"Are you planning on buying some clothes while you're here?" I asked when she arrived. "I've been watching the paper for weeks now so that I'd know where the sales are."

"I'm not sure I need anything much," she said. "Some things for the house perhaps."

But then I notice, three days into her visit, that she's been wearing the same blue denim skirt every day.

At first she tries to joke about it.

"It's the most comfortable thing I brought," she says. "You must think it's the only thing I own."

"I'm beginning to," I say. "If you like that kind of skirt, let's go and see what else we can find that's like it. You can't wear the same skirt every day you're here."

"I have other things," she says uncertainly.

Danny and I planned their whole stay in Boston, mapped out each day and arranged our schedules so that one of us was always available.

"Is today the day we're going to Bloomingdale's?" my mom asks.

"That's what I thought," I say.

"Because Gregory wants to take us to lunch."

"Let Arnold go with Gregory, and you and I can go to Bloomingdale's," I suggest.

"Do you think that's okay?" she asks.

"Why wouldn't it be?"

"Gregory's so sparing with his blasted invitations that Arnold treats them like a royal summons."

"What would you like to do, Mom?" I ask.

"Achh," she says, sitting heavily into a chair and looking quite glum. Arnold's gone somewhere so we're alone.

"What is it, Mom?" I ask. "Why can't you just go out and buy some decent clothes?"

"Achh," she says again and throws whatever it is she's carrying onto the bed. "I don't know what I want. And I'm beginning to forget things too. Simple things. I spend half my life looking for things I had in my hand just a moment before."

Then she starts to weep, sits on the bed, buries her face in her hands, runs her palm over her head exactly the way my dad used to. I've never seen her do this before.

"I'm so confused," she says. "I feel so miserable. I just want to go home."

"You're going home soon enough," I say. "Can't you enjoy being with us for the few days you have left."

"Not home to London," she says. "Home to where something looks familiar again."

The problem is that things never looked the way she remembers them. And being with Arnold is enough to detach anything from its moorings. Danny keeps saying that it's beyond him how my mother could have allowed Arnold to inflict himself on all of us as she has. But I do understand. And if she did make a mistake, for how long, and how constantly, do you reproach someone for what's clearly irreparable?

"Why doesn't she just leave him?" Danny says to Tibor and me as we stand outside the house preparing to leave.

"She can't," I tell him. "She would be miserable alone. And I think she's terrified of being penniless."

"She wouldn't be," Danny insists.

"It's not a rational thing," I tell him. "She's lost everything that defined her. Squabbles and all, she thinks he gives her something of it back."

"I can't even imagine Arnold and Dad in the same room," Danny says. "Dad would have got his measure in ten seconds and moved away as quickly as possible."

"It's not that simple," I say, and of course Danny knows it too. "She chose him to try and restore things. She couldn't have known they were too far gone for that."

My father was tall and slender, had long fingers, deep-set watery eyes, smoked a pipe, spoke softly. He wore cracked brown shoes that had been polished and repolished to a weary shine, baggy suits with pockets stretched from papers and keys, drove a battered old car. He never gave up on Gordonwood either, even long after he must have realized that he had taken on more than he could ever handle. Standing next to my mother in her handsome dresses, silk suits, fur stole, he looks especially forlorn. Danny has all the photographs.

"Why didn't someone buy him a new sweater?" I ask. "Look at this tacky old thing he's wearing here. Didn't we notice?"

"I guess not," Danny says.

"How didn't we?" I ask. "I remember that outfit I've got on. It was new and the hem was too long. And there he is in a sweater that looks so strung out even Tibor wouldn't wear it."

"Let me see," Leora demands and then adds knowledgeably: "Dad would wear it."

"We just didn't notice," Danny says. "Mom should have."

"What did we used to give him on Father's Day?" I ask.

"Aftershave lotion, probably," Danny says.

"Did he ever wear aftershave lotion?"

Neither of us know.

Danny has a picture of my Dad's warehouse. He's had it retouched and blown up and now it hangs in his office. The picture's taken from the street and in it the building appears abandoned. Many of the windows are broken, there is rust running from the drainpipes, missing pieces of casement. Each time I look at it I am surprised by the decay. It must have taken place over so many years as to be imperceptible.

"When she married Arnold," I say, "it must have seemed as if all the striving could at last be left behind."

———❦———

When it comes to Arnold, Danny, who is usually so reliable and levelheaded, becomes unrecognizable. He told me that the last time he was in London and Arnold wouldn't let up on his insistence that Danny hand-carry gifts back for Gregory's children, Danny finally took them and then dumped them in the first trash can he saw at Heathrow Airport.

"I gave them to my office mail room," he told Arnold. "Have Gregory check again with the post office in Weston."

I don't know who is right and who is wrong in it all. I couldn't help laughing with astonishment when he told me what he'd done. Now I just watch.

I'm only a couple of years older than Danny, although these days people tend to assume that I am much older, that between Danny in his restored Jaguar and expensive suits and me there's a decade if not more. But there isn't. He'll always seem like my younger brother, though, whatever the difference in our ages and no matter how wealthy and tightly wrapped he is, how much he thinks he's my protector. And, for all his wrapping, Danny's the more vulnerable of the two of us, more vulnerable in a way than my mother even. His head may be cool, but his heart never has been.

I was at the university when Danny had to do his army. All the boys got drafted straight out of high school, and Danny wasn't too happy about it. He blamed my mother for his having to go and he still does although whatever her views on the subject may have been she didn't invent conscription. While I was going to classes Danny was counting off the days until he had to leave, spending his last weeks as a civilian lying by the pool. He was also being very surly with my parents.

Baptie was crafty in how she went about doing things that were important to her.

"I have big problem with Danny," she said one afternoon. "Big, big problem."

She had cornered me in the kitchen, made me lunch, brought me tea, was standing over me while I ate. From the way she was fidgeting about it was easy to guess that something was bothering her. Baptie was transparent in that respect.

"What did he do?" I asked.

We all knew that Danny was being a bit of a problem, that until the whole army thing was over life wouldn't be quite normal again. But sometimes you had to listen carefully to Baptie to get the part of the story that counted.

"Danny is make big trouble for everyone," she said.

"How?" I asked.

It's strange how you think you can tell whether something is earth-shattering or whether someone just thinks it is. Danny wanted steak every night and would only eat at the pool, and if anyone crossed him he would react like you had eaten his young. So he was being a prima donna. Contemplating a year in the South African infantry, I probably would have been too.

"You want some more food?" Baptie asked.

"What has Danny done?" I repeated.

"He is make a big fool for himself," Baptie said finally.

She paused, busied herself at the sink, came back drying her hands.

"How?"

"Danny is make fool of himself with a farm girl rubbish."

"What farm girl rubbish?" I asked.

"Danny and a rubbish girl. A colored rubbish who don't even know her own father."

"How do you know all this?"

"I know. I know what happens in my rooms."

"What do you know?" I asked.

"What I know," Baptie said, "is if I tell the master he will beat him, and if the police find out they will take him."

That's when Baptie told me everything, or everything she wanted to tell me.

"I know this girl," Baptie kept saying. "I can see and I know. I see her next door in the sun, lying there showing herself to anybody who wants to see."

"You're exaggerating," I said.

"She likes to find boy, white boy and rich, so she can be lazy. Her mother too. Like bad women you can buy."

"Are you saying she's a prostitute?" I asked.

"Like that," Baptie said. "Like that."

We didn't like the word, neither of us. She moved away from where I was eating, went to the sink, came back with some fruit, started peeling me a pear.

I used to wonder occasionally what went on in the servants' quarters after dark. Sometimes when I was in bed I would hear gramophone records playing in the *kaiyas*, township music floating across the grass, and I would wonder what they were doing, whether someone brought food or drink, who owned the records, what they were talking about, what caused the occasional bursts of laughter. Baptie must have had lovers, or maybe she didn't, a best friend, a confidant, an enemy. She made every meal I ate for sixteen years, laughed at my jokes, when I was a child used to help me fall asleep by tickling my arms, but her room was too far away for me to know.

"Who told you this?" I asked.

"I know," she insisted. "I know. You think I don't know what happens in my rooms? You must talk to him. Tell him this is a big nonsense."

I thought about it, finding out from Danny what had happened that had Baptie so incensed, but I didn't. In fact I didn't come close. I could no sooner have discussed something like this as undressed in public. The truth is I was embarrassed, put off — how else to say it? I didn't like to think that by the muggy walls of the servants' rooms, in air poisoned by paraffin fumes, old newsprint, horsehair mattresses, pink pinafores, beds on bricks, rows of tight braids, Danny was somehow rubbing his flesh, being intimate, exposing himself. It felt like an indiscretion, life staining and humiliating, like he had crossed a line and ventured into territory that every white person knew was there but knew better than to approach. And I thought about this loose woman that Baptie condemned so completely, and about the disaffection that had clouded Danny's judgment, and I realized that this was a serious matter, after all.

That's why I told my dad and he made me promise to say nothing more and to this day I'm not sure what he did. But I've thought about it many times since then. Occasionally, sometimes not for long stretches and then several times in a few weeks, Danny mentions that girl and lets me know that he hasn't forgotten her. I don't know what he knows about my role in it but for whatever reason I'm uncomfortable talking about it, and when the subject comes up I find myself brushing it aside. What's done is done. At the time I thought it was just a matter of bringing Danny to his senses but it's obvious now there was a whole lot more to it than only that.

And then, irony of ironies, I sort of found myself in the same boat.

❧

I was at the university when the Soweto riots began on June 16, 1976. I heard about them sitting in the cafeteria having tea and toast, and soon enough the whole university was up in arms, the Student Council organizing sympathy rallies and marches through the streets to City Hall. There's this one photograph that was in all the newspapers, the one of that boy Hector Petersen being carried bleeding through the streets, that nobody could ever forget.

And it's amazing, really, what triggered it. They wanted to force these black kids to learn their lessons in Afrikaans rather than in English, to shove down their throats who was the boss and where they would all belong forever. It was like at Sharpeville in 1960 when Africans tried to protest against the Pass Laws that made them carry identity papers wherever they went. As always, the government's only response was violence.

"I sometimes feel," I told my mother that night, "that doing nothing is as bad as supporting this. I'm not sure the genteel kind of debates we're always having mean anything at all in the long run."

My mother wasn't receptive. She had a tendency — still has a tendency — to become strident very quickly. But I wasn't threatening the things she'd done all her life. I admire them. Really I do. I think her big buddy Alan Paton was a hero. I've read *Cry, the Beloved Country* a dozen times.

"Well," she said sharply, "what do you suggest as an alternative?"

"I don't know," I told her. "But it all seems condescending, doesn't it, white parliamentary politics at a time like this?"

"What are you suggesting instead?" she repeated. "Breaking the law?"

"There have to be other ways," I said.

"Well, if there are I don't know what they might be," she said. "And I've spent my adult life trying to find out."

Sometimes Leora asks me about Africa — simple things, like whether Zulu men are allowed more than one wife or whether ostriches are unique to South Africa — and I find I don't have the answers. Occasionally I ask Danny.

"Why is she asking?" Danny asks.

"Probably something for school," I say. "Do you have the answer?"

"I could guess."

"So could I. But do you know?"

"How would I know?" he says. "I went to the same school you did."

And it's true, really, that as we look back on it, try to piece together what we learned about Africa while we were in Africa, we realize that it's pretty meager. History starts with a band of Dutch marauders who came to the Cape to set up a trading station, and then the British won a war in Europe and got the Cape as part of their spoils, and then Dutch farmers who didn't like British ideas moved inland, fought with the natives, set up Boer republics, got beaten in a war, were forced to accept union under British control, finally took back the country in 1948, and then I was born, and then Danny. And also my grandfather arrived in Durban on Union Day, 1910. I forget the month.

We can laugh about it now, Danny and I, about how the only Zulu words we know are instructions, like *hamba kaiya*, which means go home, or *gajima gakulu*, which means run faster, but it's not a happy kind of laughter. More ironic. Bitter even. I don't know how many wives Zulu men are allowed to have and though I could go to the library to look it up, I won't. It's not so much that I'd like to know these things, more that I'm sorry I didn't learn them in Africa. Sorry that I never learned to talk to black girls my age and in their own language, never tried to understand how it felt to be banished in your own country, to be made to feel that your own history wasn't worth learning. I could go on.

Baptie raised me while her son was raised by relatives back in Zululand, combed my hair daily, and with love, instead of her own child's, lived in a bleak room filled with smoke from a portable stove, was the age I am now and sleeping alone night after night on a narrow bed behind the swimming pool. When Tibor goes away with one of the school's teams and I'm alone I bring Leora into my bed just to know someone's there.

"Mom," Leora says.

"Yes."

"We're doing South Africa in history and I told them the apartheid people put you in jail."

"I'd so much rather you didn't dredge that up," I say.

"The kids all thought it was neat. The teacher wants you to come in and talk to the class."

"It wasn't neat, my honey," I tell her. "And it was a long time ago."

"Does that mean you won't."

"It means I'd have nothing to say."

<hr />

There was this man, his name was Tini Makhatini, who was a student at the African medical school on Umbilo Road and who came to address a meeting of the Student Council. He was looking for volunteers to work with him on a project in Umlazi township. The kids there were having a hard time with the authorities but there hadn't been the kind of riots they were having in Soweto.

I was twenty and it was the first time I'd ever been in a black township. Eight miles from Durban and there were unpaved roads, broken-down houses, no electricity, no real stores.

"First time here?" Tini asked me.

We were in my car, the little secondhand Austin mini my father had bought for me when I got my license. Tini didn't have a car.

"Yes," I said.

"What do you think?" he asked.

I just shook my head.

"This township is a good one, honestly," he said. "Believe me. Umlazi is not the worst."

"This is all so unfair," I said.

"Unfair?"

He laughed.

"The houses are not the problem," he said. "Not the streets and not the schools and not anything you can see. The problem is what has been done with the minds of the people. Too many of them believe what the white man has told them for three hundred years, that they do not count, that things look like they do because white people are better than they are."

"How can they believe that?"

"Even the servants who work in your house," Tini said, "if you ask them, they will tell you, in one way or another, that they believe this. That there is something incomplete about their humanity."

I thought of Baptie and Ambrose, Leonard, the boy who looked after the garden, Josephine the housemaid. Perhaps it was true that we were all incapable of seeing where our roles in this society ended and we ourselves began.

"Do you know," Tini said, "how if a black person wants to work in Durban he must get a Pass, permission from the government?"

"Yes," I said.

"And me too," Tini said. "I was born in Durban but I must have a Pass. To get a Pass you have to go to this office that they call the Native Affairs Office or something like that on a certain day, and then they want to examine you to see that you do not have any diseases you are bringing into this clean city of the white people. Did you know that?"

"No."

"And so on the day the doctor is there, they make you take off all your clothes, three people at a time, and to wait in a room for the doctor to come and examine you."

I said nothing.

"On the door of the room," Tini said, "when I was going out, I saw a sign. And do you know what is on the sign?"

"No," I said.

"It said: 'Beware — Natives in a state of undress.'"

We were in a part of the township that was quite dark, the rutted streets lined with small buildings and groups of people sitting idly on the verge. I was not meant to be there, was, though I of course said nothing, becoming scared.

"This system will not be destroyed because of what white people do," Tini said. "Even those with good intentions, those who say they want to change it, they continue to enjoy the whites-only beaches and the restaurants and the other things as they wait for change to come. For them there is no urgency."

"There are many whites who hate the system," I said. "You know that."

"Of course," Tini answered quickly. "And we want them to fight with us. But for the struggle to be truly won it must be the blacks who lead it, with or without the help of white people."

We parked the car on some grass and walked to the place Tini wanted to take me. It was a long, muddy building with an iron roof and a wooden veranda running along the side. You could see he was a regular there by how warmly everyone greeted him.

"This is the classroom where we are going to," Tini said as we reached the end of the building. "The teacher is a friend. She could get in big trouble for doing this."

A young African woman came out, kissed Tini, shook my hand. She seemed shy.

"They are waiting for you," she said.

As we entered the room something shifted. At first you could see that the students were apprehensive about me, but then Tini introduced me in English and they relaxed and when he began talking to them in Zulu they seemed to forget about me completely. I didn't know what he was saying but it was clear they were enthralled. They sat forward in their desks, their eyes bright. A person could have become drunk on the air alone.

"These kids are learning nothing," he said later. "They come here every day but there are no books. Not a proper roof to keep out the rain."

"Do they need teachers?" I asked.

"Of course," he said. "That is why I brought you here."

And so I started teaching in Umlazi. My mother wasn't at all happy with the idea of my going there after dark, but it was only twice a week and Tini came with me. He would hold his discussion group in one classroom and I would be in another, helping the kids with whatever they needed help in, their math or their English or whatever. They were a long, long way behind where I had been when I was their age but I did my best, dug up my old schoolbooks, lifted pens and paper and whatever else was lying around at Gordonwood to take with me, and when I think back on all the different things I did in Durban I would have no difficulty settling on those evenings as the most rewarding. I would step into the classroom, there would be complete silence, I would begin to say something and see that they were hanging on my every word, but even as I talked I'd be wondering about them, about what was going on in their heads, what they thought about me and of my being there, how they could look across the space between us without even a hint of resentment. Sometimes it took everything I had not to stop my lesson and to start asking questions.

And there was Tini.

"Let me ask you something, Bridget," Tini said to me one night. He pronounced my name "Bree-jet." "Why are you doing this?"

"You know why," I said.

"Tell me again, then."

I thought for only a moment.

"Because I have so much. And because I can be useful."

"There are other things that need to be done, too," he said.

"Like what?" I asked.

I knew as I asked it that Tini was leading me someplace very dangerous.

"I will tell you," he said. "But later."

We were driving in Umlazi, me at the wheel, Tini with his elbows on his knees, leaning forward, watching me. We passed someone Tini knew and he asked me to stop, unrolled the window, had a long conversation in Zulu. I knew they were talking about me. You didn't have to speak Zulu to figure that out.

"Who was that?" I asked as we moved away.

"Someone I know," Tini said.

"What were you saying about me?"

"What do you think we were saying about you?" he asked.

I found myself suddenly quite upset, humiliated.

"I don't speak Zulu," I said.

"What do you think he would want to know about you, here on the street in Umlazi at ten o'clock at night?" Tini asked.

"I don't know," I said.

"You really do live in another world, don't you," he said.

"Listen here," I shouted. "I didn't make any of the rules we live by. I am who I am and I was born into it just as you were."

"But you are so used to the way things are," Tini replied, "that you can't see too clearly how they could be."

I didn't say anything for a moment, just kept driving, out of Umlazi, onto the airport road, back to my world, back to Durban.

"He wanted to know," Tini said as we started down the highway, "whether we were dating."

❦

At the end of the term I asked my mother if we could have a small party at Gordonwood for some of the students who were also working at the school.

"Why here?" she asked.

"Because there is no other place we can have it," I told her. "You know that. There is no restaurant that will let us in, blacks and whites. And the other parents won't hear of it."

"Oh Bridget," my mother said. "I worry about all this."

My dad hadn't been gone long then and somehow she seemed to have lost her spirit. She spent a lot of time talking about him, second-guessing herself, trying to persuade me it had all been an accident.

"It's not a big deal," I told her. "Just a few people."

In the end she agreed, of course. How could she not without seeming to be hypocritical? And then I wondered whether it had been such a good idea after all, what Tini and the others would say when they saw this great house in which only three people, my grandfather in his bed, my mother, and I, lived, what they'd think when they saw the servants creep away to their rooms as dusk approached.

But we did have the party at Gordonwood and it all seemed to go quite well. We stood around and talked and then someone played music and we danced, and then we had a barbecue out by the swimming pool and scattered about the garden to talk and eat. I remember it clearly because it was the night Tini propositioned me and when I said no he treated it as if it had been some kind of a joke.

"You'll change your mind," he said. "In the end they all do."

"They do?" I said. "Well then I suppose you have something to look forward to."

"No," he said. "You have something to look forward to."

I thought about it that night as I lay in my bed, of Tini Makhatini and how the children would listen as he talked, of the other boys I knew, of Baptie's room, men pulling an airplane with ropes, of men without shirts digging trenches, raising their pickaxes and then dropping them, chanting in Zulu as they worked, of a feeling that had been growing and growing that familiar boundaries were shifting. I thought of Danny and that girl from the servants' quarters, how the trip to Africa next door is filled with allure and uncertainty, and I thought that if Tini Makhatini were to ask again, this time I might give a different answer.

Then of course the police came and it all ended very abruptly indeed.

"So what did you do to get arrested?" Leora asks.

"Not nearly enough," is all I can say.

When the Security Police came I was truly a child, impervious to danger, under my mother's mantle, earnest, very callow. And then everything got stripped away in an instant, like a sheet that had been shielding the light.

At first they scared me, of course. They were good at that.

"Just come along with us, miss," was all they would say as they stood there at the front door to Gordonwood. Later, whatever it was I asked, the only answer they would give was: "All in good time, miss."

So I was standing there in the entrance hall of Gordonwood, Baptie on the stairway carrying a tray, my mother upstairs getting ready to leave for the university, and all I could think was that I wished my father were here to take care of it. Perhaps it was my last glimpse of childhood, a flashing thought that soon was gone.

"Just hold on," I said, shaken. "I'll fetch my mother."

"Send the girl," the officer said, pointing to Baptie. "We'd like you to stay down here."

"What is it?" Baptie demanded from the stairs.

"Fetch Mom," I said.

My voice was shaking, my hands as cold as ice.

But my mother was powerless too. She came slowly down the stairs, her hair unbrushed, her makeup half on, asked what they wanted.

"We have a warrant here for Bridget Divin," the man said. "This young lady admits that she is Bridget Divin."

"She doesn't have to admit it," my mother said. "She is. But what do you want with her?"

The officer recited some section of the security laws.

"That doesn't answer my question," my mother said. "I asked you what reason you had for arresting her."

"Look lady," the man said curtly. "I don't have to stand here and answer your questions."

"You watch your tone," my mother said, and it was a mistake, not the time for high horses.

"Come," the man said and grabbed me by the arm.

"You take your hands off her while I call my lawyer," my mother said, but by now things had passed the point of any civility. The Security Police answered to no one.

"You can do that later," he said. "Come on now, miss."

It was then that Baptie, maybe for the first time, realized what was happening.

"You can't take her," she said.

She was walking down the stairs slowly, still carrying a tray, her eyes wide open.

"I suggest you control your Bantu," the man said.

"Baptie," my mother cautioned. "Go to the kitchen."

"You can't take my baby," Baptie said.

Now it was clear to everyone how adamant she was. She dropped the tray on the floor — orange juice and half a grapefruit, two cups of tea, rolling around — and continued to edge towards the door.

The officer said something to his aide and the man pulled his truncheon from his belt.

"Just come along, miss," he said firmly.

It was then that Baptie attacked, flew through the air at him like a lioness, grabbed the arm of the man whose fingers were now closed over my wrist, began to pry me from him. Nothing we could say would stop her as she flailed at him, but of course it didn't last long, although it seemed to go on forever at the time. One heavy thud with the truncheon, and then another, and Baptie was on the floor, her apron soaked with blood, wailing and clutching her head.

Then I remember the inside of the police van, feeling stupid above everything else as all the neighborhood servants stood on the other side of the hedge and watched me getting loaded into this dark van, khaki with black bars at the end. The doors clanked shut, someone turned a key, and then we jerked away and I drove up Gordonwood's driveway for the last time in my life.

I don't quite know how to say this, but it was a morning without time, the only day in my life when time seemed to go backwards, when it got earlier as the day progressed, when nothing happened even as everything changed.

❦

First they drove me into the town, to the jail near the courthouse. My father's lawyer, Morton Nerpelow, had offices just next door. I could see the foyer of his building from the back of the van. A man led me into a room with an oxblood floor and one bench, told me to wait, and then disappeared. I went to sit on the floor in the corner, leaned against the wall, wondered what my mother was doing, when she and Mr. Nerpelow would appear and tell me what I had to do. I remember wondering who had decided to paint the walls of the room yellow and the ceiling a light green.

Time passed, how much I couldn't say, and when nobody came and my back started to ache I thought to start trying some of the stretching exercises I hadn't done for months, and so I moved the bench against the wall and lay on my back. I heard keys in the door and then it opened.

"Are you trying to be funny?" a voice said. I stopped what I was doing, turned, looked up at him. It was a man I hadn't seen before. He was dressed in a khaki safari suit with epaulets, long socks, *veldskoen* shoes. Two others were behind him. He looked furious.

"I asked you a question," he said. "Do you think this is all a joke?"

"No," I said. "I'm waiting for my mother and her lawyer."

"Don't you play games with us," he said.

His voice was filled with menace. If he could have hit me I knew he would have. He strode into the room, moved the bench back, walked out, and slammed the door. It was then, really, that I knew I was in the kind of trouble I couldn't get out of easily.

And yet in Pretoria, where I was driven that night, they were quite different. I knew immediately they were louts, of course, even under the initial civility, but I'd never known anyone quite like the man who questioned me.

"You do know why you're here, don't you?" he said.

I didn't.

"Why do you think?"

"I don't know what I'm charged with," I said.

"We haven't charged you with anything," he told me.

He smiled, as if he'd outsmarted me on some technicality and that I should appreciate the cleverness. He mentioned some section of the detention without trial law. I knew what he was talking about and how broad and cruel the law was because I'd listened to my mother describe it at a protest meeting when it was first passed.

"We are simply holding you for questioning."

"For how long?" I asked.

"That depends."

"On what?"

"On many things."

I said nothing.

"You don't see how serious this is, do you?" he said, lighting a cigarette and standing up.

"I haven't done anything wrong."

He puffed on his cigarette, inhaled, tossed it on the floor, and stood on the butt.

"I don't know what you want," I told him.

"Let's start with your friend Makhatini," he said at last.

"I hardly know him."

"How well is that?" he asked. "Did you have sexual relations with him? Did he stick his long, black cock in you? Slide it in and out? Did you like it?"

For a moment my body drained of feeling and all that remained was a burning around my eyes, a dryness. I looked at him, tried to remember how it had felt to walk into a classroom with Tini and to watch the children's faces come alive with affection.

"Why are you doing this?" I asked.

"Did you?" he repeated. "Did it feel good?"

The room was small and clean, quiet. You couldn't even hear the traffic from outside, another sound from the building. I glared at him, at his full lips and short black hair, the khaki shirt, epaulets, shining springbok emblem mounted on his green beret.

"Perhaps," I said.

"*Goed*," the man said in Afrikaans. "Now we're getting somewhere."

I didn't tell them anything, of course. There was nothing to tell. But it was amazing how fixated they were on my friendship, such as it was, with Tini, how much of their questioning, in fact, had to do with sex. In the end I began to suspect that it was the only thing they were interested in.

"We have your boyfriend now too," they told me once. "Wouldn't it be a pity if he tried to escape by jumping out a window or something like that, especially one high up."

I knew that political prisoners in South Africa did die that way, trying to escape they always said, out of fifth-floor windows, moving cars, trains.

"Tini wouldn't do anything foolish," I said.

"Perhaps he already has," one of them suggested.

It's disorienting being in an environment like that, surrounded only by people hostile to you, people with whom you have so little in common except that you happen to share a country, by some fluke, to live on the same ground.

"Please tell me he's okay," I said and I cursed myself but there was nothing I could do to stem the tears that seemed to find their own way up and out.

"He's as good as new," someone said at last.

After that I knew, somehow, that they would leave me alone. I wasn't a threat to them and once they'd broken through my attempt at bravado, feeble though it was, and made me cry for myself or for Tini or for who knows why, it was as if they had almost everything they wanted. In the end I'm convinced they kept me for as long as they did just to teach me a lesson. The rest of it was just bad food, boredom, a sort of torture of abandonment that seemed to have no ending and no object.

The day before I was released I was brought into a room with two men in it, one slightly older than the other, and told to sit in the only chair there was.

"How good is your Afrikaans?" one of them, the older, asked me.

"I can speak Afrikaans," I said.

"Good," he said, smiling. "Very good. Would you like some tea?"

"No, thank you," I said.

"We're going to let you go," he said in Afrikaans. "But before that you and we are going to have a little chat."

Home, I thought. Home at last.

"So listen here," he said. *"Hoor my goed, Joodse meisie."* Listen to me well, Jewish girl. His charm had evaporated. He meant to scare me and he succeeded. "There is a struggle between Afrikaner and black going on here, and you have no place in it. If you mix yourself up again we will squash you. Do you hear me?"

The other, a younger man, gestured to him to stand back and walked over to me. He sat on the table, looked at me, shook his head.

"What is it with you Jews?" he said. He wasn't being shrill or threatening. In fact he sounded curious, like he really hoped I would tell him something. "Why do you always do this to yourselves? Why do you reject every country that tries to take you in, gives you its benefits, lets you live in peace? Why do you people always have to fight somebody else's battle, bring in poisonous ideas and make yourselves so hated and rootless? Tell me, please. I am genuinely interested."

He sat there on the table waiting for me to say something, as if I was going to answer this question, provide him with a lucid explanation for his views about Jews and everything he'd always wondered about them. One of the girls in my block had been beaten. She was Indian, Shari, and somehow they'd made a mess of her. For a long moment I said nothing.

"Isn't this country beautiful enough for you?" he asked. "Haven't you people prospered here? More than anyone else, in fact. Become rich, most of you. Is there anything you have been denied because of your religion? Any city without a synagogue? Any army base without one of your rabbis? What is it with you? What is it? What? What? What?"

I said nothing, held his eye, and when he realized that this was how it was going to be he stood up and walked away from me, without another word, right out the door.

"I'm sick of all of you," the man who remained said at last. "Your mother and her insulting speeches. You and your games. Your brother and his colored girl. There's something wrong with all of you."

"My brother is in your army," I said. "Leave him out of this."

"It's all the same," he said. "You and him. People like you. You make me sick."

And so, after six months of nights on a cement floor, the pointless bouts of questioning, long days, one morning a policewoman came in and said I was going to be released. I left prison thinking I'd be home by dinner, but instead I found myself on an airplane taking me away from everything I had once taken for granted.

❧

I was twenty-two when I met Tibor. I was staying with friends of my mother's in London, also refugees but they were somehow more authentically so than I, elderly and beaten down, tired looking. Barney's brother was still in South Africa serving a ten-year prison sentence for violating the Suppression of Communism Act, and Meg, his wife, had been under almost continuous house arrest since her thirties. Barney and my mother dated back to their university days and they took me in almost as if I were one of their own children.

They had no money, were impoverished in a way I had never seen before. They lived in this really shabby row house, literally had holes in their shoes, fraying clothes, and they looked so tired and disengaged that they scared me a little.

"What's for dinner, Mother?" Barney would say to Meg and she'd take about three minutes to answer, stand up from the kitchen table, walk over to the stove in her sensible shoes, stir a pot.

"Soup," she'd say. "Fresh bread."

"Sounds good," he'd say, and bury himself back in a book.

They didn't have space for me at all in their narrow little house but even so they did nothing to make me feel this, to the contrary spoke and acted as if I'd moved in forever. But I wrote to my mother and told her that things couldn't stay the way they were and she must have asked around because in her next letter she gave me the names of other people to contact, and it was because of one of them that I met Tibor.

❦

Tibor is very tall and Slavic looking. He has an angular face, skin that's so smooth it could be a woman's, wispy fair hair that never looks quite clean, though of course it is. He is as fluent at English as I am and yet he has never lost his accent, his inability to say "th," for instance, and his insistence on pronouncing some vowels as if there were a "y" right before them. "Amyerica," for instance, or "spyontyanyeous." There are times, in fact, when he emphasizes all of this, with my mother especially, though he swears he isn't aware of it.

In all the years we have been married, though, I have never seen Tibor lose his temper, and, frankly, I can't even remember the last time we had a cross word. Tibor is sturdy and imperturbable. I cannot imagine him getting angry.

It was the sturdiness that drew me to him the first time I saw him. I was standing in the foyer of the East End YMCA in London. My mother must have done the rounds to discover who knew someone my age in London with an interest in gymnastics because that's exactly what she had come up with, the daughter of a woman my mother didn't really know who was at university in London and was also a gymnast. I hadn't been near a gymnasium for almost a year by then.

And I knew the moment I set foot in it that I didn't want to be there. I had a little bag with my kit — that was one of the things my mother had been sure to pack — but I hadn't put any of it on.

"You coming?" this girl asked.

"Maybe later," I said, and that was how I came to be standing in the foyer.

I would say it's true, to the extent anyone's life has a single high point or a single low, that it was the low point of mine. When the police came and I was interrogated and thrown into a stinking little cell it was scary and then everything seemed very bleak, but it was also different, finite, nothing I could control. This was different.

I walked over to the notice board and started reading whatever was on it, considered simply leaving and going back to Barney and Meg's house, maybe phoning this girl later to apologize. I checked in my purse to see that I had a subway token and I did, and then I stood back against the wall to think about it all. That's when Tibor came up to me.

"Can I help you?" he asked. "You look a little lost."

"It's okay," I said.

He looked at me carefully with his blue Slavic eyes, his tousled hair, his sunken cheeks.

"I coach a boys' soccer team here," he said. "You want to come watch?"

He was much older than I was, Tibor, over forty, though the smooth skin and boyish hair tend to conceal it. I wasn't open to being approached by a boy, let alone by an older man, but that wasn't what he was doing. He was trying to help, but very gently.

"Where?" I asked.

"Upstairs," he said. "You can even play if you want. It'll put the boys on their best behavior."

"How old are they?" I asked. I was almost smiling, wanted to go with him.

"They're thirteen and fourteen," he said. "Hormones with legs." Hormyones wit lyegs.

"Okay," I said.

"I'll lend you a soccer jersey," he said. "When we play inside we play with tennis shoes."

We walked to the changing rooms and agreed to meet outside, and even though I hesitated for a moment once I was alone, almost turned and ran all the way to the train station, I didn't.

He was waiting for me when I came out.

"What's your name, by the way?" he asked.

I told him.

"Mine's Tibor," he said. "Don't try the surname."

"It's all so weird," Leora, who now carries that same unpronounceable surname, has said. "Didn't it feel weird?"

It didn't. I've seen how people trust Tibor, listen to him, want him to like them. It happened to me.

Upstairs the gymnasium was filled with English schoolboys, a sea of pasty white arms sticking out of oversize shirts, thick socks at the bottom of spindly legs. When Tibor came into the room, though, everything stopped, the random movements, the shouting, and there was this surge towards us of little boys, as if Tibor had brought something with him, candy or something, that they all wanted. When they saw me they slowed down.

"Are you ready to play?" Tibor asked.

"Yes," they all said together.

Maybe schoolchildren in England are more obedient. Maybe all schoolchildren once were.

"Bridget is going to play with us," he said. "She'll play on one team and I'll play on the other."

For a moment there was silence, then a nudge or two, a stifled giggle.

"Tibor," one of the boys said finally. "Is she your girlfriend, then?"

Tibor was holding a clipboard, writing something, but he paused and then smiled.

"You'll have to ask her, won't you?" he said.

"Are you?" a dozen faces turned to me and asked.

"Yes," I answered without hesitation.

❧

Danny has zero tolerance for Arnold, which is understandable, but not much more for my mother and of course she notices. If there's any respect in which she's remained in control it's how she lets Danny pretend he's being tolerant when in fact he's being completely dismissive. She just doesn't get offended.

"You are my children," she keeps saying, as if that were enough.

Danny wouldn't admit it, of course, but there's tons of my mother in him. Even Tibor sees it and he's prepared to overlook almost any foible. For one thing, Danny and my mother think the same things are important. Take Danny's house. It's really beautiful, everyone who sees it agrees, and it's not dissimilar to the house my mother and Arnold have in London. There's lots of white stone, ebony, leather. It's actually uncanny how alike they feel. And from the outside it's reminiscent of the Dutch farmhouses near Cape Town.

"It looks like Groot Constantia," I told him when I saw the drawings.

"No it doesn't," he said hotly.

"Look at the gables," I said. "And the symmetrical shutters."

"That's not Dutch," he argued. "It's French if anything."

Danny may have one of the best collections of South African art around. He dresses beautifully, really impresses people without even realizing that he has. He has this stock market newsletter he publishes every week and though he sends it to me for free and I never read it someone told me it costs eighteen hundred dollars a year. I think he sees it all as a kind of revenge, something he does to compensate for my father. But nobody cares. Nobody, that is, except Danny.

It's like that for my mother too, to use times long past and over as a reference point, to see things against a frozen tableau. I know, for instance, what she sees in Arnold, all the wealth and power of it, but that was long ago. Now he's only a pathetic old man, really. Anything else is all illusion.

Except in her eyes.

❧

Tibor was so poor, poorer even than Barney and Meg were, but it was completely unimportant to him. I don't want to idealize this poverty. There's nothing grand about it. But it's also liberating to be convinced that you want nothing beyond what you have, that there is nobody whose opinion matters except yours of yourself. When Tibor stepped off the plane from Sofia he barely spoke English, had no money at all, had been banned from the university, and had worked as a laborer to support himself until the chance came to leave. In London he coached soccer and learned English, eventually went back to school, eventually became a counselor. He was my first true love, and has been the only.

Despite their misgivings Barney and Meg didn't object in the end when I moved in with him, and a year and two months later we were married at the Kensington Registry. My mom was offended that we only told her afterwards, but I knew what she would have said and I didn't care to hear it. When you know deep in your heart that something you're doing is right, you don't want to hear someone else's contrary thoughts echo through your decision.

Besides, she took it quite well. It was Danny who was the problem.

"How old is he?" he asked on the phone.

"It isn't important," I said. "He's older than I am."

"Isn't this a little precipitous, Bridge?" he said. "I mean, you haven't known him very long."

"I know what I'm doing," I said.

"And where's he from again?" Danny asked. "Romania? Hungary?"

"Bulgaria," I said.

"Bulgaria. Who lives in Bulgaria?"

Sometimes, I remember thinking, Danny can be the worst snob in the family. But much later, several years later, I realized that his reluctance didn't come from snobbery at all. Like my mother Danny has never really left Africa behind. Perhaps it's because he wasn't purged of it like I was. He's been left to wonder about it and to daydream, to think things are possible that really never were and never will be.

I think Danny's biggest objection to my marrying Tibor was that it closed a chapter on things, and that it did so before Danny was ready to let them go.

CHAPTER FOUR

Baptie

I GOT A TELEGRAM from Mr. Nerpelow. Mr. Nerpelow is the Divin family lawyer in Durban who also sends me my pension check each month. It comes in the same envelope from Volkskas Bank, which they now call Absa Bank. It used to come on the same day every month except the post now in Zululand is not so good. If you want to be sure your letter gets where it is going it is best to go to one of the cities like Eshowe or Richards Bay and to put it in a post box that the whites use, and then you can be sure it will get where it is going. Here in Gingindlovu you can never be so sure. When I write my letters to Bridget I send them first to my friend in Durban. America is too far to go for letters to start their journey the wrong way.

What Mr. Nerpelow said in his telegram is that Danny is coming to Durban next week.

"He is arriving next Monday," the telegram said, "and would like to see you if you can come to town. We will pay all expenses."

At first I did not believe this, and then I kept the telegram for a couple of days and it began to seem more possible. Danny has been gone for so long that one part of me says I will be sad to see if he has become an old man and another part of me says it will make me happy to see his face with my eyes again whatever he is. Also he will not be an old man. From 1978 to 1999 is not enough time to make a boy into an old man. What I am afraid to see is if he has changed from how he was, if now that he is grown up he will decide that he must treat me like a child. That is still better than the Boers, who like to treat the black people like a dog. But I do not want to see him change for either way. My Danny and Bridget were not like that before.

I told this all to my son, Eben. Eben knows Danny, not exactly like a friend but they are the same age, those two, and when Eben would sometimes come on his school holidays to stay with me at Gordonwood he and Danny were a little like friends. At first I was not sure this was a good thing, Eben seeing all these things he could not have, boxing gloves, small cars with batteries, racing carts. But I did not stop it, and also Danny would give things to Eben too so it was not always that Eben could not have.

Then later Eben decided himself that Danny could not be a friend to him. It was later, when Danny was in the army and he came home on holiday in his uniform.

"How's Eben?" he asked me.

"He's fine," I said.

"When is he coming to town?"

"I don't know," I said.

And this was a lie for me because Eben was in town, even on that day, staying with me in my room. But Eben, when he saw Danny coming down the driveway in his soldier's uniform, he told me he didn't want to see him this time, that he could not be a friend to a man in a soldier's uniform.

"He has to go to this bloody army, man," I told him. "It is the government that makes him."

Still Eben did not move.

"Give Eben my regards," Danny said when he was leaving, but when I gave them Eben said to me: "Tell him to keep his regards."

And when this Nerpelow wrote to me that Danny was coming to Durban, Eben asked: "Why he don't come here? It is much easier for him to come here than for you to go to Durban."

"Nerpelow didn't say," I tell him. "And I know these people. They will pay for everything."

"But, Mother," Eben says, "you don't know how difficult it is to go to Durban now. Before you just got on a train and went. Now you have to be very careful and the robbers will not let you travel in peace. You cannot take money with you or it will be stolen. And how can you go to Durban without money? No," Eben says, thinking that he is now a very important man, that he can tell me, his mother, what to do, "I think it is better that you do not go to Durban."

I did not take nonsense before, not from Helga or from Danny or from Bridget. I do not take it from Eben either.

"You talk rubbish," I tell him. "There are no more Pass Laws and I am free to go anywhere in this whole bloody South Africa if I want to."

"No more Pass Laws," he says. "But it is even worse now because of the troubles. There are many robbers now. It is better you stay here."

"You talk nonsense," I tell him again. "I will go without troubles."

But I know what he is talking about. There are many changes now, some for better and some for worse. In Durban there are many *tsotsi* thieves. Some of these come from other countries. What do men from Nigeria want in Durban, I want to know? I do not want to go to his country. Let him stay in his country. Why they come here? But still I am not worried. Baby Jesus will protect me.

Eben knows that I am angry with this Nerpelow. Sometimes when my pension is late I try and call his office but he does not speak to me himself. Instead I have to wait for a woman who works in his office to make some examination and meanwhile I am standing there feeding money into the telephone like it is a hungry child and she does not care. And also I tell him that in 1978 my pension was twenty-five rand a month and a bottle of milk cost eighteen cents, and today my pension is still the same, twenty-five rand a month, and a bottle of milk costs one rand. But he does not care either. I don't know even if he tells Bridget or Danny. If I go to Durban I will tell Danny this myself.

But either way it is okay with me. From long ago I have this sewing machine and I buy material in Richards Bay and make it into dresses, and there are places where they love to buy my dresses. Even one white lady — she is a schoolteacher in the mission school — sometimes buys my dresses. I charge from twenty-five rand to forty rand, depending on how much time I take to make it. So any one dress is more than one month of pension money.

But the government cannot leave you alone. Perhaps it is something in the air in Pretoria, some weed that makes government men think they have the right to go into people's lives and tell them how to live. When the whites were here they had their laws, everything based on the color your skin was, black or white, or like the Indians who own the shops, or colored. Now they are gone and the government is Zulu here but they have enough laws too to drive a person mad. And also they are less honest than the whites, I must say. Now they tell me you need a license to sell dresses, a license to make dresses, a tax number, and it's my opinion that some of that tax money they eat, whatever they say.

Eben works for this new black government doing something in an office where they say they help the farmers. Eben knows nothing about being a farmer. Also he knows to drive but even so the government gives him a car and a driver.

"For what do you need a driver?" I ask him. "You can drive better than the driver."

"It is important," he says. "So that I can work in the back of the car when we are going somewhere."

"You work in your office," I tell him. "In the back of your car you look out the window like a baboon in the zoo."

"You don't understand," he tells me. "It is something the government must do to show that it has authority."

"You don't understand," I tell him. "You are acting like the white man, and white men have more practice acting like white men."

I don't mean to fight with Eben. He is good to me. But these changes worry me a lot. If they stop me sewing, or make me pay a bribe to sew, I will get into trouble because I will not listen.

❧

It is funny that I got this telegram because I have been thinking of Bridget and Danny a lot these days. I just wrote Bridget a letter telling her.

Last week I was in my house sewing when I heard a knock on the front door and when I went to answer it I saw something that was like a picture to me, something I did not think I would see in this lifetime

157

of mine. I opened the door and there was my sister-in-law's daughter Gladys, who I of course know very well, and she is standing next to a white man and they are holding hands.

"Gladys?" I said. "What are you doing here?"

I did not mean it that way, of course. Gladys I have known ever since she was a baby and she is always welcome to come into my house. But not many white people come to this side of Gingindlovu, and none of them come holding the hand of a Zulu girl.

"This is my husband, Aunty," Gladys says. "His name is Mr. Boisey. He comes from Klerksdorp."

Now I start to speak to Gladys in Zulu.

"What foolishness is this?" I ask her. "To bring a white man to my house and to call him mister and to say it is your husband?"

"I am her husband, Aunty," says this Mr. Boisey in Zulu. "It is the new South Africa now. Black and white can be married if they love each other. Gladys and I love each other."

So I am standing there like a ghost and then Gladys asks if they can come inside and I say they can. Mr. Boisey, whose name is Adam, comes in and he asks me if I can make him a cup of tea. I am thinking that this is a clever man, this Mr. Boisey, to ask me for a cup of tea. You must be polite to a man who asks a favor in your house like that. He becomes a visitor, and you have to treat a visitor nice. And he asks in my language too, in Zulu.

"How long has Aunty lived here?" he asks.

He is not a handsome man but he has still a nice face and lots of brown hair. Gladys is a beautiful girl, very tall and nice, with big breasts like the men like and big brown eyes.

"Since 1983," I say. "I used to work in Durban for Divin family, and then Divin family left, mother and daughter and son, and they built me this house and they give me a pension too."

"Gladys told me about them," Mr. Adam Boisey says and I wonder what else Gladys told him.

But I go into the kitchen and boil the kettle for tea, and while I am there Gladys comes into the kitchen and puts the cups on the tray without saying anything. But then, just as the water boils and I am putting biscuits on the tray, she asks: "You aren't angry, are you?"

"How can I be angry. He is a nice man, even though he is a white," I say.

Things are changing very quickly in this place for these things to happen. And I think then of Bridget and the things that happened to her, how they came and took her away because of the things that she did, and of Danny and what he did.

One night, perhaps the worst of all the nights I was at Gordonwood, they had a party, Bridget and her friends. I know it was not Bridget's idea because Bridget would not have thought to do this herself. It was after this party that I knew Bridget's friends were trouble, that I tried to warn her, but she would not listen. And the worst of it was that I could not say all that I knew.

To this party she invited all kinds of rubbishes from the university, and chief among the rubbishes was this Makhatini, whose face I saw in the newspaper later. That night he was wearing a dress and only a long time later I saw a picture same like it and telling that men wear this dashiki dress in other places in Africa. But not in South Africa. Why must he wear something they do not wear in South Africa?

Before they arrived at my house Bridget came into the kitchen and she said I should not stay home that night, that I should go out.

"Why I cannot stay in my house?" I asked.

"I can do everything tonight," Bridget said, not answering me.

And of course I knew right at that time, when they came, blacks and whites, why she did not want me there. If I could see Bridget today I would say this to her: In South Africa now there are many black people who work in houses for black people. And there is something I want to tell you about that. They do not treat the people who work in their houses the same as the Master and the Madame treated me at Gordonwood. I would say to Bridget: I thanks God for Divin family in my life.

At that party after the eating they played music and I was not happy when I went into the room and saw the whites and the blacks dancing together. They did not hold each other, but even so they were dancing and moving their hips like young people do, like lovemaking, blacks and whites together.

But that was not the worst of it, what made the night so bad. What made the night so bad was that I was standing near the garage where they parked the cars, about to go to my room, and I heard two boys talking together in Xhosa, two Xhosa boys, and it was what they were saying that made the whole night so bad.

"She's got a good body," one of them said. "She gave me a number to phone her at so her parents would not know. And what about you?"

"I got two numbers," the other one said.

"How many is that for you, then?" the one asked.

"This year or altogether?"

"Altogether?"

"Fifty-four," he said. "I have slept with fifty-four white bitches and I will sleep with one hundred if I keep doing so well."

And then they whistled a little and laughed, and then I went to my room. I think they were drunk, but still I think such things are very bad. But now I also think that perhaps it was other things, bad things put on them by the Boers and how it made them feel, that is the real father of such unkindness that they make their revenge on the daughters. If the men are bad you must fight the men, not treat the daughters like a game.

And I wish these things had passed my Bridget and Danny by.

❦

I told Gladys that she and Mr. Boisey, this Adam that she is married to, should stay with me for two days because my house is bigger than my sister-in-law's house, and because she is not proud she said that she would. I made a bedroom for them, a big bed for the white man and the Zulu girl to sleep together in, and that night they went to bed in the bed I had made and I went to bed in the room next door thinking about it.

And I was thinking, this is not a terrible thing, this is a good thing. They will have children, nice children who are a little bit brown and a little bit white, with nice noses, I think, and big brown eyes. It is not such a sin, after all. And I could not help thinking how shocked I was, how angry, when Ambrose told me those things about Danny and Emily's girl, how I thought it was so bad like a crime against God even, and I told him so, and I told Emily too. Now I cannot stop thinking how you can be so wrong even when you think you are so right. Danny and that girl, I am thinking, and it is an old woman's dream I know, would have had children even more beautiful than Gladys and this Mr. Boisey.

So when they woke up the next morning at eight o'clock I was already awake and I made breakfast for them, a nice breakfast with eggs and pancakes and all the things I used to make for breakfast at Gordonwood, the best kind of breakfast I know how to make, and in the back of my mind I was thinking about other things too, other breakfasts, how I could make such a breakfast for Danny too in my house, him and whoever he chooses to bring with him. Whoever. Honest to God.

"You should not have gone to so much trouble, Aunty," Mr. Boisey said.

I knew when I said those things to Bridget about Emily's girl that they were not true, that she was not a rubbish but a nice girl, but I only wanted them to be true, thought they must be true or she would not be making trouble in my house. I think now that maybe she was good, good to like my Danny, and if because of me Bridget made Danny forget her I wish I could take it back, make it not happen. But only God can do that. Past days do not return.

After breakfast they went, Gladys and Mr. Boisey and the other son of my sister-in-law in Mr. Boisey's car to Mtunzini beach for a swim. After six, they came back for supper. Mr. Boisey was very happy for my good supper, sweets, baked pears and jelly, custard and plums, all kinds of puddings made the same way as when I used to cook at Gordonwood. Now they have gone back to Klerksdorp.

And I was thinking, watching them drive away when they left, that I did not think that I would see Danny again, or Bridget, or her angel Leora so pretty in her gym clothes that Bridget sends me pictures of, or even the Madame or that Mister Arnold in their house in London where she does the cooking for herself and makes the beds and cleans. The Boers drove them out, and now that the Boers say they have changed it is too late because one thing is true for sure. Nothing stays the same. So I wrote a letter to Bridget sending her blessings in her good country from me in my bad country.

I can see that Danny and Bridget now live in a place of peace. For sure. And sometimes when Bridget writes about the past, about the days of Gordonwood and the Master and Danny, all of us up on the hill, I am thankful she is not here anymore. Because after they left, Danny and Bridget, and only Helga and I were left in Durban, my opinion changed too about many things and it began for me to seem that my memories were not the same as I thought they were.

But I do not think it matters now. And I do not want to spoil anyone else's memories. Even when Danny wrote me his letter, the one I got after Nerpelow's telegram, the one that made me wonder how things had turned out in his life that he still was interested in doing such a thing, I decided to help him, to find the person he was looking for if I could, because things change so much in a person's life that what you think at one time is very bad turns out to be not so bad, and also what you think is one thing turns out to be quite different too.

I learned this in the flat on the beachfront where we went to live after Gordonwood was sold.

⊰✿⊱

When we moved from Gordonwood to the flat on the Marine Parade, I traded my room at the edge of the garden for a place in the servants' quarters next to the garage.

"You'll like it," Helga said. "To tell you the truth I've always been a little ashamed of your rooms here."

And it was better, this modern cement room next to the garage where the white tenants parked their cars. To reach it you took the service elevator into the basement and then followed the path past a courtyard with open drains and a large sink to a row of doors on the far side. My room looked out onto the sidewalk and my windows had heavy iron bars. From the street the building looked like a prison, not like a place where people live.

The air on the Marine Parade was filled with automobile smoke and the heavy smell of the sea. On one side of the Parade is a line of palm trees and a narrow piece of land covered with *kikuyu* grass, and on the other are the hotels and the apartments, old falling down buildings side by side with new, shining tall ones. On the sidewalk the Zulu women sell beads and ornaments for the tourists and rickshaw boys wait for people so that they can give them rides. To make the people see them they put animal skins on their backs and beads in their headdress and even paint on their faces.

The Madame chose to live in one of the older buildings.

"I think we'll like it," she said. "It gets a nice sea breeze and it's well kept." When she said something like that she would always wait for a moment when she had finished speaking and then add: "Of course it's not Gordonwood. But nothing is."

"Gordonwood is too big," I would tell her to make her feel better. "It is a place for a family, not just for one person."

"Did you ever think we would end up like this?" she would ask me.

"No Madame," I would have to say.

But my room next to the garage was actually more comfortable than the one I left behind at Gordonwood. At Gordonwood the servants lived in a dark, muddy building that had been cheaply built and not looked after by anyone. The servants' rooms, *kaiyas*, were the same like in most houses except that the *kaiyas* at Gordonwood, which was a very expensive house, were the worst of any you could see. My room was on the end where the ground sloped, and as it went down one wall had begun to move away from the others and to leave a crack which kept growing and growing. In the end the crack was so large that I could see right through it and had to push newspapers between the bricks just to keep out the insects. In the flat building's *kaiyas*, at least, the walls were not broken and the doors opened and closed as they were supposed to.

So I accepted the move to the beachfront as just another thing, nothing to be sad about and nothing to be happy about. Just to wait and see. It had been like that for a long time already. Even on the day the Master died I knew that many changes would be coming. Gordonwood was a nice house but it was so big and it needed many people to run it and it was obvious that the Madame and the children could not stay there alone. In the months after the Master's death I would often overhear them talking about what they would do, about money and going to the overseas, subjects which had never been talked about when the Master was alive. I had overheard arguments about South Africa before, for sure, mostly with the children and the Madame on one side and the Master on the other, but no one had ever spoken of leaving Gordonwood or of going to this overseas. All this was just talking talking, but it did not make a person feel safe.

Nothing changed for almost a year even after what happened to Bridget, and then within the space of a very few months the children were both gone to the overseas and Gordonwood was sold. One day there was a big sale on the front lawn, a bright red tent with chairs inside it, and things I had come to know very well indeed, almost like they were my own, had labels put on them and were held up, the big table from the kitchen, the piano, beds, chairs, pictures, and looked at by strangers. Later they were carried away by these people, across the lawn, up the driveway, out of sight. Then everything that was left was packed into large boxes, the other servants were given discharge pay, and we moved to the beachfront, Helga and I, together.

One good thing of living on the beachfront was how close we were to the sea. For years, ever since I was a girl in Zululand, I knew that seawater could heal a person of many problems. You could rub it into cuts or bites or irritated skin and overnight, even if the condition was not completely cured, it was always much better. At Gordonwood I had kept a few bottles of seawater under my bed and each time the children went to the beach they would refill them for me and Ambrose would bring them back in the trunk of the car. The water was a faint cloudy green and smelled of seaweed and the other chemicals that live and grow beneath the waves.

"Why do you want these?" Danny once asked me.

"The sea is a great place," I told him. "It has many magics in it."

I don't know how to swim and was too scared of the waves to go into the sea myself, but now that we were so close to it I no longer had to use the water only a little bit at a time. On my first day in the flat I poured what was left in the bottles into the drain and then carried them across the Parade and down to the edge of the beach. Only when

I was right at the fence did I see the sign that said the beach was for the whites only and so I had to turn around and come back to the flat. When I told the Madame what had happened she asked the superintendent of the building where was the nearest nonwhite beach and he told her that it was six miles up the road.

"This is the sort of thing that can drive you crazy," she said angrily.

But since there was nothing she could do about it she agreed to fill the bottles herself whenever I wanted, and that still was an improvement over how it had been when we had lived at Gordonwood.

The flat was on the sixth floor, overlooking the ocean. The views from the windows were good but I knew from the first moment I saw them that they would bring a mixed pleasure at best. From Gordonwood's windows you could see over the whole city, the sugar terminals at Maydon Wharf, the Bluff, the buildings on the Esplanade, out almost to the clouds that blew where the sea met the sky. From these windows you could see the sea, yes, but just one street, a row or two of lights, some traffic.

And because it was so near the ocean the air in the flat was hot and wet at the same time, and the wetness made this deep, thick smell to come out of everything. The wooden floors sweated drops of oil and smelled of sap and old polish, and sometimes from inside the walls came smells of mildew and damp cement. But there was a porch off the kitchen and on windy days, if you opened the windows on the ocean side and the doors onto the porch, a wind would blow through the apartment and fill it with a nice, salty freshness. The porch had lime-washed pillars which left powder on your fingers when you touched them and an oxblood floor that turned your feet dark red if you walked on it barefoot.

There was not much work for me to do in the flat and I did not like it, these days with large spaces in them where I had to find something to fill the time. I would wake at the same time each morning, wash in the little bathroom near the courtyard, and then I would ride up in the service elevator and let myself in. It would be quiet inside and I would make myself a cup of tea and wait for the time to prepare the Madame's breakfast and take it to her.

It had been so different at Gordonwood. First the Master would come down and tell me what he wanted for breakfast, and after that the children, and there was always such a rush, people clattering in and out, taking things, getting in my way, that I would never have even a moment to think. Only after they were gone, the Master to work and the children to school, was there any peace. After they were gone a calm would come to the house, something that felt as if it had been earned and paid for, and I would cut myself a thick slice of bread, cover it with my own preserves, and eat it with my tea at the kitchen table. At Gordonwood the kitchen table was made from a heavy piece of wood, not at all like the cheap white one we got in the flat that I could lift up and throw away with just one hand.

Everything at Gordonwood had a time and a place and it seemed like it would last forever, not be like a dream that just disappears when you wake in the morning. On Thursdays I would bake, sometimes a cake, sometimes biscuits, if visitors were coming that weekend both, and on Fridays I would go with Ambrose to the Indian market to buy fruit and vegetables, and to the butcher's, and to the supermarket. When we came back the Madame would look at what I had bought, but not carefully, and in any event I was always prepared to argue for my decisions if she did not like something I had done. I would not ever have disagreed with the Master to his face, but with the Madame it was different. These things were nothing, really. They came and went in a flash, like a summer rainstorm.

"I am not a slave here," I said once when I wanted the afternoon off and she said it was inconvenient. "If I want to go, I will go."

"So go and don't come back," she said and then almost at once felt sorry for her words. "For heaven's sake," she said. "Of course you're not a slave here."

In the flat, because there were only two of us and no longer a driver, it was not necessary for me to make my weekly shopping trips. Each day I would go to the little store on the corner and buy the few things we needed, perhaps a pint of milk or a lettuce, and there was never a need to bake or to plan dinner in advance. Usually she just wanted a salad, or at the most I might grill her a steak, and for myself I felt so seldom hungry that a piece of chicken or a bowl of cornmeal in the afternoon seemed to be all I ever ate.

As time went by I began to long for the old days to come back, for the old house with its polished wood on the walls and thick carpets from Persia, remembered how I used to walk through its rooms with a feather duster, flicking my wrist at the ivory ornaments and carvings, taking from the place a sense of belonging there and also of safety. The Master was as solid as a rock, as constant as the sea even, protected us from the police when they raided to enforce the Pass Laws, and when I was sick paid for the best care available. When Eben fell in with a bad crowd the Master paid for me to bring him to Durban from Gingindlovu so that he personally could talk to him, and after that Eben straightened out and now he eats the people's money working for the KwaZulu government.

❧

Soon after we moved to the beachfront Helga decided to stop her teaching, and then after that she went back to the university to study some more. She began to spend her evenings buried in books on Zulu history and reading old newspapers, and sometimes when I came up from my room late in the night to make myself a cup of tea I would walk into her study and find her still working, not even knowing what time it was.

"You should go to bed now, my Madame," I would say softly. Once I also said to her: "I think my Madame should find another man to take care of her."

I will admit that I was far more careful of her now, as careful as I had been of Danny and Bridget when they were very young, would never quarrel with her, treated her gently as if she were my child rather than my employer. When she called on me to ask whether her shoes matched her dress I knew that it was because she had no one else to ask with the Master dead and the children gone, and I always tried to give her my best advice. I always stayed, if she was going out, to help with her zipper or to say how I thought of her clothes, and very often when she went out at night I went up to the flat at midnight to check that she had come home safely.

Sometimes when she was writing to the children she would ask me if I wanted to add my lines at the bottom, and usually I was happy to send them a message in that way. Once though I wrote to the children that their mother was living like an orphan, hoping that they would understand what it was I was trying to tell them, sense that I was wishing for them that they would come back from the overseas and live again like a family, like they had at Gordonwood.

She was very angry with me for this.

"This will only make the children sad," she said. "I can't send it now."

I began to notice something else as well, then, how most of people's children were going to the overseas.

"Where is that woman's children?" I would ask about someone, or "Why does that man not move into his daughter's house?" And each time Helga would say: "Her daughter is in London," or "His children are overseas," and it was like no family was unbroken, that all the children had found Durban too small for their dreams, either that or had somehow given up, decided that there was something wrong in Durban that they wanted to get far away from. It was not easy for me to understand that, despite all the sadness it was causing, she was even pleased that her children had left, satisfied that they were so far away from her. Each day she went to the post box to look for their letters and I knew from how the expression on her face would change when there were letters from the children. When I went for the post first, just as soon as I came back and closed the door I would hear her calling from her study:

"Anything from the children?" and if the answer were yes her face would light up.

"Oh goody," she'd say, reaching for her glasses. "Bring bring bring."

Sometimes she would read parts of the letters to me or leave them on the hall table for me to read. When there were photographs we'd look at them together and discuss them for a long time.

"Bridget, she is too thin," I might say, "and her hair it is more curly than when she was in Durban." And then we would discuss whether Bridget had really lost more weight and whether she might have had a permanent wave and not told us.

Once I said to her: "The children should come home."

And she answered me: "God forbid."

And there it rested.

⸙

We had been living like that for four years when everything did begin to change again. First this Arnold Miro began to come and visit us. I knew this Arnold Miro and his wife because everyone knew them, so rich there in their house near Mitchell Park. I even knew the girl who worked there as their boy's nanny. Her name was Mavis and she said the wife was all right but that Arnold Miro was no good. I only visited there a few times and it was a very big house with its own road almost coming up to it. I saw Miro for myself once also, sitting on the veranda overlooking the city and talking, talking, talking, telling his jokes.

Then one day it was in the paper, on the front page with many pictures, that Miro's wife had died of a heart attack playing tennis and I didn't think anything more of it except that sometime after that he telephoned and then she told me who had been on the phone and that he was coming to the flat for tea. I did not understand then what it was all about. I should have but I did not. I think I did not want to, looking back on it.

The night he did come Helga asked me to stay late and serve the tea, though she could have done it easily herself, and both of us knew then that she was asking me to act like a parent of a young girl. Miro was no fool. He said: "You can let the girl go to bed, you know," and Helga, who seemed more relaxed as the evening went on, laughed and told me I could go to my room. But after that I came back into the flat later anyway to make myself a cup of tea at midnight and I could tell that Miro was still there, though I didn't hear a sound coming from inside.

We saw a lot of Arnold Miro after that. He came for dinner a few times and then he would come on a Saturday morning to take Helga to the horse races, which she had never been to before, and always she would ask me how she looked and whether perhaps her dress was too long or her hair tidy at the back. I knew this Miro was taking her to places she had not seen since the Master was alive, the Lido at Umkomaas and the old English hotel near Balgowan, Salt Rock and Ballito Bay, other places too. Eventually they began to go away for whole weekends, she and this Miro, and I realized that they must be sleeping together and I felt very bad for the Master even though I remembered that this was what I myself had been wishing for.

What also changed was the place itself. Signs on the beach saying that the sand was reserved for the whites came down, and then someone told me that there were not anymore two kinds of buses, red for whites and green for blacks and that anyone could take any bus, and when I checked this I found it to be true. One day I even saw a black traffic policeman right in the middle of the city.

"What is this?" I asked her. "There are black men doing the white man's job, and no more separation in the shops."

"They are changing," Helga said. "A little. I hope it's not too late."

"How can it be too late?" I asked. "These are not changes that can hurt a person."

Maybe that is true, but there were also a lot of arguments too now in the servants' quarters and often I found myself not agreeing with anyone. And it was not so safe now to catch a bus and visit friends in Kwa Mashu. It was never safe in the night, but it was becoming not safe in the day either.

"These are difficult times," Helga told me when we discussed it one evening. "I'm pleased my kids are far away."

At Christmas this Miro and Helga went together to visit the children in the overseas and for me the days that they were gone went by very slowly. I would wake each morning a little later than usual, come up to the empty flat, make myself tea and porridge, feel expectation and disappointment at the same time as I sat eating at the flimsy white table. I would stay in the kitchen for the morning, listen to the radio, and at teatime I would go to sit in the kitchens of other flats to talk to my friends and to help them with their housework if they needed. But the days went by very slowly.

Two days before Christmas I took a train from Durban to Gingindlovu to see Eben and his children, including my first grandchild, whom Eben had named Silas. Eben and I have always been close even though he was brought up by my sister in Zululand because in those days you were not allowed to keep your children in Durban. But every month I would send my money and every year at Christmas I would go back to visit. It broke my heart a little how sometimes I was a stranger to him, like a visiting aunty rather than Eben's own flesh and blood mother. But when Eben was grown he came to understand and now he has a family of his own and he understands that things are not always as simple as you would like them to be.

While I was at Gingindlovu with Eben I helped tend the corn on Eben's small patch of land and to reweave a portion of the roof of my sister's hut, but my mind was on Helga and this new thing with Miro, and I felt the same sense of moving ground that I had felt when the Master died, as if big changes which I could do nothing about were coming all over again.

❧

When I returned to Durban I went straight up to the flat and opened the curtains and all the windows to blow away the moldy smell that hovered in the air. I was surprised that I felt the relief of homecoming because I had never regarded this flat as home. And yet Helga's pictures and velvet-covered sofas reminded me of Gordonwood, of the children and the servants dusting and polishing, of dinner parties and great activity in the kitchen, of the Master in a dark suit wearing a shirt I had ironed for him. In the mailbox I found a postcard from Miro, not from Helga, confirming the date that they were coming back to Durban. It also said that he and Helga had been married in London and that the children had been there.

And I was so surprised at how I felt then. It crept up on me like a lion, this anger, without warning, and then it was so great it could almost have eaten me. I took the postcard and carried it into the living room, the room I had dusted and polished so many times, fluffed the pillows and changed the water in the flowers, and then I sat down on the sofa, something I don't know I had ever done before, just sat there in the crowded room with its fancy furniture and big chairs and I began to see pictures in my mind of all the other changes that were sure to happen now as well. There would be a move to another place, back now in a van to Miro's house, new servants, new ways of doing things, Baptie being shown how to dust like a child on her first day in school, and in it all, I knew with great certainty, I would be forgotten even by Helga, dusty old Baptie, sent back to the kitchen and to a crumbling shack at the end of the garden like that evil room they had kept me in at Gordonwood, damp and falling down. My opinions would become meaningless again, I would not read the children's letters, I would not again tell Helga that the time had come for her to go to bed. I had been tricked, I knew, tricked into thinking that I was no longer a servant but only so that I would continue to act like one. And it was foul.

At that moment I did not love this family as I had always thought I did, did not want the children to come back, to see them ever again, did not want Helga or Miro or any of the others in my life. I just sat on the sofa there, my head back against the pillows, and thought about my life.

And then I knew what I wanted, what it was that would make me feel better, and I got up from the sofa and took one of Helga's best crystal jugs from the kitchen, one of the ones that we had kept for the best kind of dinner party at Gordonwood, and started to walk down the service stairway to my *kaiya*. Some of the other servants were sitting in the stairwell drinking tea out of large enamel mugs and sharing a bowl of cornmeal and gravy and they shouted to me as I came down, offered me cornmeal, asked about my holiday in Zululand. I wanted to talk to them but I could not, could not tell them about

Helga and Miro, felt ashamed for reasons I could not explain. They were not my friends, these people, just a collection of women that I had nothing in common with. My home was not in this block of flats, not at Gordonwood, not even in Gingindlovu, nowhere. People had made a nothing of my life.

What I wanted was seawater, the rich warm water of the Indian Ocean, to rinse my mouth and pour on my hair and rub into my skin. And then I wanted to do something I had never done before, to wash it off in Helga's bathroom, to sprinkle myself with Helga's fragrant powders, to sit for as long as I wanted on a sofa in her living room and to feel the warm breezes blowing against my skin.

And I did all of those things.

❧

So now Danny is coming. He knows that I have not written to his mother for all these years, although Bridget in her letters tells me that his mother asks about me and sends her love. I know that she and this Miro live in London and it seems that there is money money money because they are always going somewhere and traveling to meet the children in different places I have only read about.

Even Eben, who sometimes has a bad temper, says that I have nothing to be angry with Helga about. This is what happened when she came back from the overseas with her new husband.

It was a Thursday in the afternoon when the postcard had said they would be coming back, and this Miro had arranged for a car from one of his factories to be at the airport to meet them. I did not know what to prepare, so what I did was bake a cake and also biscuits like I used to at Gordonwood, and also make a chicken and salads. So I was prepared for everything. Then I cleaned the flat like the day it was new, and waited for them to come.

I should have known they would not. The afternoon went by, and then the sun went down and it was dark, and I waited still and they did not come. I should have known they would go to Miro's big house near Mitchell Park, and I know it was hopeful only and not clever to think they would come to our place. But I stayed and waited, listened to the radio, made myself something to eat, even some of the chicken and salad, and waited some more. Then at ten o'clock I went to bed.

On the next morning Helga telephoned.

"Baptie," she said, and she sounded so happy, like nothing had changed, nothing was wrong. "I thought you might have come here," she said.

"To where?" I asked.

"To Mitchell Park," she told me. "You know where it is."

I said nothing, waited only for her to talk.

"How are you?" she asked. "How is everything."

"Everything is fine," I told her. "The flat is fine. I am fine."

"Good," she said. "The children both send their love. They remember you with such love."

"And me too," I said.

"They're doing so well, Baptie," she said. "Danny seems to be settling down, and Bridget and Tibor are very happy together."

"That is good," I told her.

"I have pictures," she said. "We took lots of them. I'll show them all to you when I see you."

"Thank you," I said.

"Is everything all right?" she asked suddenly. "Are you sure everything's all right?"

"Everything is fine," I said. "Everything is good."

At that moment I could hear something happening, someone speaking next to the telephone, and then I heard this Miro on the phone talking.

"Baptie?" he said.

He has a slow way of talking, of saying a person's name always as if he is asking a question.

"Good morning, Master," I said.

"Listen," he told me. "We want you to know, Mrs. Miro and me, that we will not forget all your years of loyalty before just because things have changed. Do you understand me?"

Of course I understood what he was saying. What did he think?

"Yes, Master," I said.

"Good," he said. "Now listen. What I want you to do is this. I want you to take a bus, the bus that goes to Mitchell Park, and to come up here right away. Do you understand me?"

What I didn't understand was why this Miro kept thinking I didn't understand. Did he think I had never taken a bus before? Or that perhaps after thirty years in Durban I did not know where is this Mitchell Park?

"I know," was all I said.

"Good," he said again. Then he described how to get to his house, which I already knew, and told me he would pay for my bus fare. Fourteen cents.

So I can make a whole story about how I hated this Miro and how he talked to me and what could have happened to my life after he came. But I will not because he did something else too that changed everything. It is why I am here.

The servants' quarters in his house had carpets in them, each room with its own bath, and then at the end of the little house for servants there was a kitchen with a nice fridge and a stove, a little table with chairs around it for people to sit and eat their food. In each of the rooms there was a bed and a table also, windows with curtains, cupboards built into the walls like in nice houses and also a box to lock your valuable things in. The servants' house at this Miro's was as nice as the houses many white people except those who are very rich can live in.

"Baptie," Helga said when I arrived. "How are you?"

She was standing in the kitchen, Miro next to her holding her hand, smiling at me with a look on her face that said "We know each other better than this," but not moving forward, not moving out of her white-lady-in-the-kitchen manner.

"Hello Madame," I said.

"Hello Baptie," Miro said to me, also smiling. All smiling now, even me I am smiling though I do not feel as if I am smiling. "The children talk about you all the time."

"They do, Baptie," the Madame said.

"Thank you," I said.

I felt shy, like a child again. It is not so good when a grown woman feels like a child but these are things that happen.

"Come in," Miro said, pretending now that I am a visitor in this house of his. "Come. We'll show you the pictures."

It was a very grand house, this Miro's, like Gordonwood because it was so big but also different because everything was fresh and new, smelled like honey. There were big lawns, a swimming pool you could see from the living room with a fountain, lots of marble on the floors. Also the furniture was all one color, cream color, cream floor, cream table, cream furniture, cream walls with big paintings. It was like a palace.

"Would you like some tea?" the Madame asked me. There was a tea tray on the table there, that and some biscuits. I could not have drank this tea in this living room from these fancy cups. I would have choked myself to death holding the small gold handle.

"No thank you, ma'am," I said.

And so they started to talk about their trip and their wedding and to show me the photographs they had brought back, a whole envelope of them, maybe a hundred pictures, not only of the children but also of this wedding with Danny smiling next to Helga, Bridget and this old man she became married to, other people. All along I was thinking only: What will happen next?

"I'm sorry it was such a surprise to you," Helga said. "It was a bit of a surprise to us too."

"That's okay," I said.

"Look," Miro said to me. "I want to talk to you about what Mrs. Miro and I have been thinking."

"Yes," I said.

I could tell that now the party things were over, now they could start the business of who I was and who they were, what would happen next. I could only wait and see. How could I be a housemaid in a house where they also wanted to offer me tea in the living room from cups with handles coated in gold?

"We've decided," Miro said, "to go overseas as well."

Helga could see the shock in my face, this news that was even worse than the worst news I had been preparing myself for in my mind. Nothing left. Nothing.

"Wait until he's told you everything he has to say," she said. And then she took my hand, just for a moment, and then let it go. It was the first time she had done something like that, touched me like that.

"Mrs. Miro has told me," he went on, always calling her this Mrs. Miro as if I didn't know her for a lifetime as something else, as if I needed to be reminded whose property her life was now, "Mrs. Miro has told me what you mean to her family," he said. "And to cut a long story short, she's asked me to provide for you so that when we leave you don't have to work for another family now that you've worked your whole life for hers."

"How will you do that?" I asked.

"Listen to him," Helga said.

You could see that her powers had moved, that there had been small changes in her already. She was enough of the one she had been before, but not all of it.

"This is what I think," he said. "I will be prepared to build you a house in your village in Zululand where you can go and live. If we start building it now, it will be ready in two or three months. You can go yourself and make sure they build it the way you want."

"You will give me this?" I asked.

Suddenly it was like a dream, to own a house of my own in my own village, not to live with someone else or to pay rent money to someone else.

"Yes," he said. "But I'll give you a choice too. If you want to stay in Durban near your friends and whatever, even work for someone else, you can do that too. And what I'll do then is give you a pension of twenty-five rand a month for the rest of your life instead of the house."

"I want a house," I said. "For what is there to stay in Durban?"

"Are you sure?" Helga asked. "You can think about it."

But my heart was pounding in my body. These Jewish white people, I was thinking, are different from the others. They act like the others, even like the Boers and the English, but inside there is something different in their hearts. In the last moment they change themselves, do not act like either the Boers or the English.

"I am sure," I said.

I went back to the flat that night in one of Miro's cars with his driver driving me like I was myself the madame of the house, and even that night I started to pack my things, to tell the other women in the building the fate that had happened to me. They could not believe, made me tell more than once, clapped their hands in joy for me.

But even that is not all. The next day Helga came back to the flat and went to speak to the management office about leaving. And then she came up to the flat and asked me to help her pack her clothes and also she told me that a packing company would take care of the other things, the knives and forks and plates from Gordonwood, a hundred things that people build up in a house.

We spent the whole morning working, Helga and me, taking things from the closet and folding them carefully, deciding which things she no longer wanted, what had to go to the cleaners, what was going in the suitcase. And then, when we were almost done, I turned around and she was sitting in a chair looking out the window and there were tears coming down her face.

"What is it, Madame?" I asked her.

"God, I hope I'm doing the right thing," she said. "Do you think I am?"

"The right thing by what?" I asked.

I knew what she was asking but I did not know the answer. Still today I do not know the answer.

"You know," she said. "Leaving here. Stopping work on my thesis. Marrying Arnold. Going overseas. Nothing will be the same again."

I looked at her carefully, this white lady whose children I had helped bring up, whose husband I had known so well, ironed his shirts, cooked his meals, in some ways like he was my own husband, whose death I had mourned as if my own husband had died, and I felt for her the same things I felt for myself, that the ship had come away from the pier, that it had no journey it wanted to go on, but that also there was nothing left to hold it in place.

"You have not been happy since the Master died," I said. "The past does not return."

"That's for sure true," she said, shaking her head. "And every decision one makes gets harder."

That's when she stood up from her chair and walked over to me, put her arms around me and hugged me for a long time almost as if I were her sister, her only sister or her mother.

"Thanks, Baptie," she said. "Thank you for everything you've given us."

❧❦❧

Two months later they left, went to this house in London where Helga washes her own dishes and irons her own clothes. Miro says they have someone who helps them clean the house, that this is a white lady who comes in one morning every week and even owns a car. I cannot see how that would work.

And one other thing. On the morning before they were going to leave I went to the house near Mitchell Park to say goodbye and Helga took me into this study that she had made her own with some books I knew very well spread on the desk. She closed the door.

"Just one quick thing, Baptie," she said. "Please don't tell Mr. Miro."

"All right," I said.

"Mr. Nerpelow is the lawyer," she said. "You know him. He will send you a pension of twenty-five rand a month wherever you are from my father's money. You must just tell him where you are so that he can send it."

I thought for a moment about the house they were building for me even then, of the choice Miro had given, of this lady and her good heart. Then I looked at her carefully and I knew inside my stomach that I would not see her again in this life.

That was when, in my bad country of many sorrows, I started crying too.

CHAPTER FIVE

Santi

I'M A VERY PRIVATE person. You have to be, I've found, when what you are is a contradiction, someone who lives in a country that doesn't know what to do with you. My mother is a Zulu and although she doesn't say it I know my father was an Afrikaner. I don't know how she came to sleep with him. Maybe he raped her. Maybe not. Maybe there was passion and honesty. Maybe only lies and sadness. She always refused to talk about it.

My mother was like that. She worked in the kitchen of the Arbuthnot family in a house covered with vines high up on the ridge overlooking the Indian Ocean.

"Emily's like part of the family," they would say.

It's a settler habit to say things like that. I've learned, because I didn't always know this, that there is a meaning to a statement like that. Emily was a part of the family, but not that part that could sleep in the same house and eat at the same table as the other members. She had an unwritten part, consisting of a piece of mother and a piece of father for all of them, a shadowy role that got her sent to a shadowy room at the end of the garden at the shadowy end of each day. She's dead now. No member of the Arbuthnot family came to the funeral, although three months after she was buried I did receive a letter from one of the children.

"She was like one of the family," she wrote.

Perhaps I should start over. I am not an angry person. Life has not treated me badly.

After I had to leave the school in Wentworth, a school for mixed race children like myself, I caught a train to Durban to stay with my mother. She wanted me to stay in school but it was impossible. You can't live on air. But I always knew I would get my matric exam to finish high school somehow and I did, and more too.

I called her when I made the decision to leave school. When you're over sixteen in South Africa it's your decision.

A settler lady answered the phone.

"Hello," in that singing, settler voice.

"Is Emily there?" I asked.

"Who is this?" she asked me.

"This is her daughter," I said.

Long pause.

"You know," the lady said, "we don't like Emily taking calls during the day."

"It is important," I said. "I need to speak to my mother."

Another long silence, and then my mother comes to the phone. She sounds panicky.

"What is the matter, my sweetness?" she asks. "Is something wrong at school?"

"Not really," I say. "But I am leaving school. I want to come to Durban."

Now my mother lapses into Zulu.

"You can't call in the day because Mrs. Big-bottom here doesn't like me to talk on her telephone. Mr. Drinks-too-much complains about the phone bill."

I always laughed when she spoke like that. Now I know it was a way of getting rid of her anger, letting it fly away with her jabbing words. She would curse them up and down in their presence, smile, and they wouldn't have any idea as to what was going on. So she was a rebel in her own time. All the domestic servants I ever knew were too, if you measure it that way.

"Why are you leaving school?" she says when she's done.

"Because they're saying again that they need money for tuition, and also for books, and we don't have that money. I want to get a job."

"It is not so easy to get a job," my mother says.

I can hear the disappointment in her voice. She wants me to be a teacher.

"I will get my matric through correspondence," I tell her. "Already I have the papers to fill out for it."

"That is what you say now," she says.

Then I hear in the background: "Emily."

"Mrs. Big-bottom," my mother says quietly. "Coming, Madame."

"You say you will carry on to study when you come out of school," my mother continues. "But I know what will happen. You will get a husband, and then he will make you pregnant, and then you will get lazy too. I know this will happen."

"No. No. No," I insist. "Never."

My mother laughs and then says in English: "Young girls thinks they know everythings."

I caught the train at the station in Wentworth and from there it was not even one hour to Durban station and then I carried my bag to the place where they said I would find a bus to Glenwood, the nearest stop to the Arbuthnots' house.

I'd never been there before. My mother wasn't ashamed of me, exactly. It's the opposite, really. She thought because of my Afrikaner father that I had a leg up, and that by bringing me to the grimy little *kaiya* in which the Arbuthnots kept her I might lose my toehold, my sense of self. Or at least that's what I think now. I don't know if it is true.

The train from Wentworth was filled with dust, crying children, lots of noise. I was really tired when the bus finally reached the last stop on its run, the stop before the final hill where the Arbuthnots lived. I got out, pulled my suitcase, began the walk up the hill. I was seventeen then, seventeen and six months. My birthday is May 14.

My mother had said one other thing before Mrs. Big-bottom hauled her off the line.

"I cannot tell them you are staying here," she said. "Mr. Drinks-too-much keeps saying that we can have no visitors in our rooms."

"I have nowhere else to stay," I'd said.

"No, you can stay here," my mother said quickly. "I just said we cannot tell them."

"What should I do?" I'd asked.

"You have to come in through the back way," she said. "Through a hole in the hedge that comes out just next to my room."

"And how do I get there?"

"Through the garden of this big old house on the top of the hill," she said. "It looks like a mad person's house and the people who live there don't care who stays in the servants' rooms. They won't even notice."

She was talking, of course, about Danny's house. I saw him watching me the first time, that very first day when I dragged my suitcase down their driveway and across their untidy garden.

❧❖❧

They were all revolutionaries, I swear it, long before the Soweto children started the events that uprooted the settler government and long before the killings and burnings. You could hear it in the dirty servants' quarters of the Arbuthnots. You could hear it everywhere.

It would come out in the stories.

"That bugger," Connie the nanny would say over tea. "He give me his underpants with the shit on it and I wash and wash and still it won't be clean. Then he say I don't know to do my job."

"They are like that," my mother agrees.

"So I tell him, I say, you are sixteen, you are too old to shit in your pants. Next time I will tell your mother. And also your sister."

"Weh," my mother says. "What did he say?"

"He don't like," Connie says. "So I take the clean one too, and I put dog shit on it. Then I wash and I give to him."

"No," my mother protests.

"Honestly," Connie says. "I did. But now he scared to say nothing."

And they would laugh, all of them, a laughter filled with revenge and resignation. But sometimes they would also shake their heads in wonder, just shake at how things could be the way they were.

"That bloody Arbuthnot girl," my mother said one evening. "She come into the kitchen when I am cooking food for Santi and for me and she ask: 'What is that?' And I say: 'It is samp and beans.' And she say: 'Is it nice to eat?' So I say: 'Do you think I would eat something that is not nice to eat?' And I ask her if she wants to eat some and she say, that little shit: 'Is it clean to eat?' And so I say to her: 'What do you think we are, dogs, that we eat food that is not clean?'"

"The girl is not so bad," Connie said. "It is the boy who is bad. He doesn't know nothing how to treat a person."

"But how can she think that we do not even eat clean food?" my mother insisted. "I don't know what a person can think who thinks a thing like that."

They worked hard, these settler servants, long days starting when the sun rose and ending only when the last of the brave Arbuthnots turned off the last of their bedside lamps. Then they would come down to their rooms, the dinner dishes washed, the kitchen tidied, the dogs fed, the milk bottles on the back *stoep*, and they would be so tired just about all they could do was sit around aimlessly and then drift off to bed to sleep for the next day.

And they didn't know what to make of me. I am my mother's daughter, whatever else may have gone into making me, but to them, I know, to the garden boys who were younger than I was, to Connie the nanny, even to my mother, you could see I was something else too. They would be talking, saying something treasonous, and then in midsentence they would catch me with my settler nose and my lighter skin and they would pause for a second, just a second, before continuing.

"What do you think?" I would say in Zulu. "That I am one of them?"

And then they would laugh and keep talking, at least until the next time.

In my mother's room there was a metal bed, propped up on bricks to ward off the *Tokolosh*, or evil spirit, which she said could not climb into a bed that stood on bricks, a small couch that had always been in the room with straw sticking out one end, a cupboard, a small sideboard. She also had a Primus stove so that we could cook in her room and did not have to make everything on the settler stove and then carry it across the garden to her room before she could eat it. It was not uncomfortable for us because we were used to living like that, but I knew, though she was happy for me to stay once I was there, that I could not stay too long. Sometimes the Arbuthnot children would come wandering into the servants' area and I would wait quietly inside my mother's room, just wait until they left, but each time I knew it would not be long before something happened and I had to leave. It was going to happen. All that was my worry was that I must not get my mother into any trouble.

"You can stay," she would say. "Eat their bloody food. Live in their bloody room. I am a human being too."

"And if the police come?" I asked.

"Let them come," she would say. "You are like a white."

"No," I would say angrily. "To them I am just a *kaffir* too."

"Don't talk like that," my mother would say. "You will bring bad lucks on your head."

❦

"Who is that family," I asked my mother on my second or third day with her, "who lives in the castle house next door?"

"They are good people, I think," she said. "Not like Arbuthnot rubbishes."

"Who are they?" I asked.

"The lady is Mrs. Helga Divin," she said. "I have heard that she is a lady who fights for treating people the right way in South Africa. Like Mrs. Suzman too."

I knew who Helga Divin was. Everyone at Wentworth did. She came all the way from Durban to judge the matric students' debate competition the year before, arrived in a dusty black Austin car all on her own, listened carefully to the four people making arguments, made a speech when they were finished.

"That is her house?" I asked, surprised.

"Yes," my mother told me. "Also husband and son and daughter."

"I saw the son when I came," I said.

"The daughter is Bridget," my mother told me. "She is very beautiful and also good at exercises. Baptie the cook is always boasting that inside the house there is a whole cupboard filled with trophies she has won."

"And the son?" I asked.

"I know nothing of the son," she said.

But I did, soon enough. To get to the servants' rooms of my mother's employer without them knowing it you had to cut through a gap in the hedge, cross a cement path, then go up under some vines and through an archway into the garden of the neighbors. Then if you walked quickly alongside the hedge you could be out in the street, a different street than the Arbuthnots', in a minute or two.

That was how I did it when I first arrived, and then the next day, and then the day after that.

There wasn't much to do once you were in my mother's room, of course, and I would have been happy to sit with her in the kitchen while she worked, to help her with her chores, but since the settlers couldn't know I was there I had to stay away from the house. So on the first day I sat in the sun behind the *kaiyas* and read a book I had brought with me, and then slipped through the neighbor's garden to take a walk, and on the day after that too.

It was that day, the third day I was there, coming back to my mother's room through the neighbor's garden, that I first spoke to Danny Divin. He is the one who had watched me, looked through the window on the first day when I'd been carrying my suitcase.

"May I help you?" he asked.

I was halfway across the garden, the little stretch that I would cross especially quickly to get it behind me before I reached the quietness behind the hedge, when he spoke. He was standing there, just near a little house they had in their garden next to the swimming pool, and I had not seen him. I was carrying my book, was barefoot, wearing an old cotton dress my mother had made for me a long time before.

But I felt naked.

"I beg your pardon?" I said.

"Can I help you?" he asked again.

You could see this boy, Danny, was not going to make a problem. He was tall and brown because it was summer, also without shoes, also with a book.

"I'm sorry," I said. "I was just taking a shortcut."

"That's okay," he said. He was looking at me carefully, not demanding or arrogant like some of them can be. If anything it was he who was shy.

"But where are you taking a shortcut to?"

"To the house next door," I said. "That's where I am going."

He nodded, looked down to the direction where I was going. And I could tell everything would be okay with him.

"Do you know them?" he asked, a curious look on his face. "The Arbuthnots?"

"No," I said. "My mother does. She's the cook."

"Emily?"

"Yes."

"Emily's your mother?"

"Yes," I said.

And then it struck me that this was not a good idea, this making small talk with him, that now the knowledge that Emily's daughter was staying with her in her room was out, beyond the servants' quarters, that only trouble would come of talking more. But he was not ready to let me go.

"Are you visiting?" he asked.

"Yes," I said. "I am going very soon."

"From where?"

"From Wentworth," I said. "I go to school there."

"What's your name?" he asked.

This was bad, very bad, I could tell. I had to go, to get away from this open hill of grass, back into the darkness of my mother's room.

"I have to go," I said. "Somebody is waiting for me."

And he looked disappointed, this boy. Then I saw that he was looking at me, sneaking glances down at my legs, at my arms, into my eyes, and I thought: This boy with a famous mother wants something more from me. And I thought: What does he want from me? He has everything a person could want, a big house, money, a quiet place to sit and read. Then I thought of something else and I thought: He can't want that. It would be funny if he wanted that.

I started to walk on, past him a little bit, and then I stopped for a moment only and looked back at where he was standing. He had not moved.

"My name is Santi," I said.

"I'm pleased to meet you, Santi," he said. "And you can take this shortcut anytime you want. Okay?"

"Thank you," I said.

And I continued walking then, back through the archway and down the little alley, knowing that he was watching me, thinking that he was a nice boy, that he had kind eyes, that he seemed maybe a little lonely. Or maybe that was only me, my imagination placing me in his shoes.

The things that had happened in my life until then had told me to be careful of white boys. One girl at Wentworth became pregnant with a white boy and his father was so angry he beat the boy until he had to go to the hospital. I do not know what happened to her because she left the school without telling us anything.

Once, not too long before I first saw Danny, we were going on the train, the girls in my school and I, to a netball competition for colored girls in Richards Bay. When we had been going for about one hour the train pulled into a station — perhaps it was the station in Stanger — and while we were waiting another train came into the station from the opposite direction. For a few minutes it was quiet and then we saw that the windows of that other train, the ones facing us, were filling up with boys, white schoolboys, all wearing the same uniform, dark green jackets, green and gray ties, those yellow straw hats the settler school-boys used to wear.

"Pull down the windows," they shouted and some of the girls at first did not know what to do with this, but then they saw that the boys were laughing and some of them were even a little bit handsome and so they did.

"What school are you from?" one of the boys asked.

I looked at these boys, maybe different ages, thirteen to sixteen, all in their nice uniforms, and wondered what they wanted with us.

"Wentworth," someone said.

"What's that?" they asked.

"It's a school," the girls said. "Just a school."

"A *klonkie* school," one of the boys said.

I know this *klonkie* word. It's not a polite word. It's a word the Afrikaners use for people who are mixed, white and black together. To me they looked like monkeys then, all leaning from the window, hold-ing their hats, making jokes. All I could see were their teeth, their shin-ing eyes, perspiration on their foreheads.

"Where are you from?" one of the girls asked.

"Durban. We're going home from a cricket match."

"Did you win?"

The boys began to laugh.

"What do you know about cricket?" one of them asked.

And then we could see that there were a lot of private jokes go-ing on, boys shouting things to each other inside the compartments of the other train, a lot of strange, hungry laughter.

"Why are you rude?" a girl said. "Why are you being rude to us?"

Suddenly everything changed, became ugly. Some of the boys be-gan to jeer, to make comments, sex comments.

"Where is your teacher?" my friend asked. "Who teaches you to be like animals?"

"You're the animals," they said.

And then, inside the windows, I could see that they were plan-ning something and I wished the trains would begin to move, either their train or our train, away from the station, away from these people that meant nothing to our lives.

"Show us your tits," one of the boys said. "We'll give you one rand."

All at once the girls started to shout too, also to be rude.

"You. You. Show us."

And then I saw that some of them were pointing at me, pointing and laughing.

"You," one of them said, looking into my face. "You show us. Five rand for you to show us your tits."

"You go to hell," I said.

❧❦❧

So you would think I would be a very careful, suspicious person. But I cannot be that way. It is not the way I have been born. I cannot blame one person with another person's sin, spread my disappointments far-ther than they are meant to go.

So when I went through that garden the next time, in the morn-ing when nobody was there at all, that spot where I had stood and talked to him seemed different than it had before, almost as if someone had placed an electric wire on the spot and made it jerk you when you walked over it. I thought about his eyes too, brown and very soft, and how he looked as if he had gentle hands. It's funny, really, how little things grow into bigger things when you only leave them alone.

For whatever reason I did not tell my mother what had happened. I do not know what she would have said, or if it would have made her nervous now that one of the whites knew I was there, but also I was used to living away from her and not telling her private things. And this one seemed like a private thing. And also I knew that I was foolish to think any of the thoughts I was having.

"Someone will see you," she said when she came back to her room in the middle of the afternoon. I was sitting in the sun, leaning against the wall, reading my book. Perhaps they could have seen me from the house, but then why would they have looked?

"No one will see me," I said.

"And if they chase you, where will you go?" she asked.

"I have to go soon, anyway," I told her. "I can't just sit around here while you work."

"What will you do?" she asked.

"Get a job," I said. "Also study part-time."

She shook her head.

"I think you are very clever," she said. "Not stupid like me."

"You're not stupid, Ma," I told her.

There was one thing also that I did not tell her, something I had decided when I was still at Wentworth. This business of the settlers taking everything and leaving nothing for the people, this business of women like my mother living their lives serving worthless rubbish, this business of not being able to finish school because I could not find the money while settler children went to school for free, this was wrong. And even at Wentworth I had decided to fight against the settler system. Nelson Mandela was in jail and in those days Winnie was my hero.

So it was funny then, that at the same time I hated the settlers and had a settler's blood inside me, and that I felt such anger for the white families in their grand houses around our room that smelled of paraffin from the Primus and also now looked forward to seeing the boy who had stopped me to ask questions. And then when I did see him again on the next day I knew that I had stayed in his mind as well.

He was waiting for me, I know it, even as he pretended he was not. It touched me, this. I started through the arch and then, not a minute later, there he was, almost on the same spot.

"You again," he said, as if he was surprised. But I saw that he had just come out from the house and across the garden himself.

I nodded and smiled. This time I had shoes, had brushed my hair properly, was wearing a newer dress, one I had made for myself at Wentworth. And even as I dressed, pulled the brush through my hair, something told me this was foolishness, that nothing good would come of it. I also couldn't help then thinking about my mother and the mistake she had made, if it was a mistake, in conceiving me.

"Is it okay?" I asked.

"Of course," he said. "I hoped you'd come back."

That he said this made me short of breath, but still something in my mind said to be careful, not to be a great fool. But also I was looking at him, this handsome white boy, tall and with such nice eyes, and thinking: I have not seen a white boy like this before.

"Why is that?" I asked.

"Oh, I don't know," he said. "Maybe I didn't ask you what you were reading."

"Nothing," I said, and held up the book. I don't even remember to this day what it was. Maybe a novel.

"Do you read a lot?" he asked.

"Sometimes," I said. "I am on holiday now."

"From Wentworth?"

"Yes."

"What standard are you in?"

I said nothing. I did not want to tell this boy a story, but I did not feel like telling him my whole life.

"I was in standard nine before," was all I said. "I want to be a teacher one day."

We were the same height, this boy and I. Maybe the same age too. I liked the way he smiled at me, as if he was unaware how wrong it was for him to be doing this, how much disapproval there would be for all of this, every piece of it. But he did know it. Even while we were talking a man came by, a tall man in a white driver's coat, and I could see by the look on the boy's face that he was not happy this had happened.

"Hello Ambrose," the boy said.

The man nodded, kept looking at me even over his shoulder as he went through the arch and then disappeared.

"He's my father's driver," the boy explained.

I said nothing. The truth is that in an instant, really, I was becoming impatient. I didn't want anything from this white boy. I liked the way he looked and how he sounded but I'm not stupid even if sometimes I act as if I may be. I didn't have time to dance about talking nothing with him in his father's garden even as he was ashamed when somebody walked by. I was not shy with boys, any boys, like he was shy and for no reason. I lost my virginity when I was fifteen. You cannot lose it again. You cannot lose something when you have nothing.

"I have to go," I said.

It was like a relief, honestly, to be angry with him. Now that I am older I know that feeling angry with someone does not mean you are finished with them. Sometimes you are hooked in by your anger.

He was surprised by my impatience. Something had come over me, I can't put a name on it, that said: All right, nice white boy, Mrs. Helga Divin's son. If you want something from me you must ask for it. Not ease it out like this, in little bits and pieces with nothing from you exposed, nothing to risk. For me it is risking everything even to stand for so long with you in your own private garden.

And then it was almost as if he had read my mind.

"Look," he said, "can we meet somewhere we can just sit and talk quietly without worrying about who comes and goes, what people think."

And then, as quickly as it had come, my anger went. I stood dead still, looked at the ground, moved a stone with my toe.

"Now you are looking to make trouble," I said.

"It doesn't matter."

"It doesn't matter?"

"It doesn't matter."

"I know who your mother is," I said. "I read about her in the newspaper. Do you know what all the people would say if they found you and me in a private place?"

He shook his head.

"Nobody will find us," he said. "But in any event do you really think I care about that?"

I stayed where I was, pushed an ant around with a stick.

"Also," I said, "I don't think I'm going to be here that long. I have to get a job."

"You're still here now," he said.

"And also," I said, and I have to admit that I was running out of arguments and now there was mischief in my voice, a teasing tone I had not used with a white boy before, "I have a boyfriend."

Now he looked serious for a moment only, wiped some sand from his trousers, ran his hand through his hair. I looked at him and I knew how my face must look, open, a face filled with challenges.

"So?" he said.

"And where would there be a private place?"

"It's for certain true," he said, "that nobody would want us to have privacy."

That is something I could only agree with. But now also I could not help from smiling. Something was exciting, something silly, in all of this. And it was then that he said the idea that told me he was a person who could find his way into my heart. I had thought only I could think this way.

"There is lots of privacy right under their noses," he said.

"What do you mean?" I asked.

"Late, late, late," he said, "when everybody in the world is asleep, then all of South Africa is private."

I laughed at him, this crazy idea of meeting in the middle of the night.

"You are going to make big trouble," I said. But I was laughing, and he was laughing also. I would have liked to take his hand and feel it, squeeze it, but of course I didn't.

"So?" he said.

And then I agreed.

As we made our plan my heart was beating and my knees were soft. Maybe my head was soft too, but it did not really matter.

How can there not be love when you start with forbidden things in the dead of the night right under the noses of all those sleeping people? When midnight is long past and the crickets which sing like a rushing train have all gone quiet and only the moon is above, how can there not be love? And with a boy like Danny, filled with affection and curiosity, a great tenderness that seemed as if it had nowhere to go until he found me at two o' clock in the morning, back in the garden behind the swimming pool house, back where all there is is a square of grass and a tent of golden shower creepers and bougainvillaea bushes, how can there not be love?

My mother stirs in her sleep.

"What is it, my Santi?" she asks.

"Go to sleep, Ma," I say.

"Why are you getting up?"

"It's okay," I say.

She turns over in her bed, pulls the blanket over her shoulder. Maybe for once I am grateful that she works so hard, for how tired she is. She does not move again.

"I'll be back soon," I whisper.

She says nothing.

My clothes are under a hedge outside the room, and I pull them on quickly. Then I go to the bathroom to wash myself and then I walk very carefully past the other rooms and through the gap in the hedge, back into the next-door garden. Somewhere down the hill a dog barks, and then another, and then there is nothing. From the city far below I can hear the faraway noise of engines, a bus now, a car going uphill, but they are very soft, like in another world.

Through the hedge and into the garden and it is all quite black. And I think: Maybe I am dreaming all this, because it is so unreal, from another world also, to be in this dark garden, standing alone and with no one knowing I am here in the shadows cast from the moon of a giant house that looks more like it comes from a fairy story than that it is right here on the ridge. Somewhere up there in the house, I think, the boy is also walking softly through the rooms with their thick rich carpets, down the stairs, past expensive furniture, out the door, down to meet me.

It is like a story itself, so filled with excitement, even with danger. I do not know this boy, what he has in his mind. I do not think it is for making love only that he makes this plan and if it is I will not do such a thing, on the grass, in secret, more like a punishment than a sign of love. I think of my mother too as I make my way towards where he has said he will be, what it was that may have come before that led to my being born, those things which she refuses to talk about.

He is there, waiting like a ghost against the tree. If you were not looking for him you would not see him at all. I come closer to him and he is watching me, wearing long trousers and a sweater, no shoes.

"You came," he whispers. "I thought you might change your mind."

"I thought you might," I whisper back.

He has brought fruit, a whole bowl of fruit, apricots and lichees and cherries, and for a moment I think: This is expensive fruit, too expensive, and then I forget about it as he holds the bowl out to me and we both sit, facing each other, cross-legged on the grass.

"You are very daring," I say.

"You too," he answers. "What with your boyfriend and all."

I laugh and he is laughing too, his teeth so white in the moonlight. I could kiss his mouth, but not yet.

"There is no boyfriend," I say.

"I know," he tells me.

"And what are you now?" I ask him. "So late in the night like this. My boyfriend?"

He doesn't say anything, starts to eat the fruit and then I start to eat it too. And then he asks his thousand questions, first small ones, did my mother see me, did I wake up to come or not go to sleep at all, which is my mother's room, on the end or in the middle, and then bigger questions also. What am I doing here? Where did I come from? How long am I staying? I listen to him and I think: From these questions you ask, a person would not think we live in the same country, the same world even, that you need to know how big is my room in Wentworth and how many people stay with me, and how many people are in the classes I go to, and what subjects I study, and where I am eating my meals, and who are my teachers, what color are they, where are they from. But I think also that I know nothing about this boy either, what does his school look like, what subjects does he study, how does it feel to be a settler in this country where everything belongs to you and nothing is a fight, how is it to live in a big house and have servants wash your clothes and cook your meals, drive you to your school in a shining car?

And so we talk, eat the fruit, listen to the noises. The moon is very bright and I can see his face, his serious face and his eyes, and he looks at me, talks so politely, softly, shows such an interest in every piece of my life, what things look like and where even I get the things I own and where I go. I have not before seen someone who has such great interest in every piece of my life, not even my mother.

"You ask so many questions," I say.

"I'm interested," he says. "In you."

And I think: It is funny, this, that there can be so many differences between us, like a mountain of differences, but then suddenly it becomes words only, only words, because when the words are finished there is a boy with his shining eyes and his hand on my foot, which feels nice, and there is me, with my skirt wrapped around my legs, my hand on his, and nothing more. Only words.

I did not know, honestly, at that moment, what would happen, whether his hand would move up from my foot, if I would let that happen, whether even after that night there would be more meetings, another dark walk from my mother's room into the garden filled with shadows. He asks how long I am staying and I do not have an answer, one week maybe, maybe two, and every so often he looks in my eyes, presses his lips together, nods, looks at the ground.

"I want to be a teacher," I tell him. "But first I have to get a job."

"Where?" he asks.

"I don't know," I say. "Honestly, I don't. There are not many jobs, even jobs like cleaning in a hotel. Maybe I will be a clerk or something."

"I hope it isn't far," he says.

It is then that he moves his hand, over my foot and my ankle, just touching the skin softly, the muscles in my calf, the fold behind my knee. He turns my skirt back above my knee, presses it firmly in place to show me that this is where he will stop, that I have no need to worry of what he will do, just carefully touching, touching only like he was feeling something for the first time in his life. It is difficult not to let your stomach become warm when someone touches you so carefully and with such respect.

So now there is silence, his eyes on my leg only, mine on the moon which is shining high above.

⸙

"Santi," my mother says when I come in. "Where have you been for so long?"

"Nowhere, Mama," I say. "Just outside."

She sits up in her bed, turns on the light, looks at her watch.

"Where have you been?" she asks again.

"Nowhere, Mama," I say.

She rubs her hair, straightens a blanket on the bed, folds the sheet over.

"Is something the matter?"

"No Ma," I say. "But it is late. Let's sleep."

"You don't need to worry," she says. "You are young and clever, and something good will happen for you because also God will look out for us."

I could say that something good has already happened, but even so, even now, I am not so very sure. I know what is young love, how quickly it starts, how it roars like a fire in the bush, how sometimes it leaves with no warning. I am not worried for myself because I know already how my heart works, that once it is fixed on something it stays fixed there, that whatever changes something of my heart stays fixed there like a piece of cotton wool caught on a thorn.

My mother is looking at me carefully.

"I am lucky that God gave me such a beautiful daughter," she says.

I don't know why she is talking like this. Maybe mothers have a sixth sense even when they know nothing for sure. I look down at myself quickly. My dress is folded in a bundle outside, I am in a night-gown, there is nothing to say what I have been doing.

"Now I pray," she says, "that He will make your life good also."

I lie there on my mat and think of what Danny is doing. He has held my hand until the last moment, even the tips of my fingers as I pulled away and started to walk to my mother's room, and when I looked back he was still standing there watching, standing next to the hedge just waiting for me to disappear.

I think how he must then himself walk back around the swimming pool, up to the house, through one of the doors on the downstairs and into rooms that smell of furniture polish and carpets, the stones in the wall, the ornaments and lamps and pictures with which white people fill their houses. But it is not so easy now to think of him lost in the middle of all the things his parents own. He will go up the stairs to his room, take off his clothes, go into his bed, and something of me will go with him too, something which no matter what else happens cannot be discarded. Of this I am sure.

And the next morning I do not even hear my mother get up, sleep, sleep, as she moves around the room, steps over my mat to reach her clothes, sleep, sleep, even after she closes the door and goes away. All I know is that when she does shake my shoulder I am dreaming of something, something different, maybe a boy I knew at Wentworth.

"Are you going to sleep all day long?" she asks.

"What time is it?"

"Eleven. I came on my tea break and now I find you asleep still."

"I'm on holiday," I say, sitting up. "At school we get up very early."

"Why didn't you sleep last night?" she asks.

"I slept," I say. "I think you were dreaming."

❦

It is a very delicate matter to ask questions about the white family that lives next door, most particularly about the son of the white family that lives next door. But I cannot help myself. I justify this by saying that in my experience the most reliable information about a settler family comes from its servants.

"They see me going through the fence," I say to my mother. "Are you sure they don't mind?"

She looks at me quizzically.

"If they have seen you and nothing has happened, then what is the problem?"

"I don't want there to be a problem," I say. "That is why I am asking."

We are sitting with others around a little table in Connie's room.

"They don't care," Connie says. She waves her arm dismissively. "People come and go in that house like a railway station."

"The boy in that house," I press on like a moth going around a candle, unwilling to move away, burning but trapped. "He stopped me yesterday."

Now my mother looks interested.

"Danny," Connie says. "His name is Danny."

"What did he say?" my mother asks.

"Nothing," I say. "He asked if I was lost."

"What did you tell him?"

"I told him I was taking a shortcut. He said nothing."

There's a few moments of general discussion and then Connie brings it to an end.

"They will do nothing," she says. "Even when the police come to their place because of the Pass Laws, the Master there, Silas, he comes down and sends them away."

"How can anyone just send the police away?" I ask.

"I don't know," Connie says. "Sometimes they listen to white people if they are rich. Sometimes they are frightened because they see this Helga Divin is in the newspaper. Sometimes they just go away anyway."

So I learn nothing from them, and then later my mother asks, a strange expression on her face: "This boy who stopped you. How did he look?"

"What do you mean?" I ask.

"How did he look?" she asks again.

"He looked like a white schoolboy," I say, and then I walk away.

That afternoon, the afternoon after I met Danny under the moon, I stayed away from his house and his garden. I cleaned my mother's room, scrubbed the floor hard with a brush, and then washed her sheets and clothes in a tub on a path outside.

"Can you come tomorrow night?" he had asked me.

"Of course I can come," I said. "But when will you sleep if you meet me in the middle of the night?"

"It doesn't matter," he said. "I have lots of energy."

"Me also," I told him. "But still a person needs to sleep."

"But you will come."

"I will come," I said.

But I am thinking, as I hang the sheets on the line and spread the other things on a stone in the sun, for how many nights will my mother say nothing when she wakes up and finds me gone, and wakes up and finds me back? My mother is not a fool.

※

And also Danny's father.

"He heard me coming in," he says. "He couldn't sleep and so he got up to work."

"What did you tell him?" I ask.

"That I was sitting on the lawn," he says. "I said it was hot."

"And what did he say?"

"He didn't say anything," Danny says.

We are together again like the first time except that this night when I see him it is as if a great thirst exists inside me, one that can only be satisfied with his power, his arms holding me too tightly even for breathing. And it is the same with him. I come around the corner and he is there, waiting in the dark, and I cannot stop myself from running when I see him, my legs acting on their own, and he opens his arms and we are like people who have been separated by a war or by many months of sadness.

"Santi, Santi, Santi," he keeps saying, my name over and over. He kisses me now on the neck and on the mouth, boldly now, but still it is not enough. He takes my face in his hands like a hungry person, or a lost person looking for a map.

Then the wind calms down and we walk back to the same spot we had the night before, the same place next to the hedge, and again he has brought a basket of fruit, this time mangos and peaches and some shining black plums.

"I thought tonight would take forever to come," he says.

"You came without problems?" I ask.

And now we have so many things to share, how we got home, what my mother said this morning, what his mother said, how he slept in the afternoon, how I slept in the morning, whether our faces look tired, what we did while we waited for the sun to go down. Now we have our history, Danny and me. So short but so rich.

"My heart is pounding even now," he says, and he places my hand on his chest and I can feel it, bang, bang, bang, like a little drum inside.

I sit cross-legged on the grass next to him and I notice that my skirt has risen up, above my knees, above the line he made for himself yesterday. My hem rests on my thigh and even though the moon is more faint than before my knee shines like a smooth invitation to him, a place for him to rest his hand.

And now also I have questions I have been thinking of to ask him, the chief of which is: Why me? When I think of all those pretty girls in their new white dresses in his school, all the other girls I see in their smart school uniforms, why me? This is not because I do not think a man would want me. Not at all. I know where I stand and do not stand with men, with the young trainee schoolteacher that I gave my virginity to and the others I have known at Wentworth and in my mother's village near Hammarsdale. They told me with their words and their looks what they thought. From thirteen I had good breasts and a narrow waist, long legs, the things men want. But still, this rich white boy with his famous mother, his nice gentle face and soft hands, when there are white girls that he could go with to the beach, make *braaivleis* picnic on the grass, take to the cinema, why does he decide instead to meet me in the very middle of the night?

But I do not ask it this way.

"Do you have a girlfriend?" I ask him instead.

He looks surprised by my question.

"Do you think I would be here if I did?" he asks. He lifts his hand from my knee but I take it and put it back.

"I am only asking," I say.

"Maybe I do now," he says.

He means me, of course. It thrills me but also it makes me wonder what it means, to have as a boyfriend someone who you can't even go with in the daylight. He knows, and I know too, that even if his parents allowed and my mother did not find trouble for it, even if the police did not arrest us, we cannot even go anywhere together in this country.

And also I need to hear more from him.

"But what about the girls in your school?" I ask. "How are they?"

"What about them?" he asks, but I say nothing.

"They're nice enough," he says. "But not like you."

"What do you mean?" I ask.

This is a game for lovers, these questions. They excite to ask, excite to listen to an answer. It is like eating something good very slowly, tasting it again and again.

"You are like nothing I have seen," he says. "Each time you say something it is like taking wrapping off a present. Each time."

These are sweet words, like honey, a dusting of new powder. They go for me too, say my thoughts too, and I tell him this and he looks surprised as if it were not possible, not truthful that I should say such things. But honestly I am bursting with love. I look up at the house, the strange house with crooked towers and colored glass in the windows, and instead of seeing that it is strange it looks like a beautiful thing, a chest filled with treasures.

"So what will happen to us now?" I ask.

I do not want to ask this, to show, even though he has opened his heart, that I am too eager. It is not easy to put together in one place that he is Danny, my boyfriend even, and also that he is a white boy from a big house with a father that can drive away the police and a mother whose face everyone knows. But still I cannot stop myself from asking. I have to know also, for myself. For my heart.

He shakes his head, pulls on the grass, shakes it again.

"Everyone will try to make it impossible," he says. "But it is not natural that love is impossible."

And as he says this word, love, I know for sure, or I think I know for sure, that this is a boy a girl can dream of. That this Danny will not go away, leave me flat like a broken toy or forgotten flowers.

In my room at Wentworth there is a steel bed, one table, a box in the corner for my clothes. The glass in the window is broken and they do not come to fix it, the books I have belong also to another girl. But I never think, not even once, that I do not have enough or that I want to have more. I could take Danny and move him to my room, hide him forever there, sleep with him on my bed, make love to him on my bed, and the girls in my dormitory, my friends, will laugh, admire him for how good looking he is, help me to make him comfortable. For me then life will hold as many things as it can hold at one time.

But also in my mind I do not know if such dreams are enough for a white boy.

"Whatever you want me to do," I say, "I will do."

And so we lie next to each other in the grass and watch the black clouds float above us, listen as a train makes its whistles far below, the trees shake slowly in the breeze. The time passes and I could even sleep there in the soft grass, our hands touching, our heads touching, our legs touching, only our fingers moving like seaweed in the tide. I know I could stay there forever, not move again even as I see the clouds darken and the moon fade and thoughts of morning begin to set in.

"I must go," I say.

"I know," Danny says. "In five minutes."

And then five minutes passes and I say it again, and another five minutes, but it is inevitable. I stand up slowly, brush the grass from my skirt, shake my hair.

"Can you come tomorrow?" he asks me.

"Of course," I say. "I can come anytime I want."

We kiss and make our plans and Danny says: "I will think of something."

Again he watches me as I walk back to the hedge and to the opening that I must crawl through to reach my mother's room.

This time as I get close to the cement path that will take me there I can see already that her light is on. I stand for a few minutes in the dark, lean against the wall, think about what I am going to do. I find my bundle with my nightgown in it and change quickly, rolling my dress into a little ball and then hiding it in the same place. Then I walk quietly back to the room.

The light is on but my mother is asleep. I think I will come in quietly, close the door, lower myself without a sound onto my mat and cover myself with my blanket, all without her hearing anything. Her eyes are still closed and the light is still on. I stand up and turn it off.

"Why are you up?" she says sleepily.

"Why did you leave the light on?" I ask.

"I turned it on when you were gone," she says. "I looked at my clock. It was half past one. Now it is past four."

"We were asleep with the light on," I say.

"No," my mother says firmly.

She sits up in her bed, turns the lamp back on, swings her legs over the side. She has corns on her toes from such hard work, uncomfortable shoes. One of her toenails is not the right color. I see these things from my mat on the floor.

"Santi," she says firmly. "You must tell me what you are doing."

"Nothing, Mama," I say.

"Is it something bad?" she asks. "Are you in trouble?"

"No," I say, and I laugh softly. "I am in no trouble at all."

"What is it, then?" she says.

I sit up now also and look into my mother's face. Maybe because it is so late and her face looks like a child's, shining from her sleep, I think for a moment that I will tell her everything. But I cannot even think where to start.

"I am worried," I say, "about what I am going to do now. Sometimes when I can't sleep I go and sit in the grass for a while. That is all."

"Which grass?" my mother asks sharply.

"Not this Arbuthnot grass," I say. "The grass next door."

"Did anybody see you?" she asks.

"No," I say.

Now she looks relieved, sighs, leans back in her bed. She is easily tricked, my mother, too easily that it makes me a little sad. She is thinking: So that is all. No trouble with police, or with boys, or with drugs. Just sitting in the grass.

"Can we turn out the light, now?" I ask.

I hear a click, and then there is only quiet and darkness.

⋙

And so it was that Danny and I became friends, and then a boyfriend and a girlfriend, and something like lovers, though not lovers because we were so young and because Danny was so respectful, in the deep dark grass at the bottom of Danny's garden there so long ago in the night in Durban. He came softly, and I stole away, and every night for nights on end we lay there and talked and ate fruit and made wishes and made the plans of children who are almost not children anymore.

Danny told me something right at the beginning and I did not think much of it and then when the time came close that he had to leave I thought about it more, not so much because he had to leave but because of where he was going.

"This army you are going to," I said one night. "You say you have no choice but do you really have no choice?"

"What do you mean?" he asked.

"You go into their army, the Boers' army, and you fight their war. You say you know they do terrible things and that you will have nothing to do with their terrible things, but even if you just put on their uniform and wait until your time is up, can you be sure?"

"I promise you," he says. "I will do nothing that my conscience will not let me."

"But then why do you go?"

"It is the law," he says, and he sounds surprised, as if obeying even a bad law is like gravity, something a person can never think of not doing. But if that is so what are we doing, breaking the law there in the bottom of his garden? And to bring this terrible system to its knees, in the end, we did nothing but break the law.

"If they give you a gun and a fighter from *Umkhonte we Sizwe* comes at you, how can you not shoot?" I ask him.

"What is *Umkhonte we Sizwe*?" he says.

"You don't know?"

"No."

"It is Nelson Mandela's army. The Spear of the Nation."

Danny looks very worried then. He does not know, this white boy, the name of Nelson Mandela's army. So what will he do if they aim their weapons at him?

"I will not fight," he says. "I just have to go and count the days until it is over."

"They will not let you do that," I say. "This settler army."

I have not called him, or anything that he is a part of, a settler before. Danny is not a settler. Sitting there on the red ground, the green grass, listening to the crickets in the hedges, he is as much a part of this place as anyone can be. But still. It is a settler army and I know what they do. They drive their big hippo armored cars into the townships, they humiliate and they torment, sometimes they shoot. Sometimes, even, they rape. Not Danny. But Danny will be in their uniform.

And I know this boy and I will try to understand him too, but when he puts their uniform on his lovely body it will be very hard. My friends, if I would tell them everything, would be interested, they would laugh, they would encourage me even, in everything.

Everything up to the part where Danny puts on his khaki uniform.

⊰◈⊱

It still comes as a surprise to me that so much time has gone by, twenty years since those nights with Danny in the garden. I was only seventeen but it does not seem that I was still a child, that there was anything I did not know already then. And yet those nights stand as the moment in my life when everything changed, like a boat going around a marker or a moth climbing out of its shell. I said I am not an angry person and that life has not treated me badly, but I was angry for a long time, and, I will admit it, my heart was hurt and this did change me and even the choices I have made in my life. But I had nights of such pure happiness that they have left me asking ever since: What if?

Danny wrote to me when he was away, and I know it was dangerous for him to do this. His letters went to the house of his friend called Rupert and I could walk there and ask the cook if there were letters and he would give them to me, Danny's letters in envelopes addressed to this Rupert's mother, who did not open her own post box so that he could keep them waiting for me. And when I wrote to Danny I wrote on the envelope "Santi Rupert" and not using my Zulu name, and also I was careful about every word I said. Except about love. About love I could write freely. And I did. Love will go through walls.

I will say this about Danny's letters. They were funny, filled with stupid stories about shooting pigs by mistake and fighting mosquitos, walking up and down hills for no reason, as if there was not a war at all but just some silly exercise that he had to complete, and I was ready to forget where he was and what he was doing. It was Danny, not some anonymous settler, and I did not make it a condition to love him that he become a revolutionary.

And then he wrote that he was coming home for a weekend pass, and which weekend it was, and my stomach told me that my feelings for him were very strong indeed, that Danny was bound up in my mind and also in my body and that I longed to see him as if he were a drug I had taken and forgotten but that my body still remembered.

❦

He was waiting, like he wrote he would be, just like before, standing in the darkness. And my happiness in seeing him was more than before, the things I wanted to tell him more than I could hold in, my questions growing on their own even as they sat in my head. He was suntanned, so handsome, a little thinner perhaps, his hair shaven short. But so handsome.

"When things were bad, or I was homesick, I just thought of you," he said. "I just pictured your face and your voice and thought how soft the skin is on your arms and your legs. And then the bad times were behind me."

"And me too," I told him. "I become scared that you were not real, that you would disappear."

"No," he said. "I can't disappear."

"Yes, you can," I said. "Away in their army, up there in that house, it is like you are in the sky. Even a rocket, it cannot reach you."

And then more kissing, kissing like drinking.

"I was worried you would have to leave," he said.

"I must leave soon, truly," I said. "But I can wait a little longer and also I can help my mother now too. There is nothing bad that will happen if I wait just a little longer."

"I have something for you," he said even while we were still standing there, me stroking his hair, he holding my face.

"I don't need anything," I told him.

"Here," he said.

It was a little box, maybe the size of a matchbox. At first I could not even touch it, held my hands against myself as if the box had razor blades attached to it, but he just stood there holding it out and so eventually I did take it and inside was a very thin chain with a gold heart on the end of it.

"It is so beautiful," I said. "If you put it on I will not ever take it off."

And so I turned around and he began to attach the chain at the back and as I felt his fingers on my neck my whole back began to feel like there were insects in my shirt and so I closed my eyes and let them crawl, up and down, take little bites from my spine, leave little scratches on my heart.

But when I opened my eyes and lifted my head I almost died from fright because we were not alone.

"Danny," I said, and he knew from my voice that something was wrong.

It was the man we had seen that first day in the garden, Danny's father's driver, and also a white man who I knew right away was Danny's father, standing there next to the swimming pool house, the white man and the black man next to each other, looking at us with surprise and maybe also with anger.

"Dad," Danny said, and his voice was thin and dry.

"What do you think you're doing?" the driver said to me in Zulu and his eyes wished I would just burst into flames where I stood. I could say nothing because I was still in such a shock from seeing a person come out of the darkness. Before I could think to answer Danny's father spoke.

"Calm down, Ambrose," he said. "That's not the way to handle it."

"What has she been looking for in this house, this colored thief from next door?" he said in English. "This boy does not have such ideas on his own."

"I said calm down," Danny's father said and I could tell right away where Danny got his gentle voice, his long soft hands, a fairness deep inside. Ambrose started to speak again in Zulu, saying all sorts of terrible things that I could understand and that he knew the other ones could not but Danny's father knew that this was happening and he stopped him very strongly.

"I'll handle this," he said, and there was anger in his voice now for the driver too and it made him stop talking right away.

For a moment there was silence, all except for the trees again still brushing in the wind, the clouds threatening blackness from above, although the world had changed so much. I put my fingers on my new necklace at my throat and kept them there. It felt, at the same time, like a comfort and like a mockery.

"Danny, what is going on?" his father asked.

"This is Santi, Dad," he said.

He stepped now for the first time from behind me, stood at my side, faced his father.

"Her mother is Emily," Ambrose interrupted. "She is the cook girl next door."

"For the Arbuthnots?" Danny's father asked.

He looked surprised, turned from Ambrose to me and then again to Danny, like this new fact changed something, made things worse.

"Yes," Danny said. "She's also a student at Wentworth Academy."

"How long has this been going on?" his father asked, but before Danny could answer his father interrupted.

"On second thought," he said, "I don't want to know. But this young lady has to go back to her room and you and I have to have a talk."

"You don't understand," Danny said. "You just don't understand."

And then Danny did something that made my breath just fade away, he reached for my hand and took it, and so we stood there in front of his father like that, hand in hand. Even Ambrose the driver was frozen to the spot like a statue. His father looked at me almost like he was seeing me for the first time, also at my face, our hands together, skin against skin.

"This is not clever, my boy," he said, turning back to Danny, but it seemed to me like there was a sadness in his voice, like a pity almost, and I was not sure exactly what it was for but maybe it was for many things. So we stood there, the four of us, with only the trees for music.

"This is not anyone's business," Danny said, and he was holding my hand very tightly now, his fingers like steel on mine. "And perfectly innocent too."

For a moment his father seemed unable to act, stretched between two ideas, not knowing which to follow.

"If it were so innocent," he said at last, "it would not be midnight and we would not be standing behind a hedge at the bottom of the garden."

"You know why that is," Danny said crossly.

"I'm not angry with you," his father said, but even as he said it there was anger in his voice. "I'm not sure I even care that what you appear to be doing is against the law and that if the army were to find out about it you would be severely punished. There are, believe it or not, even more important things at stake here."

Then his father turned to me and the hardness in him disappeared, just slipped away to leave his voice like a doctor doing an examination.

"Are you all right, young lady?" he asked.

"Yes sir," I said.

"Are you sure?"

"Yes sir," I said again.

"You're not in any trouble with me, do you understand that?" he said.

"Yes sir."

"You seem like a very fine young woman," he said.

"Thank you, sir."

I could hear myself as he told me these things and I answered, that I had slipped into my settler language self, the one which answers quickly and with soft tones, looks down with self-reducing respect just to bring the conversation to an end.

"But I am not ashamed of anything I have done, sir," I added.

I could see Danny turn to look at me, looked back at him.

"How old are you?" Danny's father asked me.

I told him but my voice was shivering. I could not stop it.

"And you are staying next door?" he asked me.

"Yes," I said.

"With Emily? With your mother?"

"Yes," I said.

"Does she know you are here?"

Then I felt very ashamed but even so I was pleased that my mother did not know. Perhaps no trouble would come to her.

"No," I said.

"Does anyone know about this?" his father asked Ambrose.

"I don't think so, *baas*," Ambrose said.

"All right, then," he said. "This is what we're going to do."

And then when he told us what he wanted, even though I did not like his words, he sounded like a good man, not one filled with typical settler arrogance.

"I want you to see the young lady home," his father said to Ambrose. "But you're not to be rude to her. Do you understand me?"

"Yes," Ambrose said curtly.

"And I don't want this matter gossiped about among the servants or anyone else either," he said. "Is that clear too?"

"Yes, *baas*," Ambrose said.

Danny's father took a five-rand note from his pocket and gave it to Ambrose.

"Now see her home."

Then Danny spoke up.

"This is far from over," he said. "And I'll walk her back to her room."

"You cannot go there," Ambrose said immediately.

"It's okay," his father said. "We'll wait for you here."

And that was how the night ended then, with Danny and me walking away from them, away from the house by the swimming pool, the grass by the hedge, places I never saw again in my life, the smoky sky and slow black clouds, the house like a fairy tale standing watch over it all.

We walked slowly, my Danny and me, away from the two men, back to the archway and down the little cement path underneath the granadilla vine. We said nothing, just held our hands like two innocent people sent into exile, sent into disgrace. When we reached the gap in the fence we stopped.

"Here is where I go back to next door," I told him.

We stood still then, holding each other, my heart like a stone, my skin cold like morning haze.

"They can make it harder," he said. "But nothing can make it impossible."

"Yes," I said.

"I love you," he said. "I truly do."

"And I too," I told him.

"When I come back from the army we will sort this out," he said. "I don't know how but nothing can stop us."

And I said nothing. If that were true, then time would show that it was true. But I knew there would be no more shortcuts through the big house, that soon I would be leaving with my suitcase straight across the Arbuthnots' front garden, back to Wentworth maybe, or to find a job, or to my mother's village. That night I was too sad to think about all the details, the hundreds of little details in my life. But I did feel in my heart that whatever would happen would happen and Danny would be there at the end.

So we held each other at the gap by the hedge, just held and held, and then after a few minutes we heard a soft whistle coming from the hedge where the father and Ambrose were waiting and I tried to move away but Danny still held, and then another whistle, and this time he let me go. He held my face and kissed my eyes, wiped my cheek, stroked my hair back against my head. And then he put his hand on my back and helped to be sure no thorns cut me as I crouched low and crawled into the broken hedge.

I prayed that my mother would be asleep when I returned and at least this prayer was answered. She was lying on her back in her bed, her mouth open, making small whistling noises as she slept. I stood over her in my clothes, carrying the little bundle I had brought back with me, thinking about her life and about mine, about the white man who had come into hers and then left her alone leaving only me to grow like a memory for her.

For a moment I thought too about the things that could happen in a place like South Africa, settlers and Africans coming together like branches curling round and round, drinking from each other, holding each other upright, and I felt, maybe for the first time, proud of who I was, of all the things, even of the misunderstandings and the unhappinesses and crossed paths that had gone into making me. On that night, with Danny making his way back to his father by the swimming pool house and me standing in the servants' room looking at my mother, it seemed not sad at all, but to the contrary, that life could be a very rich and interesting thing.

She woke up, my mother, saw me standing over her.

"What is it, Santi?" she asked.

"Nothing, Mama," I said. "Only that I am in love."

"Now you're talking midnight nonsense," my mother said and turned on her side.

But she was smiling, pulled the blanket up over her shoulders and stretched herself out under the covers with a sigh of satisfaction.

So I changed my clothes and put my dress and the little bundle I had kept it in back in my suitcase under the cabinet. Then I got down on the mat and covered myself, closed my eyes and tried to go to sleep.

CHAPTER SIX

Danny

SANTI'S FACE IS AN image that is never wholly out of mind. I see a young girl in the street with a certain look, little puffs just beneath the eyes, restless hair, or someone else with just the right set to the calf, and I think, Santi. Or, more improbably yet, I sit in a ski lift and wonder what Santi there in sultry South Africa would say of this, what she would think of herself all bundled up in down and wool, skis strapped to her feet, of the orange leaves and reddened barks of trees that prickle below as we sail up the side of a mountain. I wonder what she would think of me.

I would never have thought when I was younger of the speed at which twenty years passes, how it just streams by and leaves you wondering what became of it, why it is that some of the images of times past remain so vivid even as others disappear completely. And I would never have thought when I was younger that what has already happened could become, as one gets older, almost more important than what may still happen.

It wasn't that I didn't think of her further, that I didn't believe when last I saw her that it was all part of the beginning only, the first pages of a book that was destined to develop in its own way and at its own pace until the last page was turned. It wasn't that I meant to mislead her or to allow both of our hearts to be broken. In the end all those things just happened.

❦

I was seventeen when I first saw her and I had no idea where she came from or where she belonged. She wasn't white but she wasn't black either, rather a coppery brown that seemed to make irrelevant any thought of what she might be and to make who she might be all that seemed of interest. She had tightly curled dark hair and pale brown eyes, a small waist, was carrying two heavy suitcases and her shoes as she walked across my garden. I couldn't help myself but to stare, to stand against the window and to watch her until she moved around a corner and out of sight.

It wasn't only that she was tall and striking or that she seemed so very tired and yet still resilient, it was also that she was so out of context, dropped into our garden without any of the things that should have surrounded her. Mixed race, or as we called them, colored girls, especially striking and barefoot colored girls carrying suitcases, were not an everyday occurrence on the grounds of Gordonwood.

The next time I saw her I was with my closest friend, Rupert. She was walking across the garden again and I pointed her out to him.

"Who do you think she is?" I asked him.

"Maybe she works in one of the houses here," he said.

"No one has colored servants," I said.

"How can you say that?" he asked. "Maybe they do now."

She wasn't a domestic servant. She just wasn't, you could see. She was carrying a book this time, still barefoot, was moving quickly though not at all furtively, was oblivious to us.

"You're probably right," Rupert said when she passed under my window.

I noticed as she walked by snatches of things that stayed with me. Her hair was dark but also almost transparent, like a fuzzy halo in the sun. Her arms were long, her shoulders quite square. It was a hot afternoon, the sort of muggy Durban day that seeps into your clothes and leaves everything limp and wet, and yet she looked quite unaware of the heat, cool even.

"If you want to know who she is so badly," Rupert said, "go down and find out."

"You think so?" I asked.

"You have about ten seconds and then it'll be too late," he said.

So I slipped quickly downstairs, through the French doors and onto the lawn, reached a hedge she had to pass seconds before she got there herself. Even so I wasn't bold enough to do more than exchange a few meaningless sentences. But the next time I was prepared, and when I left her then at the edge of the Arbuthnots' garden I felt as if something in life that had been disconnected had shown its ability to become connected again, some mystery shown itself susceptible of understanding.

I could not get her out of my mind that afternoon. I changed and went to sit by the side of the pool, dangling my legs in the water, and then I dove in and swam a few laps, up and down, towards the house, away. I kept thinking of her graceful walk, careful voice, copper legs, curled hair. I had no doubt that this all, every part of it, was forbidden. And yet there seemed nothing stopping it.

"So what's the status of Danny's big transgression?" Rupert had asked.

"You're not going to believe it," I told him and described what had taken place.

Rupert thought about it for a while and then shook his head.

"I didn't think you had it in you," he said.

"I don't," I told him. "It's all impossible."

"Listen," he said. "If you're doing it then it's not impossible, is it? In any event, I'm sure if you are arrested you could successfully challenge the Immorality Act of 1950, which makes sexual contact across the color line a serious criminal offense. You'd be in all the papers."

"You're not being funny," I said.

"I'm amusing myself, old man," Rupert replied.

"Could I ask her to come over and swim, for instance?" I said. "Of course not."

"Who says so?" Rupert said. "The only reason to obey an inane law is that you might get caught. And who's going to catch you? There's no reason why you can't do it except that you think you can't."

"Of course I can't."

"Who says?"

"I say," I said. "The roof would fall in. Can you just imagine it? My mother? Baptie? The Arbuthnots?"

"Perhaps if you started on a less grand scale," Rupert suggested. "You don't need to begin whatever it is you're beginning with a parade."

"Perhaps," I said.

The water was lukewarm, pasty in the stickiness of the afternoon. I pictured her in the pool with me, moving through the water like a dark shadow, surfacing to shake the beads of water from her hair, diving again and fading as she neared the bottom. And then I looked up to see Ambrose standing over me.

"That girl," he said. "The one you were talking to. Her mother is a Zulu."

"So?" I said.

"Her mother is a Zulu," he said again. "Her father is white but her mother is a Zulu."

"I know that," I said.

Ambrose had started with us as a gardener and then my father taught him to drive and he became our driver and then he learned to use my father's power tools and became something of everything: repairer, finder, know-it-all.

He began to walk away, across the grass to the path behind the bougainvillaea bushes.

"Ambrose," I called.

"Yes."

"What do you know about her?"

He started to walk back.

"You leave her alone," he said.

I turned on my side and watched him walk away. It was Ambrose, I always thought, who led my father to discover my illicit affair with the daughter of the neighbor's cook, but, unlike Ambrose, my father did not seek to protect some racial or moral order. My father was not an unsubtle man, and he was not unsubtle that night either.

❦

My father waited while I saw Santi back to the hedge which separated our land from the Arbuthnots' and when I returned he was sitting on a little slope above the swimming pool. He was wearing a blue-and-white-striped dressing gown, red silk pajamas, brown slippers, sitting there with his long legs stretched out, his white shins shining in the moonlight, smoking a cigarette.

I stood over him, angry, humiliated, my arms crossed.

"Sit down for a while," he said.

My father was not one to sit in the grass, to have heart to heart talks. He was mostly withdrawn, wrapped in his own problems, his business struggles, his tug of war with my mother.

"I'd rather stand," I said. "What do you want to say?"

"You're furious with me," he said, puffing on his cigarette. "I don't blame you."

"Who asked you to interfere?" I exploded. "I'm not a child. I can take care of myself."

"Perhaps," he said. "But the truth is I'm not worried about you."

"So what are you doing here?" I demanded.

He shook his head, stubbed out his cigarette, fished in his pocket for another.

"Let me ask you something," he said. "Won't you sit down first?"

"Just ask it."

"I don't want to know how far things have already gone," he said. "I trust you were a gentleman. What I want to know is how much farther you think they could have gone?"

"I don't know," I said. I sounded petulant but it just didn't seem reasonable, the whole discussion, standing there in the moonlight with my father.

"Well, let me ask you something else, then," he said. "What do you think that young girl can expect from this affair with you?"

"I don't know that either," I said impatiently.

"Well, use your imagination," he suggested.

"I'm not playing this game," I said.

"You know," my father said slowly, "there are things in life you can dabble in and things in life you simply cannot, perhaps even people you can dabble in, experiment with, and others you must not. Don't you see that?"

We were not in the habit of having intimate conversations, my father and I, and there was something unnerving about the intimacy now, the way he seemed to have stumbled onto misgivings that might have been my own.

"If you were to think about it a little you'd come to one conclusion," he said, "and that is that you have no right to indulge your own curiosities, feelings that are otherwise quite natural for someone your age, at the expense of a person who is far more vulnerable than you are."

"You don't have to know how something is going to end before you dare to start it," I said.

"I disagree," he said.

He paused, waited for me to say something, shook his head.

"Listen," he said. "Can't you get it through your head that that girl has nothing. Absolutely nothing. Her mother is a cook, lives in a *kaiya* next door. To that girl you must look like the promised land. Do you plan to lead her there, show it to her, and then think you still have the option of changing your mind? Do you really think that?"

"You don't understand," I said. "You don't know her."

"Let me ask you still another question," he said. "I'm not going to talk about the fact that this is South Africa, whether you like it or not, and that the law says you have to leave her alone. That would be too easy. Or that you're going back to the army on Sunday, where offences like this are very severely treated. What I do ask you is what happens when you get out? What then?"

"We will work something out," I said.

"Like what?"

"I don't know."

"When you come back and start at the university, where will she be then?"

"I don't know," I said.

"And meet a whole new circle of friends, explore your independence, go places you've never been, how will that play out given that the law says, whether you like it or not, that you may not take her with you?"

I said nothing, stood for a while in silence there on the slope of grass behind the swimming pool. I had no answer that I could give him. There was no answer that was right, then and there, but we would work it out in time, Santi and I.

"This is a strange country," my father said. "But we live here. The bare minimum you can do, must do, is to be sure you don't take advantage of someone whom circumstances have made weaker than you are. I am not blind. That is a beautiful girl and I'm willing to bet she's filled with ideas and a perspective that must be new to you and very exciting too. But that is not enough. You will move on, sooner or later you will move on because you have no choice, and when that happens you will have done something very bad."

"I'm tired," I said. "I want to go to bed."

He sighed, stood up, wiped the grass from his gown. Then he tried to put his hand on my shoulder but I moved away angrily, stood a few feet from him shrouded in hostility.

"Let me suggest something to you," he said finally. "I don't give a damn what color she is. I really don't. Your mother would probably say that you should choose a Jewish girl but in all honesty things like that don't count for much with me at all."

"Well, what are you saying, then?" I asked.

"I want you to let some time pass," he said. "Get the army behind you and give that young woman a chance to rethink things. Sooner than you know it you'll be independent and able to do as you please. But while you live under my roof I will not permit what I saw tonight. Now, let's go to bed and try not to wake the women."

"I don't think I'll ever forgive you for this," I said as I turned and walked away, ahead of him across the grass.

And so I walked towards Gordonwood, our shadowy hulk of a house, back to the open French doors, through the curtains blowing slowly out into the evening, into the dark room. I stepped through them and heard him behind me, closing and then locking them, walked quickly away and up to my room.

❦

For a long time Santi's face and my dad's become linked, like overlapping photographs or pages pressed together. I would see Santi's face and then his, his earnest expression, the glow of the cigarette, the movement of his hands as he spoke. He would eavesdrop as Santi lay with me on a bed, her head on my arm, telling me what she'd seen in the day, in the dusty halls of Wentworth Academy, on the unpaved streets of Hammarsdale, sights and sounds far removed from my musty room on the third floor of Gordonwood.

I would do things differently now, knowing more, having seen the consequences of it all, but that night and the next day, my last day at home, my last day as part of a family, I did not speak to my father, refused to acknowledge him at all, answered my mother's questions curtly, avoided them both where I could. And that's how things were when I returned to the army the next day, took my surly leave of Bridget, whom alone I allowed to see me off, on Platform 9 of the Durban station.

My father died three weeks later. That was when I learned that second chances are rare.

❧

Some people like to talk about their army experiences. I can't really remember mine at all. I was assigned to the Fifth South African Infantry in Ladysmith and then sent to the Sibaya outpost in northern Zululand. There were scorpions and sandworms and not a telephone or store for hundreds of miles in any direction. The one consolation, if there could be one, was that Rupert and I were posted to the same unit.

"Too much ecology," Rupert said as we got off the Bedford truck that was taking us to our camp. "They ought to pave the whole place."

Our corporal was a great, muscle-bound Afrikaner with ruddy skin, fair hair, a flat, lowlander's face. His whole life, it seemed, revolved around things people like Rupert and I never even thought about, things like hunting and breaking in oxen and stalking jackal.

He had biceps like crane hooks and was so prone to violence — random things like smashing a can against a bedpost — that one shied from his way even as he paraded up and down the tent posturing and joking. When he showered he would walk about quite naked until the air dried his body for him, and I couldn't help thinking, as I lay on my cot listening to the raucous talk, that home was about as far on this earth as one could get from a bush camp listening to the philosophies of Corporal Van Zyl.

Rupert and I came in for his early attention. Rupert had brought a tape of Woodstock and we were listening to it one evening as we wrote home.

"What kind of music is that?" he demanded, walking up to us.

It was humid and he was stark naked. He had — and this is an odd detail to remember but it struck me at the time as proof that Van Zyl was quite beyond the things that chasten normal people — been bitten on the penis by a spider but this had not in any way interfered with his nightly prowls on the narrow path between our bunks, even as his swollen member bobbed before him like a blowfish.

"It's called Woodstock," Rupert said. "It was a music festival in America."

"Americans," he exclaimed. "They are a godless people. This music is the work of Communists."

"How can music be Communist?" I asked.

"Are you being white with me?" he demanded. I'd never heard the expression. I didn't know what the right answer was.

"I am white," I said uncertainly.

"Not with me, you're not," he said. "To me you're lower than a *kaffir.*"

"Okay," I said.

"If I hear you playing that music one more time," he said to Rupert, "I'll smash your tape recorder into the ground."

"Okay," Rupert said. His face was drained of color.

"And you too. Both of you," he added.

The colonial war against the Portuguese in Mozambique was over and a Marxist government there was struggling to hold on against an insurgency begun they say now by the Rhodesians and the South Africans. My unit roamed the arid countryside, often quite aimlessly, our only sense of danger a prickling feeling when we'd come upon little villages and stop to question their headmen. There were painted huts, chickens, plump little children, and we would descend on them like a thunderstorm, leaving nothing to chance, securing perimeters, lining men up for questioning, poking about in piles with our rifle butts. When we left each village sometimes we'd look back and see the people standing where we'd left them, not so much intimidated, it seemed, as embarrassed.

I'd wonder how it would be if ever I were called on to hurt any of them, to push and demand or, worse yet, to open fire. I knew I wouldn't do it and that the consequences would be terrible. And at the end of each patrol I'd throw my rifle and pack on my bed, count off another day, curse everyone who had anything to do with landing me where I was. My thoughts though did not protect me from the dislike I saw in the eyes of those I was a party to bullying.

"You know you've been in the bush too long," Van Zyl said one night as he paraded naked about the tent, "when you'd even fuck a *kaffir* girl. Except for these two," he added, pointing at Rupert and me. "They'd fuck a *kaffir* girl by choice."

Rupert looked at me with a wry smile.

"What else does he know about you?" he muttered when Van Zyl was out of earshot.

I remember waiting with a guard detail outside a supply depot in Matubatuba as a long passenger train came into the station and opened its doors. We watched, the six or seven of us in our mud-colored fatigues, RIs over our shoulders, as a sea of black people stepped to the platform. One could not avoid sensing the power in their number. It was like watching a river that is about to breach its banks.

"They could just turn around and drown us," Rupert said. He had been smoking a cigarette but threw it aside, was standing upright against the truck.

Van Zyl heard him.

"You scared?" he taunted. "Of that?"

"Yes," Rupert said.

Van Zyl looked across at the emptying platform, cocked his rifle, spat on the ground.

"Well, I'm not," he said.

That week we ourselves were shot at, the first time since we'd left Ladysmith. It gets very dark out in the bush. As the sun sets the growth becomes tangled, closes in on you and encases you in a woven fence of blackness. We'd come over the crest of a hill, were about to enter a village, when a single shot was fired from a cluster of trees in the distance.

"Get down," the sergeant ordered.

We already had, all except Van Zyl, who turned to face the trees with a look of profound indignation on his face.

"What is that?" he demanded.

"Down," the sergeant ordered.

"There's a *kaffir* in those trees shooting at us," Van Zyl said. He was standing there, fully exposed, looking round incredulously. "A *kaffir*," he said. "I can see him."

"Get down," the sergeant said again and lunged for him. Van Zyl fell heavily but he never took his eyes off the trees.

"I'm going to shoot him myself," he said.

"Okay," the sergeant said. Van Zyl's intensity unnerved him, you could see.

Van Zyl lay on his stomach and tried to take aim but by then there was nobody there. We split into two sections and surrounded the copse, searched it thoroughly, found nothing.

"Let's take the village," Van Zyl said.

"Take it where?" Rupert asked.

"Look," Van Zyl said menacingly, clenching his fist and holding Rupert by the collar. "I've had just about enough of you."

"Cut that out," the sergeant said.

"Jew," Van Zyl said as Rupert smoothed off his shirt.

I had been back from my weekend leave for seventeen days when the message came that I had to report to headquarters with my bag packed. I remember being alarmed, wondering what it could be.

"Rifleman Divin," the guard officer said when I reported.

"Sir."

"*Jou pa het self doodgemaak*," he barked. "Your father has killed himself. You're to catch the next train home."

"My father?" I said, standing there under the bare lightbulb of the guard house, at attention, other men around me.

"Dead," the officer said.

"How could it be?" I mumbled.

"I don't know these things," the officer said. "Report to the vehicle park immediately for a ride to the station."

And so I returned to the Ladysmith train station, sat there on a wooden bench with an overnight bag at my feet for the sleeper to come through and take me home. It was a cool autumn night, damp, dark, filled with the screams of locusts.

It was, of course, true. *My pa het self doodgemaak.* It was almost as simple as the guard officer had made it out to be. When I arrived home his office was still sealed off, uncleaned, stained, a faint smell of gunpowder sunk forever into the wainscoting.

⬦

It was on my last afternoon before I had to return to the army that I confronted Ambrose about Santi. It wasn't as if I had postponed doing it but the arrangements and the grief and the comings and goings at Gordonwood, the newspapers and relatives and well-meaning friends, filled each day.

Ambrose had been carefully avoiding me, but early on the afternoon I was scheduled to leave, already dressed in my uniform and almost ready to go, I went down to his room, knocked on the door, disturbed him as he was taking his afternoon nap. He was startled by me, perhaps by the uniform, sat awkwardly on his bed and waited for me to justify my intrusion.

"You look very nice in your uniform, *basie*," he said at last.

"Thank you," I said.

"The Master was a very good man," he said. "Everyone is very sorry for his dying."

"I know," I said.

"Me, too, I am very sorry."

"Thank you," I said.

We sat for a few seconds in silence. His room was very bare, a metal bed, a metal cabinet, a counter with a lamp and Primus stove.

"I want to ask you a question about Santi," I said. "I know she's not here or I would have seen her. So where is she?"

He stood up, raised his hands, shook them before his face as if he could wave me away.

"I know nothing of those things," he said.

"Where is she?" I repeated.

"I don't know," he said. "Honest to God. I don't know."

"Well, tell me this, then," I said. "When did she leave?"

He looked puzzled, scratched his hair, made a face. But it was all an act.

"Maybe she go nowhere," he said. "Did you watch for her?"

"She's not here, I'm sure of it," I said. "I want you to tell me where she went and what happened to her."

I sat down on his bed, looked him squarely in the face.

"It can't make any difference now," I said. "I'd like to know that she is okay."

Ambrose took his time, folded something, walked across the room to take his alarm clock off the counter and to check the time.

"The Master paid for her to go back to Wentworth school," he said at last.

"My father did?"

Ambrose nodded.

"He felt bad for her," he said. "He asked me to speak to Emily and then he made Emily go to his work in town and then he made phone calls to Wentworth and made plans for her to go back there."

"He did?"

"That's all I know," he said. "Honestly."

"Does Emily know what happened with me and Santi?" I asked him.

It was his turn to look surprised.

"Do you think if Emily know something the whole world does not know it the next day?" he said. "Emily talk more than any three other people."

"So how did he explain to her what he was doing?" I asked.

"He didn't explain," Ambrose said. "He just said he saw her and wanted to help. The Master did that for the people, gave jobs at his work, other things. The Madame make talk talk talk, not the Master."

Ambrose came and sat down next to me on the edge of his unmade bed.

"I'm sorry, Danny, for what happened. But still today I think it was the right thing."

"It's okay, Ambrose," I said, overwhelmed now with the sadness of my father's death, with Ambrose's certainty, with my own sense of being cut adrift. "Maybe it was."

Later that night, on the train back to Ladysmith, the mildewed tents and scorpions, the surprised villagers, the sun banging down on us as we staggered about in the bushveld, seemed hardly to matter anymore. They were details. It was everything else that seemed to take too long, life itself to stretch interminably with no hope of respite and no hope of order returning. I wondered if perhaps I might not make it either down the long, unforgiving years until it all, mercifully, came to an end. And soon too it began to seem as if my father's death had pulled loose the anchor knot in a fabric that would continue unraveling until the last familiar thread lay flat on the table. In a panicked telephone call I heard that Bridget had been arrested and was being held in Pretoria, and then in another that my grandfather had had a stroke, lay on a bed in Gordonwood slowly losing his mind.

So there was one more unexpected trip to Durban, this one only three weeks before my army service ended.

"Rifleman Divin," I was told in the guard room. "What is it with your family?"

"I beg pardon, sir?"

"They seem all to be dying this year," he said and as thoughts of Helga flew through my head he added, perhaps seeing whiteness in my face: "It's your grandfather. He's dead now too."

❧

It was my mother's decision to divert all the money her father had allowed her to control at his death to repaying my father's debts until every last one of them was squared away. I don't know whether I would decide the same way today, but back then it seemed the only possible decision. We would have had to sell Gordonwood immediately too except that the wave of unrest that followed the Soweto riots had caused a collapse of the property market and would have made a sale pointless. And so the conservators let us remain for the time being, but we had to send all the servants away, all except Baptie that is, and make do the best we could.

The house was impossible to maintain without domestic help and slowly, one piece at a time, my father's makeshift repairs began to come apart, the house to return to a state it had once been in, glowering, half derelict, offering only glimpses of past grandeur. On some days I would find Baptie wandering about the garden with a trowel, hunting for weeds, or Helga scooping leaves from the pool, but in the end the list of things that had to be done just piled up and we stopped keeping it. Some rooms we simply closed off, parts of the garden we just abandoned, and the house began to take on a dusty, overgrown look I actually came to like.

I suppose it was cozy, in a way, our camping there, eating when we were hungry, sleeping when we were tired, following no routine at all. Baptie moved into the house with us, left her room in the servants' quarters and had her own little suite upstairs, almost like a paying guest. It was illegal, of course, having a black woman living in our house like that, but our existence was so insular there was no chance of our being reported. On some evenings when the garden was alive with goldenrod and bougainvillaea we would turn on the colored lights in the trees and the three of us, Baptie and my mother and I, would sit on the veranda in silence and watch the glittering pool and the gazebo shining in the distance like a lantern. I remember how little there seemed to be to say.

And I realized that it wasn't only the landmarks of life that had changed but that I had changed too, had developed, in spite of all that had happened and for reasons I could not readily identify, something approaching contempt for my mother. It would not go away, could not be hidden, had something to do with my father's death and my forced march into the army, my mother's role in it all, and it surfaced without warning and on the slightest of pretexts. As we waited for Bridget and mourned our losses I began to blame her for everything,

even for Santi, how she stood for one thing and did another, advocated one way of life and lived another wholly inconsistent. And so I
berated her, ridiculed her, could not control my words even as I
watched an unbreachable distance grow between us. Even today there
is a strangeness between us that began in those months. My mother,
especially now that Arnold has subdued all that once made her lively
and engaging, is defensive with me, has said often that she knows I
think her ridiculous.

"What is it anyway between you two?" Arnold goads. "Have out
with it. Say what you have in mind, what."

I wrote to Santi at the Wentworth Academy and my letters were
returned marked "Unknown." I thought of going there to find out for
myself what had become of her but for reasons too vague and insuf-
ficient to repeat I did not. I telephoned and was made to wait, almost
endlessly and to no avail. Baptie, who understood everything when she
chose to, pretended a monumental opacity when I asked her what had
become of Emily's daughter.

And then one morning in the spring of 1977 I woke up and went
into my father's study, sat in his leather chair and watched the shadows
on the wall, smelled the mustiness of the books on his shelves, exam-
ined the nicks in his desk where the arms of his chair had hit it time
and time again, and I decided I simply wanted no more of it.

❦

I left Durban on a Thursday, an overcast, humid day punctured by un-
explained flashes of lightning. Baptie helped me pack and when we
were done she went to the kitchen and I was left to wander through
the house, to touch ornaments, books, light switches, to stand at the

windows and look out over the gardens. Even then I knew that one day it would all assume an unshakeable significance and yet I could not squeeze more into my leave-taking than I had. Looking through the living room window I saw leaves floating in the pool, that an umbrella had blown over, that the servants' quarters in the distance were completely covered with goldenrod. It was spring and the air was warm and clammy and brushed about by gusts of a bleak, rattling wind. The house, which had once been filled with activity and voices, was wholly quiet.

Baptie came into the room, stood for a moment waiting for me to turn around, then spoke.

"There is a boy looking for work," she announced. She pronounced it "wek." A boy looking for "wek."

"We don't have any jobs," I said. "You know that."

"He is the son of Emily who works next door," Baptie said.

I turned to look at her. Baptie had been with my family since I was a child, for all the years we'd been at Gordonwood, for as long as I could remember, and yet at that moment I scarcely knew what her face looked like.

"Emily?" I said.

"Yes," Baptie said. She was watching me closely. It occurred to me that, my father's instructions notwithstanding, she knew everything.

"Why has he come here?" I asked.

"He wants a job," she said.

"We have no job," I said at last. "You know we're all leaving."

I looked around the room, at the shrouded piano, stains on the walls where paintings had once hung.

"I told him," Baptie said. "But still he wants to speak to the Master."

"The Master is dead," I told her.

"He means you," Baptie said.

So I turned from the window and went into the kitchen and there he was, Santi's brother, waiting in ragged clothes at the kitchen door.

"Good afternoon," I said.

He was not properly dressed for the cold day, this boy in his tattered overalls.

"My mother, Emily, works next door," he said.

I looked at him carefully, this young Zulu boy, dark skinned, ragged, nervous, saw the vaguest of familiar outlines, the slightest of resemblances.

"Baptie told me," I said. "I know Emily."

"I need job," he said.

"We're leaving," I told him. "I'm sorry but there is no job here."

"No job?"

"I'm afraid not."

"Oh," he said and turned to leave.

"Wait a minute," I said, and he paused. We stood there on the back veranda, me in my cotton trousers and sweater, he in his khaki overalls.

"Santi is your sister?" I asked.

He turned back, hesitated, moved his cap about in his hands.

"Yes," he said.

I heard Baptie moving behind me. Nothing else.

"Where is she?" I asked.

"Santi?"

"Yes. Where is Santi?"

He looked behind me at Baptie, smiled awkwardly, stopped smiling, moved his cap again.

"Is she still at Wentworth?" I asked.

"Wentworth?"

"Where she went to school?"

"She finished," he said.

"So where is she?"

"Hammarsdale."

"What is she doing there?"

"Maybe she get job."

"How is she?" I asked.

"Santi?"

"Yes," I said impatiently. "Santi."

"Is good," he said. "Santi is good."

The boy turned to Baptie, said something in Zulu, looked back at me while he was talking.

"What is he saying?" I asked her.

"Nothing," Baptie said and walked away.

"Wait here for a moment," I said.

In the hallway was a stack of clothes I had pulled from my closets for my mother to give to the Benevolent Society when things settled down. I rummaged through it until I found a few sweaters, some shoes, a couple of pairs of trousers, and carried them back to the kitchen.

"Would you like these?" I offered.

He looked at me in surprise, at the clothes, at Baptie standing

behind me. Then he said something to her in Zulu and I waited for
her to translate, and then he said something else. It went on for quite
a while, this back and forth, until Baptie became irritated and turned
from him with a cluck of disapproval.

"He says he is not a beggar," she said at last.

"What else did he say?" I asked.

"Only that," she said.

"He said a lot more," I argued. "What else did he say?"

"Only that," she insisted.

And there we left it.

⊰⊚⊱

It was winter in Boston when I arrived and I'd come without a coat. In
Johannesburg the weather had been balmy, cloying almost, but by the
time I'd finally collected my bags and cleared American customs it had
been so long since I'd last stood in a shower or lain on a bed that the
cold sting of the air seemed scarcely to matter. Things didn't look too
unfamiliar either though the airport was huge and somehow seamy in
a way I hadn't expected. But I wasn't coming from Kabul, at any rate,
or from Bulgaria, like Tibor. Tibor didn't even speak English when he
first stepped off the plane from Sofia in London and I'd had a New
York subway map pinned to the headboard of my bed since I was thirteen. But in a practical sense I suppose it's true to say I didn't know
much more about what was in store than he did, and there was something about the place constantly whispering that all similarities were
deceptive.

I knew to avoid the far too friendly men in leather jackets standing at the airport entrance and offering to take me with them, sat by the

bus window thinking how shabby it all looked, how much was broken. In Durban if something was broken, a streetlight, for instance or a road sign, someone would call the authorities and sooner or later it would be repaired. Captive inside the leaky bus it occurred to me that someone could die in weather like this. It seemed a very trivial way to die.

I slept for twenty-six hours in a hostel near Park Square and when I woke I was ravenous. As I walked up Columbus Avenue and then ate in a little diner I realized that Boston was not like Durban in another respect as well, that in Boston a cautious person didn't try to improvise too much. In Durban you could always make do one way or another but in Boston if you counted on getting by that way you could get into a free fall with nothing under you ever, just a free fall with unimaginable consequences. Truly unimaginable.

When my visitor's visa expired I became an undocumented alien, recoiled each time I saw a policeman, felt like a trespasser, somehow, on sidewalks supposedly free. The irony of it was not lost on me either, I who in winter once had my clothes rushed to me freshly ironed so they would be warm when I dressed, who had been driven by a chauffeur to piano lessons, and to the cricket field, and then to the store to buy chocolate, I was humbled even as I was resentful. At any moment, I knew, they could send me home, back to a place that had begun to feel, in my mind at least, like a graveyard.

And then, of course, one day on a bus I met Tesseba and before too long she invited me to stay with her, and I did. For a long time until I could afford better I shared her little room with its hotplate, creaky bed, and badly sewn curtains. And if the menial routines threatened to overwhelm me, each night when I returned to her, there drawing intently over her little table, and she would look up as I came in, smile broadly, it somehow became more than tolerable, an adventure, even at times humorous. Sometimes I would find the room strewn with travel brochures or books by South African authors, and as soon as I came in the door she would begin to ask question after question, about how things looked there, how things were done, what people thought. To her Africa was as remote and unfamiliar as any place on earth, hot, an anachronism, perhaps in some brazen way exotic. And so my new life began to acquire its own rhythms.

It was during my first winter in America, in that time of unremitting penury and of a cold that robbed me of every memory of warmth, by the ineffective rattle of Tesseba's rusting radiator and a toilet that creaked and spilled water into a pan, that I found myself thinking almost constantly of Santi and yearning for her with a depth that overshadowed any homesickness I might otherwise have felt. I would lie on my steel cot, still in my secondhand winter coat and gloves, my lumberjack boots, and as I listened to the snowplows scraping along the pavement and the clatter of the sand trucks I could think only of Santi, of things I had done and decisions I had made and how I would change them if only I had one more chance to make them over.

Across a stretch of lawn, through an arch covered with vine and orange flowers, in a dark little room, Santi sleeps on a mat on the floor. But now I brook no interference, listen to no arguments, take her by the hand and lead her back out, along the cement path, out into the sunlight on Gordonwood's lawn. We stroll together, hand in hand, sit at the side of the swimming pool, our feet stirring a smoke of white ripples in the water, and as we sit, she in a white bathing suit, I ask her how it is to live in a hut with the earth for its floor, to sleep on a woven mat in a circle by a fire, to listen to men whose fathers were warriors and who know so intimately the legends of Shaka and Dingaan and the great *kraals* at KwaBulawayo and KwaDukuza. I ask her whether the maidens really walk bare breasted to the banks of the Umfolozi and sing together as they wash their skirts in its red water, whether the boys really go into the bush and stay for days as they undergo the rituals of manhood, what, in the shadows of the fire at night, the wise old men say lies in the future, how they counsel those who have been dispossessed of their land and burial grounds, what comments they have on the sorry state of things, the loneliness and despair into which the land has sunk.

And as she answers my questions the glare of the snow on the ceiling becomes the water around her and the clatter of the waves overwhelms the sounds of scraping in the street outside. For a moment again it is warm, the air smelling of fresh clay and torrents of slippery rain, of the great humid ball which rolls each day off the Indian Ocean. The light fills with the stirring reds and the golds of it, the orange sun, the mountains, the green fields of cane.

Then the cold air, Tesseba sniffing, would bring me back to the little room on Necco Street with its hotplate and narrow metal bed. I would look across at her, sitting there with her slim ankles folded under the table, her tongue between her teeth, one hand slowly moving over her sketch pad and the other buried in her hair, and the sight would awaken in me an unrequitable longing, one that has not abated in all these years.

"What are you thinking?" she would ask.

"Nothing much," I'd say. "I don't want to disturb you."

On a bench in Quincy Market I wrote my first letter from America to Santi. It began:

> My Dearest Santi,
> It's been so long — over two years already — since you last heard from me that a part of me worries that you may not want to hear from me, or that so much has happened my letter may be an intrusion. I hope that isn't so.

The letter I finally sent was much more brief:

> As you can see from the postmark I am in America now, not forever but for the time being. I'd be very interested in knowing where you are and what you are doing . . .

I mailed it to Santi in care of Emily at the Arbuthnots', and for several weeks I checked my mailbox carefully, my anxiety mounting as nothing came back, and then a month or two later the envelope was returned as undeliverable. I sent it again to the Wentworth Academy asking them to forward it, and that letter came back more swiftly, and then I wrote a new letter and sent it to the Arbuthnots themselves, a letter within the letter for Santi in care of Emily asking them if they would deliver it to her themselves, and they wrote back, a polite note, saying that Emily had died but not returning my other envelope with its letter to Santi.

And finally, one night several weeks after my efforts had come to nothing, I wrote to Rupert. We'd stayed in touch, at first quite regularly and then sporadically. He'd not yet gone to England, was still living with his parents on Queen Mary Avenue, studying commerce at the university, going to Young Progressive meetings, leafleting, knocking on doors, trying to change people's minds. I could sometimes imagine him crisscrossing the town in his little white Wolseley, past steady brick houses, black men weeding gardens, past Bulwer Park and Pigeon Valley, to Isipingo Beach, to tea and scones on a hotel veranda in Umhlanga Rocks, to the warm white waves of Amanzimtoti.

"Dear Rupert," I wrote. It was late at night, of course. Tesseba was out, her loft quite still. "I need your help. This concerns Santi. I need to find her and can't and yet I know she can't be far. I wish you'd help me."

Rupert replied:

"That's all very well. Santi from next door may be your idea of a solid lead. But being the Boy Scout I am I dutifully presented myself at the front door of the Arbuthnots and some woman received me politely enough. I dissembled about my mission (I'm not stupid, although they know something's up and were less surprised at my interest than they should have been) and I can confirm that the mother, Emily, is with her Maker. As for Santi, one of the housemaids told me that she did indeed finish at Wentworth and is now at a university or college somewhere. Did you ask me what I think of all this? I suppose not. I'm finally off to England next month. Cambridge, don't you know."

I wrote to the registrars at several nonwhite universities where I thought she might be, Fort Hare, the University of the North, the University of the Western Cape, but each time someone wrote back telling me that the person I was seeking was not there.

And then, it seemed, I had no other place to go. It wasn't long afterwards that I married Tesseba so that I could stay in America. Then the years just began to go by and my life with her acquired a pace and shape of its own.

⬥⬥⬥

It was on that last trip to London that I decided to look Rupert up.

"If he was your best friend in high school," Tesseba had said, "I don't know why you've waited so long."

"There's so much water under the bridge," I told her. "What would be the point of it?"

"Aren't you curious about what's become of him?" she asked. "Life's so short."

"I know what he's doing," I said. "He's a solicitor in London."

"Think about it," Tesseba said. "People who were best friends when they were young probably still have a lot in common."

She was right, of course. On things like this Tesseba's judgment is always better than mine.

He was easy enough to find. We were staying in a small hotel around the corner from Arnold's house in London and I simply went into a telephone booth in the lobby and looked him up. Rupert Osten, solicitor, with an inner-city address.

I called him at once.

"You're not going to believe who this is," I said when he came to the phone.

"Hello Danny," he said.

"How did you know I was here?"

"I didn't, old top," Rupert said. "Did you think I wouldn't recognize your voice even hiding behind an American accent."

"I do not have an American accent," I said.

"Who told you that?" he asked. "You sound just like an American."

"You sound rather British yourself," I said.

"What absolute nonsense," he said and I heard a mischievous chuckle I hadn't heard in many years. "You're imagining things again."

It was as if we'd left off yesterday morning and were talking again without any interval at all. I told him why we were there, he asked about Tesseba, we arranged to meet at the Savoy for breakfast.

"I'm looking forward to this," he said. "To seeing what sort of a woman you finally found who'd put up with you."

"What about you?" I asked. "Are you married?"

"I have children who're almost teenagers, for heaven's sake," he said. "Real English kids. One's shaved his hair off completely, the other's dyed his green."

"Is that an English custom?" I asked.

"Imported from you I would say," he said. "Although as usual something seems to have become skewed in translation."

The next morning we rode in a rattling English taxi to the Savoy Hotel. I had tried to prepare myself for his aging, to discount his appearance by the years, but even so I was surprised. He'd gone quite bald, all except for a steamy wisp of a thing he combed across the top of his head, and sported a pot belly. He was carrying an umbrella, though there was no sign of rain.

"Nice uniform," I said. "Does the umbrella double as anything else or is it simply a prop of some kind?"

He looked up at the sky, down at the umbrella.

"It could rain," he said. "It certainly could. And think how silly you'd look then."

Tesseba was watching all this, I could see, wondering what to make of it. And I remembered everything as we walked through the Old Bailey together, Rupert and Tesseba and I, and then had breakfast and tea at the Savoy. Tesseba didn't say much. Rupert and I, after all, went back so much farther than she and I did. He showed us pictures of his children, both with regular brown hair, of his wife, an attractive, pale-skinned woman with a wry smile.

"How did you two meet?" he asked.

"On a bus," I said. "Tess picked me up."

Tesseba smiled.

"That's probably true," she said. "He was right off the boat and a lot more shy than he is now."

"Danny? Shy?" Rupert said, looking at me. "How well does she know you?"

"Well enough," I said and then I knew what his next question would be. It always works like this.

"How long have you been married?" he asked.

"It's a long story," I said.

We ordered more tea, looked around, took stock. From time to time he'd look over at me, then at Tesseba, smile broadly and shake his head.

"Well, well, well," he'd say.

"How are your folks?" I asked.

"Not bad," he said. "Tough times there, though."

"I would imagine," I said.

"South Africa's unrecognizable," Rupert said. "Murderously violent. Explosive. It's depressing."

"What do you think of the changes?" Tesseba asked. "Surely in the end they're for the better."

"It's not very easy to be rational about it when you have aged parents there," he said. "Things were awful for so many people before, but now the streets are so unsafe my parents are virtually prisoners in their house after dark."

"It's really that bad?" I said.

"You wouldn't believe Johannesburg," Rupert said. "People don't risk going downtown."

"Why?"

"They just don't," he said. "You don't have to stop at red lights at night because there's a risk you'll be pulled from your car."

"But the Stock Exchange is there," I said. "And all the banks. And the law courts."

"Listen," Rupert said. "You have to be buzzed into clothing stores now. The Stock Exchange is a fortress."

"Who ever would have thought it?" I said.

For a few moments there was silence.

"It's hard for me to imagine the two of you as boys," Tesseba said at last.

"It's harder to realize how long ago that was," Rupert said cheerfully. He moved his hand over his head. "Though I must say I'm grateful I still have my hair."

For a moment Tesseba wasn't sure it was a joke. She looked at me, paused, and then looked at him.

"He's joking," I said. But you could see his baldness bothered him.

"I most certainly am not," he said vehemently but with unmistakable mischief. "It's too serious a subject to joke about."

"You may find it hard to believe," I said to Tesseba, "but Rupert was once a high school star. Academic honors. Sports colors. Quite the favored son."

"You flatter me," Rupert said. "What else do you remember?"

"Sitting in my mother's study talking," I said. "Walking to school. Mawkish teenage parties."

"I remember that study like it was yesterday," he said. "And that old house of yours. The clanky front door. I even remember how rank the servants' quarters were."

"They weren't that bad," I said quickly.

"They were the worst I ever saw," Rupert replied good naturedly. "The Third World right in your own garden."

I couldn't let it go.

"They may have been a bit rickety. But you're exaggerating."

Rupert looked at me strangely.

"I felt sorry for your servants, old man," he said, and then he added, trying to change the subject, "I spent some of the best moments of my teenage years in that blasted study of yours."

"I'd give anything to be back there for one more afternoon tea," I said.

"I know how you feel, old man," he said.

Tesseba took my hand under the table.

"Other than his parents and Bridget you're the first person I've met who goes all the way back," she said. "I like listening to the two of you talk."

"How is Bridget?" he asked.

"Fine."

"And Baptie?" he asked. "Is she still alive?"

"In a manner of speaking," I said. "She writes me letters but they don't always make sense."

"Don't listen to him," Tesseba said. "Getting letters from Baptie is about the most interesting thing that happens to us."

"Did you ever find your Santi?" he asked.

"No," I said. "I never did."

"Time certainly flies," Rupert mused. "It must be fifteen or sixteen years since you wrote to me about her."

I must have blushed or turned pale because he knew instantly that he'd said something wrong. But it was too late.

"Who's Santi?" Tesseba asked.

Rupert hesitated, looked at me briefly and then back at Tesseba.

"An old flame of your husband's," he said. "Back in his multiracial days. Quite lit up the African night."

"Oh?" Tesseba said. "How so?"

"Let's leave it," I suggested. "It was a long time ago."

"No," Tesseba insisted. She was looking straight into my face, a puzzled look on hers, sounded quite determined. "Really. Why was he trying to find her?"

Rupert sighed, looked at me again, shrugged slightly.

"He's never told you?" he asked.

"There's nothing to tell," I said.

"I guess there's nothing to tell," Rupert repeated.

Tesseba looked at me, then at Rupert, twirled her cup in its saucer.

"He's never so much as mentioned that name," she said to Rupert. "Why do you think that is?"

"I say," Rupert began and I could see, somewhat to my surprise, that he had become quite ill at ease. "Danny has to put his own spin on his past escapades," he said. "It's a husbandly prerogative."

"We're not actually married," Tesseba said.

Things had become so uncomfortable so quickly it was difficult to tell the precise moment it had started or the best way to put things right. Rupert looked at me, back at Tesseba, laughed, or rather gurgled, lamely.

"Life's never as simple as one might wish," he said.

"It needn't be that way," she said.

For a few moments now there was silence and then to my relief Tesseba excused herself and went to the ladies' room. She was gone a long time.

"I'm sorry if I caused a problem," Rupert said. "I'd no idea it would be a raw spot. Don't mean to be clumsy."

"It's not your fault," I said. "Who knows what's raw and what isn't."

"You chaps aren't married?"

I waved it away.

"Yes, we are," I said. "But don't start."

"After you got my letter, you kept on trying to find her?" he asked.

"I did," I said. "But I was never able to. The thing is, I suppose, that I was with Tesseba when I was trying."

"Oh dear," Rupert said. "On the other hand I'd say that even if women are entitled to be sensitive about things of that nature at some point one would expect decency demands a statute of repose."

"The point is," I said, "that even though I was never able to find out what became of Santi, I've never stopped wondering."

"I can't fault you for wondering," he said. "But at some point one's supposed simply to leave such things behind."

"And what if one can't?"

"Well, then I expect one doesn't. But it must be disruptive."

"I still think of trying to find her."

Rupert looked at me, then off in the direction Tesseba had gone to reach the ladies' room, then back.

"Oh no," he said in much the same tone one would use if a child spilled milk onto one's papers. "Let sleeping dogs lie, old man. Let the dead bury their dead. Let bygones be bygones."

"I can't," I said. "I need to see what happened, how she turned out. I need to know for myself. It just doesn't go away."

"Leave the poor girl alone," Rupert answered. "For her own sake if not for yours. Just let it be."

"My father said pretty much the same thing, once," I told him.

And then Tesseba returned and we said our stilted farewells and hailed a taxi back to Sloane Square. We rode for a few minutes in silence.

"Sometimes it seems that I don't know you at all," she said at last.

"Oh come on, Tess," I said. "Let it be."

"It's not only what just happened," she said. "Can you even understand that I don't care why you want to contact some woman in South Africa. I care that you think it's important to keep it so secret from me. I'm tired of it, of your little holdbacks, of wondering why it is that things with you always feel so tentative and incomplete. You do believe, don't you, that there's something else waiting for you, something I'm obstructing, that sharing any of it with me could spoil it all."

"No," I said. "I don't believe that."

"You're used to me," she said. "And you like me. You really do, I know. But I don't know if this is the kind of love that will satisfy me as I become a little old lady."

She said it simply, sadly, without accusation. I looked down, then at the back of the taximan's head, then at the strange way the seats are arranged in London taxis, a regular seat and then two hinged jump seats attached to the back of the driver's partition.

"Of course I love you," I said.

She shook her head.

"You don't really even understand what I'm talking about," she said. "Perhaps it's time for you to resume your real life, the one I seem inadvertently to have interrupted."

That afternoon she said she wanted to spend some time alone at the Tate, and then when she wasn't back by dinner I became alarmed and started searching for her, first through the Tate and then in the streets and restaurants around it. She hadn't returned by midnight and I couldn't defer telling my mother and Arnold about it beyond that, and they called the police, filed a missing person's report, while I spent much of the night roaming the streets hoping to spot her by chance, willy-nilly, among the rambling crowds. I didn't.

She called the next morning from a hotel whose location she wouldn't disclose, wouldn't speak to my mother or to Arnold, told me that she was fine, apologized for disappearing. She told me to go on without her, that she'd meet me at the airport on the day we were scheduled to leave, that she needed the time alone.

"Are you alone?" I asked.

"I just don't want to talk anymore now," she said.

And there we left it. We flew back together, but not in adjoining seats. It was shortly after that that she and I separated.

⊰⊱

Tesseba's expression hardens when I tell her that I have decided to go back to South Africa. She folds her long, dark legs under her skirt and rocks slowly in her chair as she thinks.

"I don't get it," she says.

"You don't get what?"

"Don't you deflect me like that," she says. "I don't understand why you're doing this. It would be ridiculous if it weren't so dangerous."

"It's not dangerous," I say. "I'm not going to do anything that's dangerous."

"You heard the same things I did about how things are there now," she says and gets up from the chair. "And it's not only that the place is dangerous. What Arnold wants you to do is illegal. You could get caught."

"I'm not going to do anything that could get me caught."

"But you could go to jail for this if you were, couldn't you?" she insists.

I think about lying. Tesseba is easily misled. But I can't do it now.

"I suppose so."

"So?"

"There's a risk to everything."

"You're going to risk getting thrown in some South African jail just so that you can prove a point to Arnold Miro."

"That's not why I'm doing it."

Unlike my sister and brother-in-law, who don't ever seem to argue, Tesseba and I have our moments. And yet this is different. We argue about trivial things like who's being indecisive about a restaurant choice or whether I take some of her friends seriously enough, and of course the subject of our marriage itself, such as it is, is a topic we don't take lightly. But Tesseba never makes me feel foolish. So this is different.

"I'm not going to do anything dangerous," I say again.

"Who are you trying to reassure?" she asks. "Me or you?"

I say nothing.

"It's our money," I say. "Even if Mr. Mandela takes the whole lot in the end, I'd like to know how much he's taken."

"This isn't the time for black humor," Tesseba says, and then catches herself. "Any humor, for that matter."

"Look," I say again. "The money's ours. I can't just ignore it."

"You could," she says. "And besides, you're far too old to go traipsing halfway around the world on an errand for your mother."

"Oh come on, Tess," I say. "Don't take cheap shots. This has nothing to do with my mother."

"She asked you to go," Tesseba insists.

"Can you really picture my mother handling this kind of thing?" I ask.

"Let Arnold go," she says, and then laughs. "At least you'll know it's being stolen for a good purpose."

"Besides," I add, "Durban is the place I grew up. I'd like to see it again, just one more time, before it changes forever."

"And you're forgetting one other thing," she says.

"What's that?" I ask, knowing from the tentative way she says it to expect an idea she knows will make me bristle.

"It's blood money," she says after a long pause. "Money made on the backs of real Africans."

"It is not blood money," I say angrily. "And we were real Africans too. It is neither less nor more honestly come by than any fortune accumulated anywhere."

Tesseba's eyes narrow, she purses her lips, rocks faster backwards and forwards in her chair. She's not amused or impressed with my supposed compromise either. I'll go for three days only, and if I stay on Boston time I won't have a problem with jet lag when I get back. She hears this without looking up.

❧

Tesseba sits in an armchair across the room and watches me as I pack. It's dark outside and cold. I take clothes from my drawers, fold them and place them carefully in the bottom of the case. She crosses the room and lifts a red flannel shirt I've never worn.

"Why are you taking this?" she asks.

"In case it's cold."

"Isn't it hot in Africa?"

"It is."

"I pictured you wearing this out west," she says. "In the Grand Tetons or somewhere. When I bought it I almost bought you matching hiking boots."

"Red plaid boots?"

Tesseba has talked of driving across the country, staying in pokey little motels with decor that will make us laugh, eating in strange diners, seeing Yellowstone Park, Santa Fe, Wyoming, Tahoe. Perhaps someday I'll want to do these things.

She unfolds the shirt and drapes it over her shoulders.

"I just folded that," I say.

"Or this one," she says, lifting another from the case. "This one would be perfect in the Grand Canyon."

She shakes out the folds, holds the shirt up to me, nods.

"Just perfect. Imagine how much fun we'd have on a raft floating down the Continental Divide."

"I'm not sure that's a river," I say. "I think it's just a place on a map."

"Or this," she says, ignoring me and twirling a cotton sweater in the air. "You could wear this when we go to Old Faithful."

"We could probably use a raft there."

"Okay."

"I really do have to pack," I tell her. "You're messing everything up."

Tesseba stops moving and stands thinking for a moment with the sweater now draped over her shoulder.

"Sometimes you really bug me," she says, dropping it on the bed.

She walks from the room and as she reaches the door and is about to become lost in the darkness of the hallway I remember how the house had felt without her, experience again how it had been with her gone.

"Tessie," I say as she moves into the darkness. "I really do care, you know."

❧

When I'm finished packing I go in search of her and find her drawing at the kitchen table.

"Let's go for a walk."

Tesseba is always up for walks and bike rides, little adventures of any kind. She disappears and returns with her windbreaker and walking shoes and soon we're out the gate and going in the direction of the old estates. It used to be an evening ritual, these walks among the mature gardens and fusty stucco walls. She takes my hand and clasps it between her elbow and her waist. I don't remember when we stopped doing this.

"Are there places in South Africa that look like this?" she asks.

I don't know anymore. As we walk past the graveled drives and ivy-covered gates I think how in Durban the houses are built of brick, the trees are mightier, the bushes less manicured. There are monkeys instead of squirrels, *kikuyu* grass that scratches your feet, plants with leaves shaped like an elephant's ear, creepers alive with insects. The roofs are made of a dull red tile.

Tesseba stops in front of a house with an ornate loggia and stands shredding the petals of a dead flower.

"I can be okay about your going," she says. "If you promise to be careful."

"I will be," I say.

She pauses, thinking, shreds a final petal.

"And if you need to find the people who still mean things to you, I'm okay about that too."

"Thank you," I say.

Two days later she drives me to the airport in her new Mercedes. It's quite cold, an unseasonable night. We don't say much as we follow the turnpike into town, drive through the tunnel, enter the airport. She parks the car and we walk to the terminal together. I have only one small case and a bag with my suits. Tesseba slings the bag over her shoulder and takes my arm with her free hand.

"I think I might buy some flight insurance," I say as we pass a machine that sells it.

"I don't want you taking chances," she says.

It's not the flying, of course. Airplanes don't scare me. But at certain moments it feels as if memory has an undertow that can pull one back, refuse to release.

I fill out the form as she waits, under next of kin I write "Tesseba Metropolo."

"I don't want to be listed as your next of kin," she says over my shoulder. "Bridget and your mother are."

We stand together on the causeway leading to my gate. I hold the policy in one hand, an overnight case in another.

"Let's not argue," I say.

She takes the policy, folds it, slips it into her pocket. Then she puts her arms around my neck, pulls me closer, buries her face in my coat. Her hair smells sweet and comforting.

And then there is waiting and flying, disorienting meals, night and day. We land on an island in the middle of the Atlantic, refuel, drink tepid tea under a swirling roof fan. I think of the story my grandfather used to tell, how when you flew from South Africa to Europe in the old days airplanes would be taxied around the apron by black men pulling ropes. He thought this was a great joke, my grandfather. And then we reboard and fly again, I manage to sleep, awaken as the sun appears across the clouds and we pass over the craggy brown hills of Angola and Namibia.

We reach Johannesburg and I find the gate marked "Durban Flights Only," wait again, fly again. And then, after dozing off, the pilot's voice wakes me and Durban is below us.

"We're flying over the Valley of a Thousand Hills," he drawls. "I've offered many times to send my mother-in-law on vacation there so long as she sees the place properly, which I understand takes a week on each hill."

The passengers smile. It is a joke that would not go down well in Boston.

And then, there below in the distance, waves break against a barricade of rocks, briefly coat a cold stretch of beach, feed a great cloud of vapor which hangs over the spires of the city. This sight, this vision of a mist-shrouded outpost, spreads itself like an overlay on every city I enter.

In my pocket is a copy of my last letter to Baptie:

Dearest Baptie,
As Mr. Nerpelow has probably already told you, I'll be in Durban for three days in two weeks' time and I hope you'll be able to come and to see me. But I have one favor to ask of you too, a big one that might require you to come to Durban early. I want to ask you to help me look for someone.

When I see you I'll tell you why. In the meantime, please don't say anything in the letters you write to Bridget. . . .

❦

To my great surprise it is Morton Nerpelow, my father's friend and lawyer, whom I see awaiting me at the airport. I glimpse him as I wait for my luggage to arrive in the customs hall, see him anxiously peering through the glass, bobbing first this way, then that. I know it is an illusion but the people all seem familiar, as if I know them, or if I do not actually know them know a great deal about them. And yet of course I do not.

"Uncle Morton," I say to the man as I step through the door and he stares at me. He begins to make a gesture and then stops and stands with his hand frozen in midair. I see that his hands are shaking, notice immediately that his clothes are quite worn. Despite the heat he wears a cardigan with large brass buttons and leather patches at the elbows. He lowers his spectacles, looks at me carefully.

"I would have sworn, for a moment," he says in that familiar, deliberate voice, "that it was Silas Divin walking through the doorway. You have his walk and eyes, the same sallow complexion."

He takes my hand in his, so cool and dry in this swampy air, and shakes it for a long moment.

"It was kind of you to come," I say. "But unnecessary."

"If there is anything I can do for you while you are here," he replies, "anything indeed that your father would have done for you, I will do it and with a greater pleasure than I can convey to you."

And then, now that he has made his statement and with a brusqueness that has always been typical of Nerpelow, he turns and begins to walk away. I reach into my pocket and find a note that Tesseba has left for me to discover. It mimics the language on the cover of my passport:

> The Secretary of State of the United States of America hereby requests all whom it may concern to permit the citizen of the United States named herein to pass without delay or hindrance and in case of need to give all lawful aid and assistance. Tesseba requests all whom it may concern to remind the citizen named herein that there is at least one person who wants him back just as he is, unchanged, unencumbered, unenwealthened.

In the Durban aerodrome, with Nerpelow two steps ahead of me, the admonition seems comic. He turns to see me smiling, hesitates, and then continues walking. I look at my watch and though it is late afternoon here know that Tesseba must be preparing her lunch. She tends to steamed vegetables and tofu with snippets of chicken thrown in to silence me.

We exit the building into a startling brightness. Taxis and buses wait at the curb and through them I see that very little has changed. Silas in his whining relic of a car could come hurtling to a stop at the side of the road and nothing would be out of place. Helga, her hair lacquered into place, heading for some convention or other, could step to this sidewalk at any moment and walk confidently away with Bridget at her side.

"You will find," Nerpelow is saying as we wait for a clearing in the traffic, "that most of the landmarks are still here."

I see evidence of drought, stretches of scrub turned yellow by the sun, how the red sand itself seems bleached a jaundiced ocher. It all looks very different than I had imagined. I see a group of black soldiers on the corner and an army truck parked in the shade between two threadbare trees.

Nerpelow still walks ahead of me, talks now of the drought and of its effects on his garden, and when we reach his little car I am discomforted by the prospect of a long drive at such close quarters. But we set out, round the familiar perimeter, head towards the coastal road. I look across at him, mouth firmly set, clutching his steering wheel as if it were made of rope. As he drives he flexes his jowls and his gray moustache rides up and down. I remember how he would not, when I was a boy, visit Gordonwood without a flashlight in case the dusk might make his walk up the pathway too treacherous.

"Marvelous new highway," Nerpelow says. "Did they have it when you left?"

I honestly cannot recall. I had thought I would know every inch of this place, find my way anywhere in an instant. Now I honestly cannot recall.

"Of course," he goes on, talking more to himself than to me, "to you Americans these must seem like very small potatoes."

"Frankly, it looks very American to me," I say.

"Tell you what," he says. "Let's take the old road in. Then you can really see how much has changed."

And so we drive past the highway entrance, stop at streetlights, turn, double back, find ourselves on Umbilo Road, rows of Indian stores on either side, caught in heavy traffic. The buildings are muddy, their windows streaked with dust. Africans on bicycles weave between the cars, shout messages to each other, seem indifferent to their own safety as they brush against the moving traffic. It looks a little like any Third World country, busy, cacophonous, pungent, dirty.

"I wonder how you'll find things," he says. "I sometimes think the newspapers make too much of our troubles. People just want to live their lives, after all. Except for the lunatics. And who needs to read about them?"

Nerpelow is quaint, in the end. The men with whom I do business in Boston would eat him for breakfast. And yet I would entrust everything I own to him on a handshake.

We reach the center of the city and he finds a parking spot on the Esplanade. With much backing and edging he gets his car into the space to his satisfaction. As I step out I smell the thick, muddy waters of the harbor, the hot aroma of vegetation and petroleum. Nerpelow behind me carefully checks that his car is locked, turns the key at each door, removes it, tries the handle twice more. The trees are tall and gray against the sky of early evening and the harbor is quite peaceful and silent. He walks solidly beside me as we cross the Esplanade and walk past the great stone gates of the Durban Club.

I did not remember that it was so warm in the autumn. There is a cool breath about but the air is heavy with a hidden spray of moisture and the wool in my flannel suit has lost its soft fold, become limp and scratchy. This griminess must blow in from the sea, the wind sweeping foam from the waves and hurtling it among the buildings. Fumes and heat distort the tower of the university, there high on the ridge.

"I will walk with you to your hotel and leave you, my friend," Nerpelow says.

A police car comes rushing by, its sirens blaring.

"Watch your step," he cautions as if I had never crossed a road before.

We enter the Royal Hotel together, Nerpelow and I, he straining to carry my briefcase, and as we climb the stairs a midget porter in white uniform and turban approaches us and takes my baggage. I follow him as he waddles ahead through the foyer, the briefcase dangling from one hand, the bottom of my case scraping the floor. That too is a tradition here, midget bellhops. Now I remember.

"You look so like your father," Nerpelow says again.

An Indian at a marble counter fills out his forms, carbon paper, ledger books, things I have not seen used in commerce for years. I hand the man my credit card but Nerpelow takes my hand.

"We'll pay for this from the trust," he says. "No point spending good dollars when you may as well enjoy your family's funds while you're here. They're not much good anywhere else, I'm afraid."

A potted palm tree rustles. The Indian continues writing.

"We'll talk about that," I say to him, and he cuts me off as if he has been waiting for such an opening.

"No, we won't," he says sharply.

Another midget now lifts my suitcase, he strains, it is bigger than he is, the first takes keys to my room, and together they lead the way back through the foyer.

"I'll leave you here," Nerpelow says. "You should know that your woman Baptie is on her way here. We're trying to keep track of her, but of course it isn't easy."

"Where is she?" I ask.

"I don't exactly know," he says. "Somewhere en route, one hopes."

We walk a few steps farther and he adds: "Perhaps later in the evening, if you feel so inclined, we can meet at the club for a drink before dinner."

I follow the midgets, past a window displaying diamond jewelry, another with carvings of ivory and verdite, African heads fashioned from ebony, tiny toucan birds made of dyed monkey skin, and wait with them for the elevator.

⬦

The room is large and its walls are paneled with yellow wood from trees a colorful guest book says were planted years before specifically for use in this hotel. There is a television set, a desk, prints of native chieftains in waterstained frames on the walls. Above the bed is an old map of the city, the Old Fort at its center, the ridge where Gordonwood would be built still uncharted. The harbor with its sandbar and bluff is carefully drawn with red dots showing the channels and lines of the tidewater. Although cooler air hisses from the vents in the wall there is a faint odor of stale smoke, of mildew, and of a damp, unreachable dust.

The midgets return with ice, a bowl of fruit, the evening newspaper, then again to turn down my bed. It is so hot in this yellow box of a room, unbearably humid but at the same time dry and parched. I look around the room, at the television set, at the stinkwood desk. It all seems unspeakably forlorn. I open the telephone book and turn to Divin. There is one, a distant relative of my father's, but no one else. It's strange that we should not be there too, as if we had all just disappeared, or died.

Then I look under Arbuthnot and begin to dial.

"Hello," a young voice says.

This is strange, oddly humiliating. It's as if no time has passed at all.

I begin to explain. My name is Danny Divin. We used to live next door. Yes, she says. She remembers vaguely. She was a little girl herself. They've divided the house into maisonettes now, a two-family. She lives upstairs with her husband. Her father's a widower and lives downstairs. You had a maid called Emily. Of course she remembers Emily. Emily died in her sleep so long ago. Why do I ask? Well, Emily had a daughter, a colored girl, and we were friends all that time ago. Now I live in America. I'd very much like to look her up. Can they help? We'd so much like to. I don't think so. I'll ask my dad. Please, wait. Now, I've asked him. We can't help. What did you say your name was again?

So I replace the receiver, sit on the edge of the bed, page again through the telephone book seeing how many names I recognize, how many businesses are the same. I've come so far to do some sleuthing myself and now, one phone call later, I am out of ideas. When last I saw Baptie she was in her fifties, greatly overweight, stood alone on the sidewalk dressed in her starched pink uniform, white apron, and bonnet. She had been in our home for most of her life and yet she took her leave of me as if I would return by nightfall. Maybe Baptie will help. And if not Baptie, maybe I am destined to go home never knowing. There would be something poetic in that anyhow.

≈≈≈

Dinner with Nerpelow at the Durban Club drags, seems almost interminable.

"So what do you think?" he's asked a dozen times.

"I just arrived," I say. "It doesn't look that different."

"Oh, it's changed, all right," he says knowingly in his dry, parched voice. He has a crumb on the end of his moustache. It rides up and down as he talks.

"So I've read," I say.

"Who knows where it will all end," he says. "Everything will either go down the drain or it won't. It's out of our hands now."

"It never really was in our hands," I say.

"Well," he says with some finality, "as much as I hate to admit it, your mother and her colleagues were quite right all those years ago. I wish more people had listened to them."

"Did you agree with her, back then?" I ask.

He looks at me strangely, takes a sip from his wine glass.

"No," he says finally. "No, quite frankly. I didn't."

Dinner is served by an Indian in a starched white suit. He has a red sash across his chest, a cloth turban. We could be in India, only a hundred years ago, and I wonder why Nerpelow has brought me here. He must know I haven't forgotten that the Durban Club doesn't take Jews, lets them eat here as guests only on sufferance. When my uncle Barnes somehow got himself admitted as a member, the whole Jewish community thought he was a traitor.

And, affectionate though I am towards Nerpelow, I decide not to let him off the hook too lightly.

"I've never been inside here, you know," I say.

"No?" he responds. "Well, many people haven't."

"They wouldn't have permitted it in the old days," I say. "Considering their policy on Jewish members."

"The place has a certain atmosphere," Nerpelow says and nothing more. I'm not even sure whether he hasn't said it with a measure of approval.

It all calls to mind something else from long ago, the instinct to let things be. What should I do? Challenge him? Stalk angrily from the club? Make a scene beneath the moldy portraits of Queen Elizabeth and her collection of dowdy old colonials, force crusty Nerpelow in his scratchy tweed jacket to concede that all this is unacceptable to me? If this place were in Boston they'd snap its liquor license by breakfast and have it closed by lunchtime. But it isn't. And if it were I'm not so sure I'd turn it in.

I order a shrimp cocktail and watch the yachts bob about in the marina across the Esplanade.

"Your hors d'oeuvre, Mr. Divin," a waiter says at my elbow and when he's positioned the plate before me and left I ask Nerpelow: "How does he know my name?"

"Standard practice," he says. "Knowing the names of dinner guests. Employees know the names of all the members and also their professions, preferred wines, preferred tables, family members, and so forth and so on. We insist on it."

I don't respond. The place does seem so safe, so tranquil and insulated. It's not hard to see why fossils like Nerpelow seek refuge here. Let them, for heaven's sake. It'll end with a bang soon enough. I look around. Some of the fossils are my age, not much more. Maybe I'm a fossil too.

Nerpelow is talking politics, describing how things have changed, how serious a problem crime has become, how much taxes have gone up and the bureaucracy has become inefficient, how unreliable the police have become. I listen but I am just not interested. Of course it has changed, I want to say, and this is just the start of it. Mandela let you off the hook but at this moment we are sitting on land that many people believe was stolen from them. There may still be a further accounting.

"An avalanche is about to hit this building, old man," I'd like to shout. "Can't you hear it?"

But of course I don't. I have other things on my mind. I could walk from here to Gordonwood, literally walk to a place that has been in my thoughts so constantly for so long. I could walk there, up onto the ridge, look down at the turrets myself, the cold stone tower and balustrade. I could stand by the pool and look across at the pool house, the hedge that shields the Arbuthnots' servants' quarters. But for the moment I am trapped, sit listening to Nerpelow.

"Not only that," he is saying, "but they have affirmative action here too, you know. Just like you chappies in America. I don't know what I think of that. I mean, surely if a man is qualified to do a job he should be hired, wouldn't you say? Makes no sense to give it to another fellow just because he happens to be black."

He thinks awhile, pulls on his moustache, tells me his views oblivious to any irony in them, and I half listen. A waiter brings our dinner, lamb chops and potatoes, recommends a wine, Nerpelow orders. The food is really very good. Across from us other people eat their dinner, talk quietly, from time to time share a subdued joke. I can hear their accents, this lazy, flat South African sound, and it is like a call from another life.

❧❧❧

I sleep fitfully but dreamlessly. In the morning I call Nerpelow's office.

"Mr. Nerpelow has arranged with the bank for you to get some currency," his assistant tells me. "How much would you like?"

"How much can I have?" I ask.

"As much as you need," she says.

"And Baptie?" I ask. "Have you heard from her?"

"No," she says. "My guess is that at some point she will just arrive."

"And there's no way of getting in touch with her?" I ask.

"I don't know how you would do that," she says.

After breakfast I make another call, this one to a number I've carried in my wallet for over a month.

"Natal Plastics," a woman's voice says.

"Is Mr. Meyer there, please?" I ask.

"Who shall I say is calling?"

"He doesn't know me," I say. "I'm Arnold Miro's stepson."

"Please hold on a moment," she says.

There's a pause but for a few seconds only.

"You must be Danny," a man's voice says.

"Mr. Meyer?"

"Call me Sel," he says. "Did you just get in?"

"Yesterday."

"Where are you staying?" he asks.

I tell him.

"Nice place," he says. "Used to be better."

"I'm hoping you can give us some advice," I say. "Arnold tells me you have experience with some of the problems my family's facing."

"But of course," he says. "But of course. I've known Arnold Miro since we were kids. How is the old bastard?"

"The old bastard is fine," I say.

"Give him my regards."

"I will."

There is a moment of silence as I wait for him to lay out what I must do.

"Arnold tells me you're with Morton Nerpelow," he says. "Is he still in practice?"

"Apparently," I say.

"You should look around, you know," Meyer says. "He's not going to be of much help to you."

"Well," I say haltingly, "he's been our lawyer for a long time."

"Certainly I understand that," Meyer says. "Certainly I do. We can discuss it when we meet. Are you free for dinner later in the week."

Now I hesitate. This is either not as complicated, or much more complicated, than Arnold has said it would be. Tell me, I want to say, how to get my money out of the country. Tell me what to do and how much I must pay you and then let's go our separate ways. Instead he is busy giving me directions to his house.

"I'm only here for three days," I say. "I have to get back to Boston."

"Three days." He sounds surprised.

"I have a business to run in Boston."

There is silence on the other end of the line.

"So what business are you in?" he asks. I can sense that what he wants now is to get my measure, that and to stall until he has.

"Financial services," I say.

"Financial services," I hear him repeat. "In America they make money doing things nobody's ever heard of."

I suppose you could say he is being rude, but then there is an uncouth, bantering surliness that passes for friendliness too, in some circles. It is just about the only way Arnold communicates with his peers. Perhaps that's what it is, I tell myself. And I have come too far to take offense.

"I manage money," I say slowly.

"Do you have your own business?" Meyer asks.

"It doesn't really work that way," I tell him. "I'm on my own but I work with a number of institutions."

"Like who, for instance?" Meyer presses.

"Universities. Pension funds."

"What have they got that needs to be managed?" he asks.

So what am I going to do? Explain to him about endowments? Charitable-giving deductions? 401k plans?

"It's rather complicated," I say instead.

"Americans," Meyer chuckles. "So what else? Are you married? Any family?"

"I'm married," I say. "But I have no children."

"An American girl?"

"Yes."

"You sound totally American to me," Meyer says.

I don't respond, and for a moment the line is silent.

"Can you help?" I ask.

"Do you have your own transportation?" Meyer asks at last. "It's not the best idea to take a taxi even if you can find one."

"I'm picking up a car," I tell him.

"Well, why don't you come here today," he says. "To my office."

He sounds displeased, angry that I'm being so curt. But I don't want to chat with him, do the Arnold shmooze, spend an evening being entertained in his home.

"I might as well tell you now what I would start by telling you later," he says.

"What's that?" I ask.

"Get rid of Nerpelow," he says. "I don't have time to waste tripping over Morton Nerpelow."

"What do you mean?" I ask.

"What do I mean?" he says. "What do you think I mean?"

He sounds quite rough now, this Selwyn Meyer. I don't really know what I have done to offend him either. I guess in the end there is not much room for gentility among those who operate at the margins even as there is a surfeit of it at the Durban Club.

We make our plans, I confirm where it is I must go to meet him, using cryptic language he explains his terms. When I hang up the telephone it is as if I have been released from some kind of servitude. But I am not done yet. Dialing slowly, breathing deeply, I call Nerpelow's office one more time.

⬦⬦⬦

I find him behind a great mahogany desk, frail looking in his cardigan with its large leather buttons, peering at me sharply from beneath thick white eyebrows. As I walk into his office he seems filled with energy, a feisty, eighty-year-old man quite prepared now for the task at hand.

"I knew Arnold Miro when he didn't have a penny," he says.

"And he hasn't changed that much over the years. What you see now is what you always saw."

"Did you have much to do with him?" I ask. "On a business level."

"Oh no," Nerpelow says. "No, no, no. Much bigger scale than anything I did. I never made much money for my clients but then I never lost any for them either. Not my job, you know. I'm a lawyer, in the end. Just a lawyer."

"I've come to know him quite well," I say. "He's not a very nice man, is he?"

Nerpelow looks at me over his glasses.

"Your mother always knew what she was doing," he says. "I trust she did in this instance as well."

"What do you think my dad would have thought of him?" I ask.

"Your dad knew him, of course," Nerpelow says. "Didn't care much for him. Like chalk and cheese, your mother's two husbands. Chalk and cheese."

An African woman in a pink uniform and no shoes brings in a tea tray and he begins pouring tea.

"There's something I have to tell you, Uncle Morton," I say at last. He looks up from the tea tray, silver pot in hand, scrutinizes me, continues pouring.

"What is that?" he says.

"I'm going to be moving our affairs over to another firm," I say. "It is in part something my mother wants, you know, to streamline her affairs with those of Arnold. And also it has to do with currency issues and the rest of it."

He continues pouring.

"Maybe you can understand the pressures," I say.

Still nothing. I stand, walk to the window. The tide has left the harbor, exposed the great sandbank between the Esplanade and Salisbury Island.

"I'll just say this once," he says to my back. His voice is so dry, so familiar. "I may be an old fool, but sometimes it's preferable to be an old fool than a young one. I know what people are doing. I know what Arnold Miro is said to have done. Your father would say to you now what I'm about to say, and that is this: I would have no part of it and I advise you as strongly as humanly possible to have no part of it either."

"I don't see I have much of a choice," I say. "These are funds my mother could put to good use."

Nerpelow rises from his chair, walks to the window, shakes his head slowly as he looks out over the harbor.

"There are some people to whom no amount of money is enough," he says. "I don't know your circumstances and don't want to, but something tells me you haven't failed to live up to your expectations. If I can't persuade you that what your stepfather has laid on for you is wrong, let me try to persuade you by telling you it's dangerous. Truly dangerous."

"I know the story," I say.

"Five to ten years I believe is the penalty," he says, "against which the wholesale confiscation the statute allows will begin to look very trivial indeed."

"Uncle Morton," I say. "I appreciate your advice. Truly I do."

There is a long silence and then Nerpelow returns to his chair, lifts my cup from the tray, offers it to me.

"We can have all the papers ready for the transfer by the end of the day," he says.

And then he asks again about my mother, about my sister, about Boston, steadfastly refuses to discuss any further business.

He has his hand on my shoulder as we wait for the elevator cage to appear behind the brass grille. My last sight of him is of his shoes as the cage descends, cracked leather polished to a worn sheen.

⟡

I drive slowly, survey the buildings, see how they have changed, how storefronts have been repainted, how little there is that is newly built. Once ripe gardens are the color of straw, medians once filled with flowers are barren and windswept. I see the rebuilt railway station, the old Indian Market, a building my grandfather once bought and sold.

I have not allowed myself to lapse from formal dress and my wool suit clings to my body, dank air puffing from within my jacket as I move. As I head across the town and up to the ridge I think of Nerpelow and my dad, how they used to sit for hours discussing business around the dining table at Gordonwood, were always polite to each other, subdued, and then I remember once seeing a hint of intimacy between them too, my father taking Nerpelow's reading glasses from him and putting them on as he tried to decipher a sentence.

"Better, old man?" Nerpelow asks.

"They do help," my father says.

The next day Nerpelow's driver delivers a pair of glasses, just like his, to our front door. I will soon be my father's age. If he were alive today he would be an old man.

The roads lead uphill, Moore, Manning, MacDonald. There are trees where there once was grass, huge oaks, a willow brushing the pavement. I am prepared for almost anything now. I will park beside

Gordonwood's stone pillars, walk down the driveway between hedges that lurch inwards and creepers that grow inches every day, will approach an old stone building that to others might look shabby but to me will not. Inside I will notice the patches of dampness, how they discolor the ceilings and leave a moldy odor in the air, will find scratches on the floor where familiar pieces of furniture once stood. I picture the faces that will accompany me on this tour, owners who have allowed me in, if at all, only on sufferance, suddenly proprietary.

And then I reach the steep hill, the last climb to Gordonwood, up past the house with the vines, past the house with the many-layered brick walls, past the Arbuthnots'. But when I reach the crest immediately I know that something is wrong, something is missing, the two red pillars for a start and then the hedge, the gate, where the spires should be nothing, only sunlight. Someone has taken it down. Gordonwood, creaky, pepper potted, crumbling Gordonwood, is gone. Quite gone.

I park the car at the curb, climb out, walk slowly across the road. There's a brick fence now where the tall hedges used to be, no trace of the red stone pillars. They have combined two lots, ours and that of the people behind us, and at first the whole thing looks like a field, just flat grass behind the ugly wall. And then I see a sign, "Gordonwood Mews," and a driveway that starts in a different place a little higher up, and then a row of townhouses set back on the knoll where the gazebo used to be. Where the house stood, where its footprint was, there is nothing. Just grass.

It is midday and the sun, almost overhead, casts bitter shadows forcefully at the ground. Behind the row of new houses is an African woman washing clothes at an aluminum basin. She sits on a dirty wooden stool, barefoot, the basin locked between her knees. She hums as she works. There is no one else about, just the houses, a parked car or two, an expanse of grass. She looks up from her washing as I approach, watches me carefully as she slowly rubs a garment against her corrugated washboard. She is wearing the pink and white uniform of domestic service, there are suds on her sleeves, her glasses are misted over from her perspiration. On her head she wears a scarf, around her ankles are ornaments of elephant hair.

"Good morning," I say.

"Good morning."

"Do you work here?"

"Yes."

"How long have your worked here?"

"Not long," she says.

Now she eyes me with open suspicion.

"Who do you want to see?" she asks.

"No one," I say. "I used to live here."

"Oh," she says and keeps on washing.

"Before they built these new houses," I say, "there used to be one big house here. I lived in it."

She nods, keeps on washing.

I remove my jacket and loosen my tie, sit beside her on the grass. The shoulders of my jacket are almost too hot to touch. If anyone comes home now they will find me sitting with their washerwoman in the sun, jacketless and wet with perspiration.

"Why don't you sit in the shade?" I ask the woman after a few minutes. She does not look up, rubs the collar of a shirt against the board.

"It's the same to me, shade and sun," she says after a pause. "If you like I can fetch you a glass of water from the kitchen."

I would, and replacing her wash in the basin she rises and walks slowly towards the house. She moves with difficulty, as if her joints had been stiffened, her large hips clock forward first to one side then to the other. I follow her and just as we reach the house I ask: "How long have these new houses been here?"

"They are not new," she says. "They have been here long time."

"Do you know when they were built?" I ask.

"No, Master," she says.

She asks me to wait at the door while she goes for the water. Baptie as well at Gordonwood had her guests wait at the kitchen door while she made them tea, and there they congregated, talking loudly, at home around the concrete steps which led up from the backyard and into the house.

"Did you know Baptie who used to work here?" I ask her when she reemerges.

"No, Master," she says, and walks painfully back to her washing.

It proves difficult to converse with this woman. She continues to regard me with misgiving, casts an occasional glance at me beside her stool on the grass as if my decision to plant myself there was somehow inexcusable.

"Do you know the Arbuthnots who live next door?" I ask, pointing in their direction.

She keeps washing.

"Maybe the Madame will be home soon," she says.

I am making her increasingly uncomfortable, I can tell. And

there is no need for it. I am just wasting her time, being a nuisance, an interloper. I stand up.

"Just one more question," I say. "Do you know if any of the servants at the Arbuthnots' have been there a long time?"

"Maybe Connie only," she says and keeps at her washing.

I walk away from her, down the lawn, over a piece of ground which is more or less where the swimming pool used to be although there is no sign of it, not even a dent in the grass, past a ghost of a pool house, an absent hedge, an archway. But before me I see the fence, the same old wooden fence with a hedge growing beside it. There used to be oak trees here, trees stooping over the grass like rheumatic old men, with monkeys in the branches, little things like squirrels that would hover over you in a manner I think they thought was menacing. They would taunt too, occasionally throw things like acorns or seed pods down on your head. If I had to walk beneath a tree and knew they were there I'd carry a pocketful of stones in case they became too bold. They would see me scoop them up and keep their distance. I look up. No monkeys. Only sky. No need for stones. The gap is gone, of course, but now there's a door, a full, hinged door almost exactly where the gap used to be. I open it and go through.

It is strange really, given how completely everything on the other side of the fence has changed, how little seems to have changed here. The same dank cement path, the same little rooms, the same skunky smell. I make my way to one of the rooms and knock on the door. No one answers, so I go to the next.

"Yes," a woman's voice says. "Wait."

I wait.

The door opens and I find myself facing an elderly African lady in a pink housemaid's outfit.

"Yes," she says.

"Is Connie here?" I ask.

"I am Connie," she says.

I look at her carefully and there is nothing familiar about her face. She watches me expectantly.

"I used to live next door," I say. "A long time ago."

"Divin family," she says knowingly and without emotion.

"Yes," I say. "I'm Danny Divin."

"Weh, weh, weh," she says. "You very grown up now. Like an old man almost."

"You remember me?" I ask.

"I remember," she says. "Baptie my friend."

"Do you still see Baptie," I ask.

"How can I see Baptie?" she answers. "Baptie live in Zululand. But I hear about her. My friends tell me about her."

"She's coming to town," I say. "Maybe tomorrow. To see me."

"Weh," she says again.

"I want to ask you something," I say. "About Emily. You know Emily?"

"How can I not know Emily?" she answers. "I work with Emily a long time."

"I'm looking for someone," I say. "Emily's daughter, Santi."

"You know Santi?" she asks.

My heart leaps, really it does, to stand face to face with this woman who knows Santi.

"Yes," I say. "Now I'm looking for her."

"If you want Santi you can find," she says. "Santi is not lost."

"Well, I haven't been able to find her," I say.

"Santi is important person now," Connie says. "Sometimes she comes to visit, but not often. She is a teacher. Also an official of African National Congress."

"Where does she teach?" I ask.

"She is a teacher," Connie says. "At the university."

"What does she teach?" I ask. "What department?"

Now Connie looks puzzled.

"I don't know," she says. "You can find her there."

"Connie," I say hesitatingly. "Is she married?"

"Weh, weh, weh," Connie says. "Why do you ask this?"

"I'm curious," I say.

"You ask her, then," Connie says and starts to chuckle to herself. "Weh, weh, weh."

"You won't tell me?" I say.

"Santi can tell you," she says.

❧

It is two in the afternoon, Durban time, and seven in the morning in Boston. This notion of keeping Boston time is becoming very disorienting. I could fall asleep so easily, have a tight, buzzy feeling in my head, but then sleep is also something I cannot risk. Three days is so short, zipping by at a pace that leaves me breathless.

My sordid little deal with Meyer is done. He can't save everything but for a cut of thirty percent he'll see over four million dollars delivered to my bank in Boston by the time I get home. All I need to do is to

sign a paper that allows him to withdraw the funds from places Nerpelow has invested them, and it will be over.

"When do you withdraw the money?" I ask him.

"Why?"

"Will I be out of the country when you do?"

"Look," Meyer says. "I've done this dozens of times already. If you
don't want to do it, don't."

"I'm just asking," I repeat.

"You've got to sign in front of a bank official," he says. "In South
Africa."

"So the whole process begins while I'm still here."

Now Meyer's really short with me.

"You asked me to do this," he says. "I've gone to a lot of trouble.
Everything's set up."

I shudder at the risk, am openly hostile to Meyer, but it's done.
He'll meet me at my hotel in the morning with his sheaf of papers, his
bad hairpiece, his oversized Rolex watch. We'll walk to the bank. I'll sign
the papers. If a swarm of police don't descend on me then, end this all
quite forcefully, it will be done. It is like a dream, in a way, one that my
strange schedule of sleeping and waking is not doing anything to end.

From the ridge I head over to the university, to the tall tower of
the university. At the registrar's office I look up Santi and there she is,
lecturer in economics, with an office in the student union. I stand at
the counter, my jacket over my shoulder, take down her number. She
still has the same name. When I call there is no answer. I fold the piece
of paper in my pocket and walk back out to the car.

The campus is almost all African. When I left it was almost all
white. Nobody pays any attention to me. I get in my car and drive

back to the Royal Hotel. I park the car in the Albany Garage and walk up one of the side streets to the hotel entrance. There is a musty, air-conditioned smell in the air, stale, like age itself or used-up air. Up in the elevator to my room, where the red light on the telephone is on. I call the desk.

"Good afternoon," an Indian voice says.

"Good afternoon," I say. "I believe I have a message."

"Just a moment, please," I hear.

A few seconds pass.

"There's a Miss Baptie here to see you," he says. "She's waiting in the lobby for you right now, as a matter of fact."

I look at myself in the mirror, beads of perspiration on my forehead, my suit patched with moisture. In the bathroom I pull a comb through my hair, wash my face and rub it hard with a towel. Then I turn off the lights and leave the room.

The elevator takes forever to come, even longer to descend, but then as I step from it there in the lobby is Baptie. She is breathless, ill at ease, looks constantly around as if she were in danger of attack. I approach her slowly, my eyes fixed on her face, my shoes clicking on the marble floor. She looks at me without recognition, her face a blank slate, her eyes empty. She smells strongly of thatch, of paraffin, of the hot dry wind of the veld.

"Baptie," I say.

For a moment she is poised between emotions, stands quite still, her face frozen.

"Look at you," she says and then repeats it over and over. "Look at you. Look at you."

I put my arms around her, feel the cotton of her scarf against my cheek, her spikey hair, the softness of her forehead.

"You haven't changed at all," I say.

"Nonsense," she says and clucks. "I am an old woman."

"You haven't changed one little bit," I say.

"And you," she says, "you have become a real man."

"I'm getting old too," I say and she laughs.

As we walk out the hotel I remember that I haven't called the university again, worry that I may miss Santi, that she will come into her office, work at her desk, and then at the end of the afternoon turn out the light, close her drawers, head off home.

"How are you?" I say again. Something in me feels desperate, out of time, foolish.

"Being old is no good," Baptie says and then she stops walking, turns to me, begins to run her hands through my hair, over and over, to touch my face and my chest.

"Danny, Danny," she keeps saying. Her eyes are red, her nose is running. I reach into my pocket for a handkerchief, give it to her, and she wipes her eye delicately with a corner of it, just a corner, and then holds it without knowing what to do.

"I can't wash this for you now," she says.

"Never mind," I tell her.

"Let's go and sit somewhere," I say. "We have so much to catch up on."

There's not much one can do with an elderly African lady on an autumn afternoon in Durban, South Africa. We walk across to the town gardens and sit for a while on a bench where the "Whites Only" marker has been so recently removed there is still an unpainted patch where it once had been. I sit down and she sits next to me, in the shade of the Cenotaph commemorating the city's war dead. I show her my photographs, give her those I have been carrying in my wallet, ask her about her little house, her pension, her son.

"KwaZulu business is rubbish," she says. "The Boers made big trouble and now big trouble will last for a long time. Until after I am dead, I think."

"Maybe not," I say. "Maybe Mr. Mandela started to make things right."

She looks at me incredulously.

"He is an old man," she says. "And when he is dead, who will look after us?"

And as we talk it seems to me that it is only Baptie, all the years notwithstanding, all the anguish, all the memories, who belongs here, only Baptie, in the end, who is rooted here, as rooted indeed as Silas, as my grandfather, as others who will never leave. We have passed over like shadows, flitted by, are gone. The years have passed and Baptie, sewing at her ancient black machine, squatting as she eats, showing her feelings with extravagant gestures and much clapping, remains embedded in the hard red ground.

So we talk, about Helga and Arnold, their house in London, she asks about Bridget and Leora and Tibor, where we live, how far from each other, how often we are together, whether Leora really looks like her picture.

"The Madame learned to cook?" she asks.

"So she says," I say.

"I do not believe. Cook and clean up. Nonsense."

"She cooks. Honestly," I say.

"You say, but still I don't believe," she says.

And then we both start laughing, laughing at the thought that my mother could be doing laundry, cleaning, cooking.

"Weh mameh," Baptie keeps saying. "Weh mameh."

And then I see that the sun is beginning to go down behind the old post office and realize that my time is running out.

"Did you get my letter?" I ask her.

"Yes," she said.

"Do you remember Emily?"

"Of course I do," she said. "Emily and Connie and those stupid Arbuthnots."

She begins to laugh.

"Those people were so stupid," she says. "They didn't know how to treat anybody. Now she is dead and he is all alone and the daughter is married to a man who beats her."

"He does?" I say.

"He is a bad man," she says.

"I was there this morning," I tell her. "I didn't know Gordonwood was gone."

"I knew," she says. "Not long after the Madame left they pulled it down."

"Why didn't you tell us?" I ask.

She pauses.

"I didn't want to make you sorry you left," she says. "The past cannot come back again."

"No, it can't," I agree.

"So what did you find there?" she asks. "At Gordonwood?"

"They made flats out of it," I said. "Garden flats. They call them mews."

"Like a cat," she says.

"Like a cat."

"I have been inside one," she says. "I asked a servant there to show me. It is too horrible."

"Small?"

"Small and horrible."

"I went to the Arbuthnots' also," I tell her. "I saw Connie there."

"She is still there?" Baptie says in surprise. "I think she is too old to work."

"No," I say. "She's still there."

"And what did she tell you?" Baptie asks.

"She told me a little bit of what I want to know."

"About Emily's daughter?"

"Yes."

"I know why you want this thing," she says at last.

"You know?"

She moves her head but not to say yes, just moves it slightly, says nothing.

"What do you know?" I ask.

"I heard something," she says.

"From who?"

Again she says nothing.

"It's so long ago," I say. "It doesn't matter."

"Things in the past, they were not all the way they should be," she says.

Now I am at a loss. We sit together in the sunlight, Baptie and me, not saying anything, looking ahead of us at the Cenotaph, the pigeons, the traffic moving slowly up the street.

"I need to find her," is all I say.

Baptie reaches into her pocket and pulls out a purse, a wrinkled leather pouch with a brass clasp. She opens it carefully, takes out a piece of folded paper, hands it to me.

"Here," she says. "This is where she is."

I open the paper, read it. It's only an address and a telephone number, in town, not far away.

"This is where she lives?" I say.

"Yes," Baptie answers.

"Where did you find it?"

"From Ambrose," she says. "He works for the bus company now as a driver. I sent him a telegram."

"Ambrose still works in town?"

She nods, for a while says nothing. And then, without warning, she begins to shake her head, slowly at first and then with determination.

"I'm sorry for these things," she says.

"What things?" I ask.

She says nothing but her head keeps shaking. Her pink scarf moves rhythmically, will not stop. And then, because I can think of no other way to show my feelings, I ask her to pick anything in the world that she wants that I can buy for her in the next hour. She hesitates, for some minutes is quite lost in thought, and then she asks with some embarrassment whether I will buy her a paraffin lamp and I say of

305

course I will. We rise and walk together to the Indian shops where she assures me we will find one.

She stands meekly beside me in the store as the Indian shows us his selection, demonstrates how they are lit and how the mantle will suddenly begin to glow and to cast as much light as an electric bulb. I watch Baptie as the Indian explains, worried that she will become confused and that my gesture will backfire and burn down her little house, my mother's gift to her. But she says she understands and so I buy the best lamp in the store, some extra mantles, a bottle of paraffin. Yet it still seems a pitiful gesture, less money, indeed, than one night at the Royal Hotel.

"What else," I ask her as we walk back into the street, the lamp under my arm, she carrying the mantles and paraffin, "what else can I get you to take back with you to Gingindlovu?"

Now she does not hesitate at all, asks for fabric so that she can sew dresses from it and sell them at the gates of the factories in Eshowe. And so we enter another store and there two Indian ladies watch with apprehension as I instruct them to give Baptie everything she wants.

"From which price range, sir?" one of them asks.

"Whichever she wants," I say.

And as I wait in the dowdy little store I can see Baptie selecting fabrics and that her selection is gathering momentum, watch as she begins frantically to pull bolts of material off the shelves and to pile them haphazardly on the counter. I stand chilled, the Indian women try to steady the pile as it mounts until it is almost two feet high, contains hundreds, perhaps thousands of dollars of material. I step forward, the sense of loss now overwhelming, place my hand on Baptie's shoulder, startle her, suggest that she has chosen too much. And I see then that her face is wet with tears, her lips quiver as she continues reaching up and blindly tearing the colored fabrics from their shelves.

"You have to put some back," I say softly.

She looks at me blankly, at the fabrics, the confusion she has created, up at the empty shelves.

"I don't want these ones," she says. "They are cheap rubbish."

Later, in the quiet of my hotel room, I imagine Baptie sitting in some dusty train as it moves through the stricken countryside. My gifts are on the seat beside her, a reminder only of what is hers and what is mine and of children whose pictures, now soiled, are wrapped in her handkerchief. With luck my visit will fade from her memory like some further modern insult and will leave her again to dream of us, of an endlessly benign Silas, of innocent children, of royal friends, of baptisms and ordinations and sanctifications, of pillars of fire and the peeling back of the heavens, of rain and atonement and forgiveness.

"Hello," a voice says. It is hers.

"Santi," I say.

"Danny."

"How did you know?" I ask.

"I heard."

"How?"

"I heard."

"Santi," I say again.

"Hello Danny," she says.

"I'm approaching forty," I say. "Are you also?"

She laughs.

"I stayed the same," she says. "But what are you doing here?"

"Several things," I answer. "Seeing how things turned out for you is one of them."

There's dead quiet on the line now, the sort of quiet that stills all thought.

"Why?" she asks finally.

And I could explain it to her, to her of all people, but I need to see her face while I am doing so, to be sure I have a mirror in which I can see if I am deluded, if I have allowed myself to stray from the path of reason.

"Several reasons," I say.

Her voice is the same but her accent has changed a little, isn't quite so African now, is more English, more South African sounding.

"How long are you here for?" she asks.

"Well, that's the catch," I say. "Just two more days."

"Do you have no family here now?" she asks.

"None," I say. "I heard you lost your mother. I'm sorry."

"And I heard what happened to Bridget," she says. "My mother told me. I'm sorry too."

"She's married and has a teenage daughter," I say. "It was a long time ago."

"And you?" she asks. "Are you married?"

"It's a long story," I say. "Too long for the telephone. Are you?"

"I was," she says.

There are a lot of silences in this conversation.

"Can I see you?" I ask again.

"When I heard you were here I wondered whether you'd call," she said. "I hoped you would and then I hoped you wouldn't."

"I have called," I say.

"You're looking for trouble, you know," she says.

"It didn't stop me once before."

"And my heart got broken."

"And mine too."

Another pause.

"Where are you staying?" she asks.

"The Royal."

"Oh."

Silence.

"Can we meet for coffee?"

"Perhaps later," she says.

"Nine?" I suggest.

"Later," she says.

"Ten?"

"Later."

And then I get it, realize that I do understand something about this girl still, and after all, that in some fundamental way we are not dissimilar.

"You mean late," I say, "when the whole world is ours."

◄◊►

They all advise against it, the bellhops and the counter assistant, Meyer himself when I check in with him and he asks what my plans are for the evening, but long after the sun has finally disappeared, the traffic outside the hotel slowed, the crowd in the patio bar dissipated,

I leave the hotel and drive slowly to the beachfront, past the City Hall, outlined in lights like a tottering old wedding cake, the library, the museum, past the car dealerships and the hole-in-the wall tea shops, the silent warehouses and shuttered discount stores. There is very little traffic and the streets are deserted.

"It is not safe," they all say. "Foolhardy."

Behind me I hear the clock above the post office strike one, a train pulling out of the station, ahead is the steady rumble of waves as they break on the beach. I pass the aquarium, the old Edward Hotel, the children's pond, the beach baths. The Cuban Hat is gone, as is the Nest, places where when we were children we would sit in the backseat of my father's car and drink milkshakes to the sound of the waves, in their place buildings I do not recognize, a nondescript restaurant, a new parking lot, a new seawall. I park the car, cross the street, climb over the wall, feel the sand under my shoes.

She is there, where she said she would be, sitting on the seawall. She is dressed in a long skirt, a sweater, sandals, wearing an ivory bangle, a hairband, a watch, a belt, a ring. I see her and she sees me and neither of us say anything as I walk towards her and she waits on the wall, watching me, her arms at her sides, her hands on the stones.

I reach her, stand before her, look carefully at her face, into her eyes. She returns my gaze. She has not changed, hardly at all.

"Hi," she says.

There are the faintest lines at the corners of her eyes, like spiderwebs, no more, and at the edge of her mouth, the skin of her neck is softer, less taut, as if it has been powdered only, not stretched. Her hair is longer, instead of falling in tight curls about her face it is swept back, held in place by her hairband. My throat is tight.

"You haven't changed," I say. "You look exactly like I remember you."

As I say this I realize it is not completely accurate. She is darker than I had remembered, as if memory itself had lightened her skin, changed her from what she is to something else. Now I see her again as she truly is, in the light cast by the moon on the sea, in the velvety air of the seafront.

"You're the same too," she says. "Perhaps not so thin. It suits you."

"I thought I wouldn't find you," I say. "I'm not a very inventive detective."

"What did you try?" she asks.

"I went to the Arbuthnots'," I tell her. "Connie is still there and told me you worked at the university but she couldn't say where you lived. Baptie found you for me."

"Connie knows where I live," Santi says with a smile. "She looks after my children sometimes."

"Children?"

I try to look calm, benign, interested. I need to sit down.

"Two," she says. "Fourteen and twelve."

"What about Mr. Santi?" I ask.

She smiles, shakes her head slowly.

"I'm not sure I'd be here if there were a Mr. Santi."

"Tell me everything," I say. "From the moment you stepped through the hedge until now, everything that's happened."

"It's not such a long story," she says. "And you can probably guess most of it anyway."

"I don't know," I say. "I've invented a hundred lives for you."

"And me for you," she says.

I shake my head. We both sit on the seawall shaking our heads. And then I take her hand but she withdraws it gently, leaves it on her lap.

"It's beautiful here," she says. "It's not always like this. If I'd told anyone where I was going they'd have thought I'd lost my senses."

"That's what they said to me," I say. "Maybe I have."

"I don't think so," she says.

So I ask again for her to tell me everything and she begins, but I must prod her on, and every so often she stops and says: "And what about you? I'm telling you everything and you just ask and ask. Like before too. Now I remember this habit of yours."

"I'll tell you everything," I say. "But you don't stop yet. I've wondered so often."

"It's been very difficult, here," she says. "Hard to keep on track, not to fly off course in anger and do something stupid."

"I would read about it," I say. "And I would wonder where you were in it all. What you were doing."

"You can't know how it was from so far," she says. "Even then when we were young and played in your garden, even then I myself did not see all that a person has to see to understand. Before, when there were their stupid laws and all the things every day that hurt a person, apartheid laws, it was bad. But in the last few years things became much worse with bullets and burnings and with violence. I don't think you can understand that from reading a newspaper only."

"Perhaps not," I say.

"When they shot into a crowd and someone was killed or hurt, it hurt here," she says and touches her heart. "It hurt as if a brother or a sister had been hurt when I saw pictures of people crying and children with blood on their clothes."

I say nothing.

"This country has made us all pay a terrible price for our freedom."

What can I say. I listen to her, this slow description of things I've read about, wondered about, seen pictures of, but the truth is I know so little. And I read it all not so much with pain as with apprehension.

"Now that change has come perhaps the end of the suffering really is near," she says. "But I cannot allow myself to believe that we are safe yet. Too much has happened for the insults and the bad times to be buried in the joy that came with casting a vote. What can we do in six months or six years in the face of so many generations?"

"There's been a good start," I say. "Why are you so despondent?"

"I'm not," she says. "I'm fine. The truth is that hearing you were here and looking for me has made me look back and wonder why everything happened as it did. I was in love with you. And this whole tangle, the disappointments and the heartache, for me they're all tied together."

"They are for me too," I say.

"No," she says. "Not in the same way."

I'm not going to argue with her, turn this into a political discussion. Perhaps it can only be a political discussion.

"Maybe you are right," I say.

"I am right," she says, and laughs, shakes her head, lays the hem of her skirt against her knee and flattens it. Her ring is of silver, flat and engraved. "You left, but still life went on. And so many things can change in a lifetime."

"What are your children's names?" I ask.

"Albert and Winnie," she says. "For Luthuli and Winnie."

"Do you have pictures?"

"No," she says. "Why do you want to see them?"

"Don't you think I may be curious as to how your children came out?"

She thinks about this.

"And you," she asks. "Why no children?"

"That's a long story," I say. "Sometimes I think it has to do with South Africa. Sometimes I think it even has something to do with you."

"How with me?" she asks.

"Now you're playing with me," I say. "You know what it all meant to me."

"No, I don't," she says. "And if what you say is true, then why didn't you try and find me?"

She jumps off the wall, stands in front of me, raises her arms, raises her voice.

"Why?" she repeats. "If it was important. You could have found me. I didn't go anywhere. You did."

There is no easy answer.

"So much happened," I say. "When I got to America all I thought about was you. But then I couldn't find you."

"Did you try?"

"Of course," I say. "But you were gone."

"I was here," she says. "At the university in Durban. They started allowing colored people in and so I came. I used to see your mother sometimes walking on the campus and I'd think: I'm going to go right up to that woman and talk to her. But of course I didn't. I was afraid she'd send me away like a child having a bad dream."

"I wish you had," I say.

"No," Santi says. "I'm pleased I did not. When someone walks away from his heart he has to walk back to it himself. Someone else cannot come running to bring it."

"It's more complicated than that," I say. "You know it is."

"For a long time I prayed that you would come back," she says. "I believed that you would. If someone had told me that you would not, I would not have believed them. Even when you did not find me I believed that you would try, that something was keeping you. And then slowly I realized that even if you did try you did not try hard enough. And I was right."

And it's to that question, really, whether I did everything I could have done, that I have no answer. I suppose I could have written to my mother and asked her to help, to Baptie nineteen years earlier and asked her. There were other things I could have done. But I didn't do them and I know why. It is not difficult to see, as I stand here in the dark, what it was that kept me from finding her. Those nights, those irretrievable nights, offered a clear view of something I hadn't seen before. Bridget always says that we grew up next door to Africa and while I can't say whether she was ever tempted to see what Africa might hold, for me, just once, just then, I looked across and then I stepped back. And the consequence of it is that the place now, with all its texture and mystery, has moved far beyond the reach of a person like me. Even the memories, it seems, are furtive and borrowed.

I try and tell these things to Santi and she listens as she stands there on the sand, moving her feet slowly from side to side, digging a ridge between them. I look down at her legs, her long brown legs, at the way her skirt blows to the side in the breeze, at her narrow waist and I would kill, truly kill, just for a chance one more time to take her back, to recapture the things she once thought of me, the feelings that ran between us. For a while she says nothing, walks slowly up and down in the sand before me, her hands behind her back, her skirt billowing, and then she begins to walk off along the beach and I walk quickly to catch up with her.

"You talk as if we had left you behind," she says. "In fact it was the other way around."

"Back in those days," I say, "even when it seemed that freedom was a long way off, you must have known that the future here belonged to you. For me freedom seemed to be only in places like America and England."

"I cannot even imagine how it would be to live away from here," Santi tells me. "And perhaps that is the biggest difference between you and me."

We pass the restaurants, the public pool, the children's pond. Soon the beach will end in rocks.

"What happened to your husband?" I ask.

"I left him," she says. "It's a long story. We were too young when we married. He is in Cape Town."

"What does he do?"

"He was elected to Parliament."

"Things certainly have changed for you," I say and she laughs.

"They have changed," she says. "Now there is a lot to do."

As we walk I look across at her, can't indeed keep my eyes from her, and I begin to feel that a balance has become unexpectedly upended, leaving me bashful where I had not expected to be bashful, admiring in a way that moves me away from her.

"What are you doing here, really?" she asks.

I can't tell her, of course. How could I? Spiriting away our assets before your ex-husband confiscates them? Preventing my grandfather's bounty from being the dowry of piccanins?

The air is wet even as it is warm, bathes me in a fine steam that leaves my skin clammy, cold even. I feel something slipping away from me, something I want to hold, something valuable. And I know what it is, for sure, why it is Santi who has brought this so clearly home. I had always thought, for all those years in America, that I could not be home there because my true home was elsewhere, that no matter how well I came to know the streets of Boston, the side streets and short-cuts and corner stores, no matter how well I fit in, I would always know another place better, recognize other quirks quicker, feel more at home somewhere else. And that, it turns out, is not true.

I have had, all my life, this series of recurring dreams about South Africa and one of them, Bridget says, she has had too. She and I stand together in the shade of the warehouse while my mother and father play a game with Leora. They throw a ball between them and she tries to catch it but never can. And so they throw it, back and forth, back and forth, as Leora jumps pointlessly between them. And as we stand back and watch I call out to them to let her play too, to drop the ball just a touch so that she can reach it, and they look across without acknowledging me, continue to throw, oblivious to us. I want to intercede further but know I can't. It is then that I begin an endless sigh. Tesseba has learned when she hears it to lean over and waken me.

"What's the matter?" Santi asks.

"I don't know," I say. Then I add: "But I do know this. I have not spent a single day out of love with you."

We stop walking and now she takes my hands, both of them in hers, faces me.

"And me," she says. "And me too. You were my first love and the way you found me and then made such plans to be with me touched me in a way no one else has. And so I never wanted to forget you."

She starts to walk again, slowly, touches her throat and then reaches inside her sweater. I watch as she lifts her hand, reveals a chain with a fragile heart on it, the gold glinting against her fingers in the moonlight.

"Even to this day," she says, "I do not take it off. For you, but not only for you. For all the things that go to make up dreams, for the moments in my life when I thought that happiness had no boundary."

"It seemed to have no boundary once," I say.

"We were young," she says and laughs.

"I have completed so many sentences for you," I tell her. "We have had so many discussions. But now I see how inadequate my imagination has been."

"Not imagination only," Santi says emphatically. "This really is a new South Africa. Many exiles are coming back. Maybe you will come back too and we can be friends. Real friends. See where we finish when we are not the servant girl from next door and the boy from the castle but adults, equals each with our own scars. That is where everyone must now start again in this country of ours. Everyone. There are too many problems now, problems no one even thought were possible, but there is also an openness, a belief everyone shares that it is up to us, that we can create a country that fills our dreams and more. I do not doubt my dreams. You should not doubt yours."

I think of this, of coming back here to this place, this heartless town, selling my house with its carefully chosen antiques, its wonderfully bright rooms, my business, my car, of saying goodbye to my friends, closing down my life and coming back to this arid place, stamping ground of a time so long gone by and so unhappily remembered. I think of Tesseba, of evening walks around the old estates, of the creaky monastery near the reservoir, the mossy grass and rich green firs, the Greek church, the hidden park behind Olmsted's museum.

"A long time ago," I say at last, "when I first reached America, a girl married me so that I could get permission to stay. And then, as time went by, I began to feel more than gratitude. Her name is Tesseba."

Santi has a little Mazda car, silver with some rust on the fender, a dent in the door. I open it for her and she leans against the car frame as I stand beside her holding it open. We both look up. The sky is black, pitch black, except for the clouds, which are quite white.

"It is a pity a person can only live one life," I say, and she laughs.

"I think one life is enough for me," she says. "We are different people now but still inside of you is the person who was the love of my life."

Then we stand awhile and I slip my arm around her waist, draw her close, kiss her on the lips and it is all vaguely familiar, the shape and taste of them, the feel of her cheeks, the slope of her neck, the firm smoothness of her hair. We part and she gets into the car, looks for her keys, places them in the ignition.

"I have to go," she says.

She starts the car, closes the door, rolls down the window.

"So if you ever come back again, now you know where I am," she says.

I nod.

"Bye, Santi," I say. "You will always be the girl of my dreams."

She puts the car in gear, begins to move, looks at me through the window.

"Perhaps that is where I belong," she says. "Only in your dreams."

❦

I walk back along the beach, kicking the sand as I go, listening to the warm roll of the waves. Near the pier where the snake museum used to be I climb over the wall, walk back towards my rented car on the Marine Parade. It is a great gold Mercedes-Benz, covered now in a hazy dew that makes it look as if it has been frosted, preserved for some later use. I get in and close the door with a clunk, start the engine, pull away from the curb. It is three o' clock in the morning. There is no one around.

Everything I have come for is over now. Selwyn Meyer will be at my hotel in the morning with papers for me to sign, there is an Indian tailor who has made me a half dozen cashmere suits, the only thing I could think of I wanted to buy with all this blocked and useless currency. For Tesseba I will buy some jewelry, something delicate and as expensive as she will agree to wear.

The Marine Parade is empty. On one side are the great holiday hotels, the Blue Waters and the Maharani, the Elangeni and the Malibu, the old Edward, white pillared, mannered, once the most elegant hotel in the city. We went there on birthdays, to the Chinese restaurant on the top floor, the Mandarin, the smartest restaurant in Durban. They served us eight courses, one after the other, with chicken substituted for pork.

I turn right and drive slowly up Smith Street, past the Lonsdale and Ivy's Curio, the car dealers and Indian cafes, scrubby two-story Victorian buildings, colonial holdovers overlooked in the scramble to build, the brightly lit City Hall barricaded against car bombs, the Old Mutual, Town Gardens, Eagle Star Building, the Technical College.

And then I keep on driving, up onto the ridge, past Curry Road and Musgrave Road and Essenwood, along North Ridge Road to the Jan Smuts Highway, out past the old Tollgate, the tennis courts and 45th cutting, out past Sherwood, Westville and Cowie's Hill, past Pinetown and Kloof, Hillcrest, up the steep road cut into the mountains which drop precipitously onto the city and end in sea. And then I turn back, down behind the Indian suburbs, Chatsworth and Cato Ridge, past Kwa Mashu and Umlazi, find myself south of the city and so I turn around again and head back in, through Amanzimtoti and Reunion, Lamontville, Mobeni, Jacobs, Greyville, along Umbilo Road, up Francoise, past the Tesserarie Swimming Pool and the King Edward Hospital, and I'm just driving and driving, past sights that were once so familiar I scarcely saw them, that now I know I am seeing for the last time in my life.

So goodbye, Carmel College, goodbye, King George the Fifth Avenue, Botanical Gardens, Pigeon Valley, Berman Bush, goodbye, Berea Park, Entabeni, St. Augustine's, Congella Park, Old Dutch Road. All I want now is to be home, truly home, back where I belong.

"Is it safe?" I'd asked Meyer. "I mean, is there any risk involved?"

He'd laughed, slapped me on the back.

"Of course there's a risk," he said. "Do you think the government likes you doing this?"

"What is the risk?" I'd asked.

"Of being caught? Slim to none. If we're caught. They'll throw the book at us."

"What are the chances of that?" I asked.

"I've been schlepping money out of South Africa for years now," he said. "They haven't caught me yet."

I think of Nerpelow as I drive, of his jacket with its patches at the elbow, his sturdy manner, how implicitly my father trusted him, would have signed his life over to his keeping, how I have allowed myself to dismiss him. Nerpelow's world is dead, or it is dying, swept away by forces whose time has come, but his sensibilities are not altogether obsolete either and his disapproval carries a stigma that I can see, can feel, and it is enough to stop me in my tracks. Even in a sea of ambiguity, when all bets are off, all reference points gone, there is still a right and a wrong.

The sun is beginning to rise over the sea, to color the sky a dull shade of pink. One more day and one more night here, but now it seems unbearable. And the thought that I am running a risk, no matter how slight, of not being home, forever out of this place and walking again in the streets of Boston, is too much to contemplate. I think of Tesseba preparing for bed in Boston, of how she lies on the floor each evening to do her yoga, raises one leg straight into the air, then the other, raises her waist with her hands, breathes deeply, closes her eyes. I think of how she takes off her clothes, pulls one of two chosen tee shirts over her head, an oversize pink one I wanted to give to Goodwill or a blue one I bought her years ago, climbs into bed, presses against me until I feel her breasts and thighs tight against my side. I think of how she is irreligious but crosses herself at news of disaster, rebellious except against her parents, unconcerned with appearance and yet always wholly wholesome. I think of how when I come home on some evenings she is standing at the door, her arms outstretched, her eyes closed, a broad smile on her face, an open, accepting, gleeful smile, waiting only for my kiss to draw her firmly into my embrace. There is a part of Tesseba's life that she has given to me and I have not accorded it the sanctity I do memory.

And I think of my hotel room back in the city, dank, empty, smelling vaguely of stale smoke, of moisture, of carpeting. I am a fool, I swear it, feel like a fool, am too blind to see the nose on my face. I love this woman and always have, and I love being with her, and being with her in America, and America too, and I have learned to see the world through her eyes when mine are clouded over, and have done so without even knowing it, and that is who I am.

As the sun begins to rise I turn the car around again and head for the airport, past the Woolgrowers' cooperative, the Lyric Theater, the flour mills, the factories at Jacobs. Ironically I see, as I pass through, a sign for Natal Plastics and I go a little faster, raise the window to close out the cold air.

The city begins stirring to life. I am going home.

⋘⋙

There is an eight o'clock flight to Johannesburg, a connection, and then home to Boston. I'll take it.

"Any luggage to check?" the ticket agent asks.

"No," I say.

"No luggage?" she asks again.

I pull my wallet from my pocket, check my passport, traveler's checks, everything I need to get home. Let the lousy Royal Hotel keep the few soggy suits I brought with me, the bellhops share the unworn cashmeres, let Selwyn Meyer curse his wasted time, the bank keep its money. Helga doesn't need it, I don't, Bridget probably doesn't even want it. I want nothing, nothing but to be home, in Tesseba's embrace, back in my life and out of this. I will not return loaded down like a carpetbagger with soggy artifacts, diamonds no one needs, suits filled with moisture, an ivory stand, a dogwood head, a verdite carving. I do not want them, do not need them, will not have them simply because they are mine for the asking.

The restaurant is busy and I realize how scruffy I must look. There is sand in my pant cuffs. I need a shave. I order coffee and sit at a table by myself at the window.

—❦—

Higher and higher and higher and we scream through the clouds, break into the sky and shudder home. There can be no one on this craft who does not feel, at least in some deep part of him, relief to be leaving a place which is home to such ambiguity, not one mind that does not, at least for an instant as the jet soars into the atmosphere, think of the heat and the drought below, familiar faces left behind in the midst of overpowering uncertainty.

Below the fortified farms become again just dry brown buildings, antlike in the distance. Their roofs drift away with the ocean as the aircraft tears homeward through space. I recall the words of the judge as she swore me to citizenship in an unventilated Faneuil Hall, that I would bear arms, that I would honor the laws of the United States, whatever they may be, that I would abjure and reject forever all allegiances to princes and potentates, foreign places, foreign oaths, save to my new country. I look out the aircraft window. Its faithful wings bob up and down in the air currents. This is a good airplane. It is taking me home. I take from my pocket the little piece of notepaper with Santi's phone number. It seems that it has been an age, not just a morning ago, that Baptie handed it to me. I put it in my pocket, lean back in my seat, begin to doze, fall asleep.

And then I awaken and there is orange juice and a warm bun on the tray before me, coffee, a smiling woman distributing customs forms. I reach into my pocket and take the piece of paper out and read it in the light of day. As the aircraft dips through the clouds, below in the sparkling light I see the upper edges of buildings, the sun glinting through the arches of the city, the otherwordly glow of morning. There is my building, there is my bank, there is Rowes Wharf, the silver washboard of the Federal Reserve. And I tear the paper, slowly and carefully, into a hundred tiny pieces and press them, a few at a time, into the tray at the edge of the seat.

We begin to sink, down and down until it appears that the aircraft will land in water, and then, without warning, a runway appears below us, a shriek of rubber, a thrust, and we are down. The ficus plant in my office is over five feet tall. I hope my secretary has remembered to water it. Next week is my mother's birthday. I will surprise her with a giant bouquet, a call, a renewed silent promise to let her be. Automobiles with flashing lights and steam billowing from their tailpipes race alongside the aircraft as it moves gracefully to its berth. Men in down vests and heavy gloves stand below my window and wait to open the hold. I am home, and I am safe.

The airport building blinks in the distance, and somewhere behind the mirrored windows, over the heaps of snow, behind the crowds of people, wondering where she has put the car keys, her face alight as it always is, always could be, when I return to her, Tesseba waits.

The craft pulls to a stop, people stand, the lights dim. And then we file out, through a snap of cold air and through the soggy jetway. I walk quickly across the vast arrivals hall, take my place in a line for "Citizens Only." A man in a blue uniform takes my passport, slides it through his machine, hands it back.

"Welcome home," he says.

Downstairs a customs official looks at me carefully, wrinkles his brow.

"You travel light," he says as he waves me through.

The doors swing open and I see a line of faces, the black tiles of the floor, colorful banners hanging from the rafters. A man wheels a trolley loaded with boxes just in front of me. For a long moment I do not see her.

And then I do. Against a far wall, beyond the busy crowd, Tesseba is waiting. She is wearing my red flannel shirt, the one she bought for me to wear as we gazed at the Grand Tetons, looks wind-blown, distracted, a little apprehensive. I stop walking, wait for a moment to take her in there beside her slender reflection in the sky-high window. She is looking into the distance, she is a stranger to me, I have never met her, I do not know her, she is waiting for someone else, she is not mine.

And then her head turns and she sees me. Her face is transformed. Happiness covers her. I am ready for her. I am ready for her. I am ready for her.